Praise for Rick Ludwig

Maui Mystery Series

"If you're yearning for a page-turning tale of suspense and skullduggery, look no further. If you're hoping for some crackling dialogue and vivid descriptions, you'll find them here. And if you're yearning to go that land of myth and mystery in the middle of the Pacific, let Rick Ludwig take you. Along with the beauty, he'll show you the dark side of paradise. Don't miss it."

— William Martin, New York Times-bestselling author of *The Lincoln Letter*

Soul of a Sleuth carries all the flavors of a good Hawaiian poke. Sprinkled with aloha, Ludwig mixes Maui's rich culture in with its global connection to keep the crimes committed tangled in tension.

— Elaine Gallant, author of *The 5th C*

Ludwig spins a fast-paced tale of mystery, intrigue, and even a little magic, set in the backdrop of an island paradise in his third book in the Maui Mystery series, *Soul of a Sleuth*. This book is a thriller from start to finish, but it's also a beautiful homage to the resilient island of Maui and the township of Lahaina that was devastated by fire in 2023. If you like fearless protagonists, spine-tingling suspense, and pulse-pounding action, check out this fantastic series!

— Betsey Kulakowski, Bestselling Author of
The Veritas Codex Paranormal Thriller Series

Just finished *Soul of a Sleuth* and enjoyed it thoroughly!!! It's always nice to return to familiar characters and see their story play out. One of the best parts about this one is that it rewards people who've read Ludwig's previous work. The first few sections were kind of revisiting the earlier cases, making the third act hit all the harder. Seeing them all intertwine was pretty great —and finally getting closure on Thanatos is really nice to see. I think this is the most spiritual novel Ludwig has written, which says something since the last one was about a guy writing a novel in the afterlife. It's really respectful and thoughtful and doesn't pander. It really adds to the atmosphere for the final confrontation at the end.

— R. J. Johnson, award winning author of
Dreamslinger

Soul of a Sleuth

Maui Mysteries
Book 3

Rick Ludwig

Soul of a Sleuth

A Maui Mystery

First Edition

Copyright © 2024 Rick Ludwig

Published by Babylon Books

For Jon

A note on the spelling of Hawaiian words

After moving to Maui, I learned a great deal about the history and culture of the Hawaiian Islands. I respect this ancient and vibrant culture and have tried to reflect this in everything I've written in this beautiful place. But I am neither a native Hawaiian nor a speaker of the language. Though I have learned a few phrases that I am not too embarrassed to speak aloud, I faced a challenge in spelling Hawaiian words.

Two characters are used in proper Hawaiian spelling that may be unfamiliar to those new to the language. These are the *'okina* and *kahakō*.

The 'okina can be approximated by an apostrophe but is an actual consonant and represents a glottal stop. It may occur at the beginning or in the middle of a word and changes the pronunciation and meaning of words. An example familiar to many non-Hawaiians is the name of the island Lāna'i (Lah-nah-ee), which is very different from the word for a veranda or covered patio, lanai (Lah-nigh). Throughout the novel I have used a reversed apostrophe to represent this important consonant.

The kahakō indicates vowel length, which changes meaning and the placement of stress. In other languages it is referred to as a macron and represented by a line over a vowel. An example of how these can impact meaning in a Hawaiian word is the word kāne (kaa-nay) which means male, while the same word without the kahakō, kane (ka-nay), means skin disease.

In this trilogy, I have elected to use both the ʻokina and kahakō. I apologize to Native Hawaiian readers for my other limitations.

I have also attempted to use the standard method for distinguishing non-English words, using italics for the first occurrence of such words, except for place names.

Another characteristic of the islands is the common use of pidgin in friendly banter. I have learned that there are subtle differences between the pidgins used on each of the Hawaiian Islands. What I have tried to capture, on occasion in this novel, is probably closest to the pidgin I heard on Maui. I have tried, phonetically, to capture the essence of this joyful and constantly evolving language as I heard it spoken. Born from the desire of each wave of immigrants to this lovely place to communicate with each other, despite vastly different native tongues, Hawaiian pidgin is an essential component of daily life here in paradise. One very common aspect is a tendency to end most sentences with, *yeah?* It's kind of like ending a sentence on the mainland with, *right?*

Prologue

Wednesday, October 30, 2013, 5:00 a.m. Central European Time (CET)

Agent Andreos Calliopoulos always arrived early to his office at Europol Headquarters in The Hague. Starting the day without interruption made reviewing information so much easier. By the time everyone else trickled in, he was up to date on the status of every investigation in which he was involved, and a few in which he wasn't—officially.

Each day, when he arrived, he allowed himself a strong cup of espresso. The jolt of caffeine recharged those *little grey cells* that his fictional role model Hercule Poirot used to wax poetic about. The bushy fur on his top lip was a far cry from the elaborate moustaches sported by his Belgian hero, but Calliopoulos was the son of a Greek fisherman and proud to represent. With steaming cup in hand, he reached into the incoming mail basket on his desk. A colorful postcard from Singapore caught his eye. *Who'd be travelling this late in the year?*

Turning the card over he found the note was written in English—not terribly unusual. But the handwriting . . .

My dear Agent Calliopoulos:

I hope that this card reaches you in advance of a festive holiday being celebrated in many parts of the world at this time of year. The North Americans call it Halloween. In Latin America it's El Dia de los Muertos. I prefer honoring the departed to tricks and treats.

You could never accept that the trivial person killed on the Acropolis was a god. Good for you. Thanatos indeed lives. My mission is far from complete. I know we shall meet again. But leave that heathen at home this time. He and his puny gods bore me.

Thanatos

Part One

Evidence

"Extraordinary claims require extraordinary evidence."

— Carl Sagan

1

Tuesday, October 29, 2013, 6:05 p.m. HST (Hawaiian Standard Time)

Detective Sergeant Keone Boyd lingered outside Brandy's Bar and Grill in Wailuku looking at his smartphone. When his new partner, Angela Beyers, hesitated at the door, he glanced up from the screen. "Need something?"

"Aren't you coming?" Angela asked.

"Do I need to?"

"Could be more than one of them in there, you know."

Keone knew Angela hated it when she thought he was testing her. "Total confidence in you, *Tita*. Go get 'em." Keone intentionally used a Pidgin term that could mean both little sister and tough, independent woman.

Angela rolled her eyes but entered the bar.

Though they were both now detective sergeants, Lieutenant Alcala made it clear who was in charge when he teamed them—shortly after Keone returned from his honeymoon and Angela completed physical therapy. Keone was sure Ange didn't mind. His suggestion to Alcala had helped her achieve her dream of becoming a detective.

Working together made it clear to him that his partner wasn't the only one learning new and better methods. She had interpersonal skills that balanced his tendency to withdraw around people. But he still needed to get her to trust her gut more.

Shortly after Angela entered Brandy's, Randy Opaka pushed his way out through the exit. Keone calmly tripped him, sending the man sprawling down the bar's front steps. In a single motion, Keone slapped one cuff on Opaka's wrist and the other on the bent pole that served as a handrail for the front entrance.

"Howzit, Randy? Have time for a little chat?" Angela's informant Blue had told them Scooter Morales was in the bar but hadn't mentioned Opaka.

There was more than one.

"I'm one busy man, but I always make time for you, Sarge," Opaka said as he took a seat on one of the steps. "You no hafta chain me up."

"Sergeant Beyers warned me that you can move pretty fast when you want to."

"Dat lady cop your new partner or sumting?"

"That's right, Randy. But you already know Sergeant Beyers, don't you?"

"Yeah. She shut down my business."

"I believe you were in the process of helping a murderer get off the island at the time."

"I din' know dat old man killed anyone. I just helping a friend." Keone found Randy's attempt at honesty laughable but kept a straight face.

"I read your testimony. Didn't believe it then. Don't believe it now. Neither did Sergeant Beyers."

"Yeah. But the jury sure did. She misses shit. You need teach her mo' bettah. She nevah even see me in dere." Opaka pointed to the entrance. "She head straight fo' dat bah."

"I'll note that in her next review. But *you* saw her. That's why you left so quickly. Were you afraid she might have a few questions for you?"

"I just got someplace ta be."

"Uh-huh. Lucky for you, I have some questions, too. A colleague of yours in the transport end of your business just turned up dead. Thought you might know something about it. You've worked with good old Hopper Alavezos, haven't you? He was almost as good at driving illegal merchandise as you are at flying it."

"Dat's real sad. I like dat guy."

"Good. Then you'll be happy to help us with our investigation."

"Sure. Sure. But you no gotta trip me. Dat hurt."

"No, *that* didn't hurt. But try to jerk me around a little more and you'll learn a whole lot about hurt."

Keone watched Opaka's gaze travel upward over his six foot seven, two hundred seventy-five-pound frame. Opaka would take his threat seriously.

The dive's door flew open, hitting the frame with a bang. Keone yanked Blue Herrera's hand from the doorknob and swung him into an arm-lock. "Hey, Blue. Looks like all my friends are here tonight. Why don't you have a seat next to Randy while we wait for my partner?"

Keone shoved him down hard on the concrete steps and hoped, for Angela's sake, he hadn't cracked her informant's tailbone. But he had to make Blue's collar look as real as Randy's. Too bad the dumbass didn't think to exit through the back door. They could have avoided this charade.

"Randy and I were just talkin' story about your old buddy, Hopper. You hear what happened to him?"

Blue looked uneasy but kept his mouth shut.

A few minutes later, a disheveled Angela Beyers shoved Scooter Morales out the front door. The blood dripping from the corner of Keone's new partner's left eye suggested Morales reacted negatively to her questions. "Too bad you decided to hit me with that beer mug and run, Scoot. I just wanted to ask some polite questions. Now I've got to arrest you for assaulting a police officer. Come on."

She dragged Scooter down the stairs past Keone, while Randy and Blue sat quietly at his feet.

"Nice collar, partner."

Angela looked daggers at Keone and perp-walked the drug-dealer to their unmarked cruiser.

2

While Angela booked Scooter Morales for assaulting a police officer, Keone placed Randy and Blue in separate interrogation rooms. By the time Angela came down the hallway, Keone was waiting with a gauze pad to clean the slash above her left eye.

She pulled away at first, then let him dab the blood from her eyebrow.

"Ange, what happened?"

"He just sliced my forehead—and my pride."

Keone felt a little guilty about his partner's injury. "I didn't expect the little shit to react like that. He's usually a coward."

"My fault, not yours."

"He's fast. You did a good job snagging him."

"Did you know Opaka was in there?" Angela asked.

"Just a hunch. That's why I waited by the entrance."

"I'm glad you collared Blue. The other two might have smelled something."

"That's what I thought. Good thing Opaka came out the front. You must've been keeping an eye on the back exit."

He suspected she hadn't been, but decided she'd learned enough lessons for one night.

"You want me to interview Blue?" Angela asked.

"Yeah. I'll take Randy, and we can double-up on Scooter in the morning. He's not going anywhere."

"Sounds good."

"And Ange. I meant what I said when you came out of the bar. You did good, Tita."

Keone saw Angela try to suppress a smile before he strolled into Interrogation Room Two to find Randy Opaka sitting behind the interview table, right hand cuffed to a curved rod embedded in the table.

"What the hell, Boyd?" Opaka shouted. "It agin the law to walk outta one bah now?"

"You were running, Brah. And that's a dangerous road crossing. I probably saved your life."

"Well, I din' really know Hopper dat well."

"Just enough to say . . ." Keone flipped open his notebook. "'Dat's real sad. I liked dat guy.'"

Opaka stiffened. He clearly hated hearing his own words thrown back at him, even in Pidgin.

"You know Dave Walden and used to know Koa Kaleho. You think either of them had a reason to snuff Hopper?"

"Kaleho did. Your partner would never have caught him if Hopper hadn't squealed. But he's beyond getting even."

Not mentioning Dave, Keone thought. *And he's not using Pidgin anymore. Must be thinking before he speaks, now.*

"Oh, that's right. She took him out when she caught him about to fly off the island—with you."

"I only got two months. I paid my debt to society. I can't afford to do background checks on every client."

"What about Walden?"

Randy paused—too long. "Barely knew him before you and

that Fed took him out of circulation. I heard he was on the mainland somewhere."

"Where'd you hear that? From Hopper?"

Randy's expression told Keone all he needed to know. But he'd continue asking questions to keep the drug pilot from figuring that out.

<hr>

ANGELA FOUND BLUE IN IR ONE, STANDING BUT SECURELY handcuffed to the interview table.

"Didn't yo' kanaka partner know enough to let me go? I'm thinkin' you should maybe look for one new snitch."

"Sit down and shut up." Angela sat down directly across the table from her confidential informant and glared at him. "I guess you never considered what Opaka would have thought if Keone gave you a pass? Did you?"

Blue followed her directions and, once seated, remained very quiet.

No smart comeback this time, eh, Blue? Angela thought.

"Maybe I'm thinking you knew about Hopper's accident a little too fast. Just how did you find out about it?"

"Oh, Sarge. Word got out before you even found the body. Whoever killed him was sending a message. That's why he left the body outside that Safeway, across from your station. He knew one of us would see it and tell the rest. Whoever did it wanted anyone tempted to rat him out to understand the consequences."

The stitched-up mouth and missing tongue did make that fairly clear, and Blue's dropped the Pidgin. "What makes you say that, Blue?"

"I heard the stiff's mouth was sewed up."

"Anything else?"

"Just where he dumped the body, like I said before."

He's probably telling the truth. I don't see Blue getting his hands dirty. In her notebook she wrote, *He's more apt to be a victim if this killer is targeting squealers.*

"Do you know anybody Hopper might have ratted out?"

"We both know he sang about the old guy that shot that haole friend of yours up at ʻIao. You took care of Koa Kaleho, though."

But not his grandsons.

"Anybody else?"

"Well, he did a lot of work for that Iceman, Walden. But I heard the Feds got Waldo a while back."

Keone's case.

"Can you think of anybody else, maybe somebody who's alive and on the island? I'm getting impatient, Blue."

"He worked mostly the Wailuku pakalolo growers and the ice dealers in upcountry, like Walden."

She tossed a legal pad to Blue and handed him a dull pencil from her pocket. "I want at least five names from each group. Use good penmanship and I'll consider cutting you loose."

"Damn. You know I hate this shit."

"Ten bucks for each name that checks out. Don't try to con me, either. I'll be right back."

Angela quickly left but slowed when she spotted Keone leaning against the hallway wall.

"Get anything from Blue?" he asked.

"Well, he didn't do it, but he's scared someone might think he ratted, too. I'm getting a list of possibles from him. How'd it go with Opaka?"

"He didn't do it either, but he knows something. He could be involved with the killer. Did Blue say anything about the grandsons?"

"He mentioned Kaleho had a motive but didn't say

anything specifically about Kāne or Manolo." She hesitated. "You'll find it out from my interrogation report anyway, so I might as well tell you. Blue mentioned Dave Walden."

Keone smiled.

"Listen, big guy, you know Walden's a non-starter."

"Because he's in witness protection, I know. But what if he isn't?"

"Did you hear something from your friend in the DEA?"

"Not yet. But until I do, I'm keeping good old Dave on the list. I've got a funny feeling."

Lieutenant Tony Alcala caught up to them in the hallway. "I see you two have been busy. What's the story on these three? Alavezos case?"

"Sergeant Beyers can fill you in." Keone's smile never slipped as he turned to Angela. "Here are my interview notes. I'll get the list from Blue and cut him loose for you before I leave."

"Thank you, Sergeant Boyd. Have a good evening." Angela could barely keep the sarcasm out of her voice. She knew Alcala would keep her for at least an hour, recounting their actions. Then she'd have to write up both Keone's notes and her own before she could head home to Linda.

"Come on in, Beyers," Alcala said as he walked toward the open door to his office.

As she followed, thoughts tumbled around in Angela's brain.

Alcala's a strong leader. And I'm glad he's less formal around me since the shooting. Just. Please. Don't let this get weird.

Before beginning the debriefing, Alcala turned to Angela. "How is your friend Nancy Lister doing these days? She was very shaken when I called after you were shot." Tony grabbed a folder from his desk, slid into one of the two upholstered chairs in front, and gestured for Angela to take the other.

"She's doing very well. She and her daughter just published her husband Rob's book about his life, and it's selling very well. She's also moved to a new condo complex near a friend that she works with." Angela was used to the casual way Tony tried to open a debriefing, but hoped he'd stay away from a certain subject.

"Oh, she got a job. That's good. It sounds like she's moving on. Where is she working?"

"At the Macy's in the Hyatt Regency Hotel."

"I'll have to stop by and buy an aloha shirt. By the way, I want to tell you again how very pleased I was with your work on that case."

"Thank you, sir." *Don't want to go there.* "Now about this case."

"Right to business, eh? Have a hot date tonight or something?"

"Just tired, sir. Anxious to get home."

"Understood. Okay, do we have any idea why someone decided to silence Efren 'Hopper' Alavezos?"

"The way we found his corpse this morning told us a few things, sir," Angela replied, relieved to be back on topic.

Alcala opened his folder and flipped through the documents inside. "Found across the street from this very station. Double pop in the head. Probable time of death: two to three a.m. Tongue cut off and jammed down vic's throat. Lips sewn together with fishing line. Okay, someone wanted to send a message."

"The funny thing is Hopper Alavezos was a grower and

transporter, not a snitch. I only got information from him that one time and had to work for it," Angela said.

"The Lister case. I remember."

The memory of rushing between her boss and Koa Kaleho's pistol flashed in Angela's mind.

"Hopper was with Koa Kaleho the night of Dr. Lister's shooting," Angela replied. "After they sideswiped Rob Lister's car, the old man complained about Hopper's driving and said he'd walk home. But, when I interviewed him, Hopper remembered Kaleho walked in the opposite direction from his house, toward the park, carrying a heavy duffle bag. His testimony helped us tie Kaleho and the weapon to the location."

"But Kaleho's dead. Thanks to you. Did Alavezos work with anyone else he could have informed on?"

"He hauled some reagents to crystal-meth labs a few times, sir. Aside from that, he stuck with agricultural products, mostly pakalolo."

"The marijuana's small-time stuff. But the ice labs . . ." Tony paused. "Do you know which labs he supplied?"

"Only one, so far. David Walden's."

"Walden. Shit. Let me summarize. You and Keone have two suspects for the killing. One of them is dead and the other is in witness protection a few thousand miles away. Is that about it?" Her boss didn't hide his disappointment.

"We're working a couple of theories, Lieutenant," Angela replied hurriedly. "Kaleho's grandsons are still alive and one of them, Kāne, idolized his grandfather. He's also had a few brushes with the law, including one involving Hopper."

"You said a couple of theories. I'm guessing the grandson's your angle since you worked his grandfather's case." Tony paused again. "Unlikely, but it deserves a follow-up. What's Keone's take on this?"

"He's checking with the DEA to make certain Walden hasn't skipped."

"And?" Tony asked.

"Still waiting to hear back, sir."

Tony shook his head. "What about Alavezos? What's he been up to?"

"Pretty much nothing. He just got out of jail a week ago for a hit and run."

"Detective Kalani's case."

"That's right, sir. Some hotshot lawyer found a technicality and got his sentence reduced." Angela rolled her eyes.

"Did we make any mistakes?"

"No. The technicality involved the judge. Lindsay's case was solid. It's just the timing of his release . . ."

"You're thinking Alavezos' release was convenient for whoever wanted to off him. You better follow up on the lawyer and see who paid his fee."

Angela hesitated.

"Go ahead and follow up on that grandson and let Keone disprove the Walden theory so you can both put your full attention on real suspects. What about the three you brought in tonight?"

"Keone brought in my CI, Blue Herrera, to cover Blue's ass for giving us the tip on Scooter Morales. Scooter used to work with Alavezos and Kaleho in the old days. I've had some recent reports Morales is trying to recruit at the grandson's school in Wailuku."

"Okay. What about Randy Opaka?"

"He just happened to be in the bar where we found Morales. When he made a run for it, Keone . . . uh . . . prevented him from running into traffic. After a few questions, Keone decided to bring him in for a more in-depth interview.

You may remember Opaka was also involved with Kaleho and the Lister case."

"I remember he was about to fly Kaleho off island right before you saved my sorry ass in that cabin at his airstrip."

Angela remained silent.

"Keone probably thinks he flew Walden over from witness protection so he could kill a guy he barely knew. None of this makes sense. Alavezos must have some other connections. This looks more like a mob hit than anything else."

When Tony paused, Angela rose from her seat.

"Oh no, Detective Sergeant. We're not done. Tell me everything you and Keone saw and heard from the moment you reached Brandy's. And leave nothing out."

Damn it, Keone, Angela thought as she dropped back down into her seat and re-opened her notepad.

3

Julie Boyd loved to bake. Her pies and cakes tantalized the taste buds. But, aside from a few casseroles, she struggled to create actual meals. Early in her first marriage to Dave Walden, he hired a cook. She had no input on this decision, but Dave made her feel inferior about it. Like everything else.

She pushed the disturbing memories of her ex-husband out of her mind, replacing them with thoughts of her near-perfect marriage with Keone and her sister Janet's new-found happiness with Mike Fowler.

Once Julie and Keone returned from their honeymoon and combined their furniture in Keone's condo, Janet dedicated herself to sharing the basics of meal planning and preparation with her sister. Julie was now capable, if not accomplished, aided by Keone's preference for hearty fare over culinary masterpieces.

When Keone called to say he was heading home and offered to pick up something, Julie was already making Texas-style, Flamin'-hot chili. "You just get your butt home. Dinner will be ready when you get here."

She tasted a spoonful and felt the burn. She also felt a little guilty about making Keone's favorite dish, given her ulterior motive. Julie and Angela had conspired to entice Keone to talk about two things that were bugging him. Julie was tasked with the one from their honeymoon and Angela the one from work.

She moved nimbly about the tiny kitchen, set the table in the living room, and made sure a beer schooner was chilling in the freezer. But her mind wandered back to their cruise of the Mediterranean. The first half consisted of Rome, Naples, the Amalfi Coast, Pompeii, and Athens. The second half would have taken them to lovely islands and the Mediterranean shores of Turkey. But after the murders and Keone's pursuit of a killer, they'd decided to forgo any more cruising for a while. They flew from Athens to Venice and spent their remaining days there before returning to Maui. Remembering their final romantic night in Venice brought a smile to Julie's lips.

The honeymoon was amazing—except for the secret Keone kept from her between Naples and Athens. When a killer was captured in Athens, Keone told her the whole story and apologized. She forgave him and decided she would never again ask him to avoid talking about work. She knew he might have to keep information secret during certain investigations, but he agreed to tell her when there were things he couldn't share.

Deep in her thoughts, Julie jumped when she felt Keone's massive arms surround her.

She turned and kissed him on the lips, then pointed him toward the bathroom. "Take off that jacket and shoulder holster, wash up, and then come have a brew."

Keone followed her instructions, then returned to take a deep draw from the oversized, chilled schooner of Longboard

Lager she placed in his hand. He inhaled deeply and pulled out a chair. "Do I smell chili?"

"With no beans and plenty of heat."

"Ah, Texas-style. You're one kine good wife."

"Good?"

"Okay, great. I'm in a generous mood."

"Progress on the case?"

"A little. I enjoy working with Ange."

"Still making her do all your paperwork?"

"Busted. But I am the senior detective."

Julie loved Angela and knew how grateful her friend was to be learning from the best. She brought Keone a huge bowl of chili and, while she dished up her more modest helping, made her first announcement. "I finished *Hawai'i Anna Goes on a Moku Pe'a* today."

"That's great." Keone laid his spoon down and looked into her eyes. "I'm so proud of you, Julie. You even used the Hawaiian expression for taking a voyage in the title. You had to ask me for the Hawaiian word for hospital for your last book, but you came up with *Moku Pe'a* on your own."

"My lessons with your Tutu are going well. I love to hear her speak Hawaiian like her ancestors when she teaches me about the island's mythology. Pele is her favorite of the gods, but I kinda like Maui, even if he is just a demi-god."

"She's your Tutu too, now. You learned moku pe'a from her?"

"Yep. I like the way it sounds." She knew Keone was relieved that his family had accepted her so warmly and that she was back to writing full time. After the publication of her first book since the honeymoon, *Hawai'i Anna Goes to the Haukapila*, she jumped right into this new book, which contained locations from their honeymoon cruise. "Speaking of taking a voyage."

"Uh-huh," Keone said, quickly spooning in another mouthful of chili.

"I know you don't want to talk about it, but it's been three months, Keone."

"I thought you loved our honeymoon."

"Oh, you know I did. I had the time of my life." Julie meant it, too. "So did you before Naples and after Athens."

"I've apologized a million times for what I did those three days." Keone looked down at his empty bowl.

"And you told me everything about the murders and your role in the investigation, eventually. But you brought something back with you. Something that still bothers you. Please talk to me."

Letting out a huge sigh, and getting up from the table, Keone said, "Okay, I'll tell you what I've learned from Europol while we clear the table."

"That's a start."

By the time Keone finished his detailed report and they'd moved to the living room couch, Julie was confident everything that he'd told her was complete and accurate. "I'm sorry your friend Andreos got in trouble, but even you felt he played a little fast and loose with the facts."

"There are worse things than being reprimanded. But I think what really bothers him is that he couldn't save that last girl with the antidote."

"And the fact that the guy you two caught was just a henchman and not the crazy that thinks he's a Greek god," Julie added.

"I think even his bosses at Europol realize that, now. But they still won't let him back on the case." Keone shook his head.

Julie snuggled closer to her husband. "Have you talked with Andreos?"

"We've communicated by email, but I suspect his communications are being monitored."

"Isn't there anything more you can do?"

"I've asked my friend at the DEA, Tom Freeman, to monitor communications within the intelligence community about any killings matching Thanatos's M.O., but he hasn't seen anything yet. I'll let you know if I hear anything more from him or Andreos. No secrets."

"No secrets," Julie replied and gave Keone a long kiss. "Now, how about helping me bring out the coffee and dessert."

"Do I smell lilikoi crème brûlée?"

"Yes, and before you ask, big guy, I made you two." Julie knew there was still something bothering Keone. But she'd pushed enough for one evening, and Angela was in a better position to tease out the other one. *Baby steps.*

"Oh, Keone. There is another reason we're celebrating tonight," Julie said.

"Oh, what's that? Something else from the honeymoon?" Keone sported a huge smile.

"You know, being married to a detective has its disadvantages. Still, just to make it official, my Ob/Gyn confirmed the ship's doctor's suspicion. I am pregnant. He estimates a due date in late April or early May."

"You've made me one happy kanaka." Keone lifted her in his arms and swung her around.

4

Tuesday, October 29, 9:45 p.m. HST

Linda Carroll never expected Angela to be home at a specific time. She knew better. Ange often joked that Lin's skill at creating meals that tasted almost as good re-heated was one of the reasons she kept her around.

Linda knew it had been a rough day when she spotted the bandage over Angela's eye. "Who'd you piss off?"

"Just some punk drug dealer in a bar. I'm fine."

"Still hungry?"

"Starving. Give me two minutes to get comfortable," Ange said, taking off her clunky work shoes.

When Angela reappeared, Linda set a plate of samosas and a steaming bowl of hot and sour soup in front of her. She studied her friend quietly as Angela ate.

Angela glanced up nervously a couple of times but said nothing, even when she finished eating.

Linda cleared the table and brought coffee. "Have you thought about what we discussed last night?"

"Yes, I have."

"And?"

"Lin, I need more time. What we have is wonderful, but a wedding would raise so many flags with so many people."

"It's not the nineteenth century anymore, or even the twentieth. People are permitted to love whoever they want. Keone told you the MPD would support us. And so would our church."

"But not my family's church."

"Ange, the new pope has been very open to gay people attending mass."

"The pope's not the problem. It's my Popi." Her voice cracked on the last word.

"You don't know that. Your sister accepts us."

Angela looked down at her coffee. "I took a great risk when I told her. But she loves me."

"So do your parents."

"They do now. But once they know . . ."

"Is there any other reason? Friends? Neighbors?"

"No. Our friends and neighbors respect us for who we are. My folks' friends and neighbors are a different story."

"You aren't ashamed of me, are you?"

"Hell, no. You're my life. You know that. After I got out of the hospital, we both realized we were more to each other than friends and housemates. And the last few months have been fantastic. We've always shared our hopes and dreams, but I was afraid sharing a bed might spoil our friendship."

"It didn't."

"I know. I know. I just . . . Something happened today with Tony. I'm not sure how to handle it."

"What?" Linda's felt her eyes open wide. "You think he's got a crush on you?"

"You think so, too? At first, I thought he was just grateful for me taking that bullet for him. But tonight, while I was giving my report, I got a strange feeling."

"I was just kidding." *I like Ange's boss but never considered him a competitor for her affections.*

"Well, he's been acting . . . different."

"That doesn't sound like him. Are you sure you're not imagining something?"

"What if he asked me out? How weird would that be—for everyone?"

"I'm sure Keone would talk to him for you."

Angela shook her head. "No. That would embarrass them both. I need to tell the lieutenant myself."

"When?"

"Soon. After that, I'll tell my folks and we can set a date. You're my family now. Everyone needs to know that."

Linda held her tight, tears filling her eyes.

The nightmare came so often since the shooting that she almost expected it.

There she was, covered in body armor, watching Tony tease confessions out of Koa Kaleho, both for shooting Rob Lister and for a series of murders and attempted murders in San Antonio decades earlier. Tony helped Kaleho off the bed, Koa's feet tangled in the ragged blanket, and he hit the floor. Kaleho rolled into a sitting position with a pistol pointed at Tony Alcala's chest, but it wasn't Tony. It was Keone.

No.

She leapt between them, but the face changed. No longer old and wrinkled, it became the face of a child, not Kāne or Manolo—a baby. A familiar voice shared a thought in her head:

Protect them both.

Two years ago, she would have laughed at the thought of having visions. But, before she came to in that hospital, she'd felt a presence and heard a voice in her head. A voice that resonated with the bizarre case she'd pursued to discover who shot her friend Nancy Lister's husband. The same voice she'd just heard. The voice of Calla.

She and Nancy had talked a lot since then. Mostly about the manuscript they'd found on Rob Lister's computer. Nancy later incorporated Rob's manuscript into a best-selling book about her and her daughter's experiences during and after the shooting. In the manuscript, Lister described his shooting and something more, something impossible. But forensic analysis proved the manuscript was written after Rob was shot and lay comatose in the hospital. The file was saved on their computer after Angela drove Nancy to the hospital. No one was home, and no evidence of forced or unforced entry was ever found. The only fingerprints on the keyboard were Rob's. And they weren't smeared, as they would have been if someone wearing gloves had typed something after him.

She thought back to the first time Keone returned to the station after his honeymoon.

"Hey, Ange. When I called you from Greece after you were shot, you said something odd about an ancient Greek you'd met named Calla? Was it just the meds you were on, or do you remember that?"

"Of course, I remember that. Calla was a key character in that manuscript that led me to catch Rob Lister's killer. He was the spirit guide of Rob Lister in his afterlife. Rob figured out that Calla had been born in Ancient Greece when Socrates was still alive. Why?"

Keone looked at her as if she had just said the sky was green. "The detective I worked with from Europol was supposedly a descendant of an ancient Greek fisherman from Piraeus, who was present at the death of Socrates and was called Calla. As a result, his name was Andreos Calliopoulos. But why should I be surprised. The serial killer we were chasing claimed to be the Greek god of non-violent death. A guy named Thanatos."

Now it was Angela's turn to look confused. Tony had interrupted them at that point and the topic hadn't come up since.

Linda had told her to let it go.

She'd tried and failed. Now odd questions surfaced in her mind.

Is Keone in danger? Who's the baby?

5

Leaving Scooter Morales in a cell overnight did nothing to loosen his tongue. Angela could feel her partner's disappointment.

"C'mon, Scoot. Just tell us what you know. You've worked with everyone who ever knew Hopper. If you didn't know something, why did you bust my partner in the chops?"

"I don't know nothing. I barely knew the clown."

Keone slammed his fist on the desk so hard, Angela thought it might break. She could barely keep a straight face when he growled, "I hate bad grammar."

"Wha . . .?" Morales was confused.

"If you *don't* know nothing, then you know something. Didn't you ever take high school English?"

"Huh?"

"What do you know, Scooter?"

"Nothing."

"You just contradicted your earlier testimony. Which is it? Do you, or don't you?"

"What?"

"Know nothing."

Angela covered her mouth and bit her lip to keep from laughing.

"Yes?" Scooter Morales said, completely lost.

"Let me ask a different question, Mr. Morales." Angela jumped in before Keone could strangle the jerk. "Last night, before you hit me, you admitted to knowing Hopper Alavezos. Did you ever work with Koa Kaleho?"

"I knew who he was, but I haven't sold pakalolo for years."

"Do you know Koa's family?"

"I know his grandson, Kāne. Seems like a good kid."

Finally.

"Have you seen Kāne recently?"

"Not since he started seein' that shrink. His mama's keepin' him on a short leash."

Keone took over. "Then how did you know he was seeing a shrink?"

Morales hesitated. "Word gets around."

"Like word about Hopper's mouth being sewn up?"

"Yeah."

"Where did you hear about that?" Angela asked.

"Some guy. I don't know his name."

"What did he look like?" Keone leaned toward Morales.

"Average."

Angela took a turn. "Height? Weight? Hair color? Age? Race?"

"I told ya, average."

"What is an average age, race, or hair color, Scoot?" Keone's tone reflected growing impatience.

"You know. Age—twenty, thirty, maybe forty. Race—mixed."

"And his hair color?" Angela asked.

"He wore a hat."

Angela looked at Keone. They'd been at this for almost an hour with nothing to show for it. Scooter was stonewalling them.

Keone stepped outside the interrogation room and returned with the officer who would take Scooter back to lock-up. "Say hi to Dave for us," Keone said as Scooter started to get up.

Did he fall back into that chair for a moment before he jumped up?

Angela couldn't be sure.

When Scooter was gone, Angela said, "Keone, I know you still think this has something to do with Dave Walden, but it's a long shot. I called Kāne's mother and arranged to talk with her and her husband this morning. Wanna come?"

"Yeah, if you'll come with me to talk with some of Walden's acquaintances in Lāhainā."

"Deal. Maybe we can get something solid to loosen Scooter's lips."

"Yeah. Like a crowbar." Keone grinned.

They swung by their desks, picked up their gear, and headed to their unmarked Lincoln Town Car. Angela knew she'd be driving. She always drove. But this time, she had a reason. She knew the way by heart.

6

Wednesday, October 30, 9:30 a.m.

Esther Kaleho Hernandez and her husband met Keone and Angela at the front door of their little home in the ʻIao Valley. Keone noted they were one of the lucky families whose home wasn't washed away by the recent flash flooding. The deluge had damaged the National Park and the Kepaniwai public park upstream from their house, before sweeping through the rest of the valley. Building a little higher up on solid rock had been an excellent idea. Their home stood alone above the recently restored highway.

Keone had never met the family. The Lister case occurred while he was on his honeymoon. But Tony had told him about Angela's diligent work on the case, including the initial theory that the shot that killed Lister was fired by accident by the actual shooter's grandson, Manolo.

Elvin Hernandez wrapped Angela in a bear hug before they could even enter the house. "Detective Boyd, your partner saved my family."

Esther Hernandez shook Keone's outstretched hand. "Her name says it all. She's an angel. Please. Come, come."

Keone could tell his partner was uncomfortable with the attention.

She's visited them more than once since the end of the case, Keone thought.

"Mahalo for welcoming us into your home, Mrs. Hernandez." Keone accepted a glass of mango iced tea. "Mr. Hernandez, you were on Oʻahu when your father-in-law shot Rob Lister, is that right?" Keone moved right into the interrogation.

"That's right. I couldn't stand to be around the bastard."

"Is there some new information about the case?" Mrs. Hernandez asked.

"Maybe," Angela replied. "Last year, you helped us identify and locate some people who were involved with your father. Do you remember?"

"I told you about that pilot, Opaka. The one that tried to get Dad off the island. Oh, and I let you know Dad spent time with that truck driver, Hopper."

"That's right. Randy Opaka and Hopper Alavezos. Have you seen either of these men recently? Maybe talking with one of your sons?" Keone asked.

"You mean Kāne, don't you? I understand. He was in a bad place when his grandfather died. But he's been getting help since then. He meets twice a week with a therapist. Having Elvin home has made huge difference, too. Kāne's almost the same, happy boy he used to be."

"I'm happy for him. But, back to my question." Keone needed to keep this on track.

"No. I haven't seen either of them since the day Dad died. Elvin, you saw their pictures in the paper. Have you seen either of them since you got back?"

"No. The only people I've seen around this place have

been the boys, that shrink, the tutor we got to help Kāne with his schoolwork, and a butt-load of construction workers."

"Before you ask, the tutor's name is Mrs. Ochoa and she's almost seventy," Esther added as the front door banged open.

"Ah, here's Manolo," Elvin said.

The boy gave each of his parents a hug.

"Look who's here, Mannie." Esther pointed to the detectives.

"Angela," he shouted. "You need one hug, Auntie."

"Aloha, Manolo. Howzit?"

"Got early release today fo' I give my report first."

Mrs. Hernandez waved Manolo to the couch. "Sergeant Angela and her partner Sergeant Boyd have been asking us some questions. Have you seen Hopper, uh, Mr. Alavezos or that pilot Opaka here or at the school?"

"No, ma'am. Not for months. The last guy I saw hangin' around the school was Scooter Morales. He was talking to some boys, tryin' to get 'em to work for him."

"Was Kāne with the boys?" Angela asked.

"Yes, ma'am. But before I could get ovah dere, Kāne knocked Scooter on his butt and said, 'I don't do drugs no more.' He left Scooter lying on the ground and came ovah to me. All the other boys came, too." Manolo's face lit up with pride for his brother. "Kāne's a different person since Gramps died and Popi came home. We're friends again."

"I'm glad, Manolo," Angela said.

"Mahalo nui iā 'oukou a pa no ke kokua," Keone said, thanking them for all their help. "We'll still need to talk with Kāne, just to close the loop."

"Could you meet him Monday—at his appointment? I'll give the therapist permission to answer any questions you have. His appointment is over by four p.m. Here's the address and phone number." Esther Hernandez reached into a drawer by the phone and handed Angela a business card from the therapist.

"Have any of you seen a man named Blue Herrera?" Keone asked.

Elvin answered first. "He's pretty much a fixture in Wailuku. I've never seen him out here, though. Has he been by your school, Mannie?"

"Nevah. The only place I evah seen him is outside Brandy's."

"Manolo Hernandez, what were you doing at that place?" Esther sounded shocked.

"We used to have to go get Gramps there some nights. You know . . . when he got sleepy. I haven't been there since then. Neither has Kāne."

"We look forward to talking with Kāne on Monday. Have a happy Halloween. Aloha," Keone said as Angela led him out the door.

BACK IN THE CAR, HEADED CROSS-ISLAND TO LĀHAINĀ, Angela waited for Keone to comment on the interview.

"We need to talk with Kāne and see if that was all a big smokescreen. It sounds plausible, but a little too neat to me. What do you think?"

"I hate to say it, but I think they're telling the truth. I got to know Manolo and his mother very well. I think I'd know if they were lying." Angela couldn't lie to Keone either.

"Have you got a plan B?"

"Lieutenant Alcala suggested I follow up on the attorney that got Alavezos out. But I've got nothing else." She also didn't think Keone's hunch would pay off, but she was willing to wait and see. "Who are we going to see in Lāhainā, big guy?"

"Some folks who knew Dave Walden."

"Did you hear back from your DEA friend, Freeman?"

"Uh, yeah."

"Well?"

"The DEA thinks Dave's dead."

Angela waited, and finally said, "But?"

"But they don't have a body."

They were quiet for the rest of the ride. Angela concluded Tony might be right about their theories but kept her opinion to herself. She wouldn't rub it in if Keone didn't.

"Let's eat," Keone said, pointing to Dickenson Square, a shopping area a block off Front Street.

"Lāhainā Coolers? Last time I ate there with you, you ran off to interview the folks at Sam Loftus's office upstairs."

"Dave Walden had his law office here, too. But I'm just here for the burritos."

"Uh huh. Pull my other one, partner. You want to talk to Max."

Keone slid into a parking stall and led them through the outside seating area and up to the bar.

"Hey, Max. Howzit?"

"Well, look who the tide dragged in. Hey, Keone. Hey, Ange. I heard you two were working together now."

"I'm never surprised by what you've heard, Max." Ange smiled as she climbed onto a barstool.

"You each want the usual?"

"Sure," they said in unison.

Max first brought two giant smoothies. "No booze. I figure you on duty."

"Good guess," Angela said.

"So, start asking your lolo questions while we wait for your burritos."

Angela took a sip of her smoothie, letting Keone take the

lead. "You know I don't ask crazy questions. Except when I have weird-ass cases, which happens more and more often these days. Have you seen Hopper, Scooter, or Randy Opaka around recently?"

"Funny you should ask. You remember Lee Marder, Sam Loftus's friend?"

"Yeah."

"He manages the whole complex, you know. And he said he thought he saw Scooter around recently, talking to an old acquaintance of yours. But I told him he was lolo. Just a sec." Max hurried through the kitchen and out the back door to return with Marder in tow.

"Hey, detective. Good to see ya."

"Aloha, Leroy. Good to see you, too. I'm sorry about how things worked out with Sam. I know he was your friend."

"Best friend. But he's a'marchin' to that different drummer these days. I visited him once after they moved him to that asylum, or whatever they call it. The store was open, but the shelves were bare."

Angela joined the conversation. This was exactly what Julie had asked her to follow up with Keone about. "They moved him to that facility in Haʻikū, didn't they? Island Calm?"

"Yeah. That's what they call it. They can paint it blue and call it Thursday, but it's still a frickin' nut house. And both of you need to call me Lee, okay."

"Sorry, Lee," Keone said. "I haven't seen Sam since before we left on our honeymoon. He was in bad shape then."

"Well, he's talking again, but he's still not making any sense. Says he's not the guy who hurt your wife. Says that guy's gone and he's back. It's so sad. Anyway, Max said you was askin' after that little shit on the pink scooter?"

"Yeah. Did you see him?"

"Well, I thought I did. But I also thought he was talking to someone, someone who ain't around here no more." He removed his glasses and scrutinized them. "These specs may need some adjustment. If you know what I mean."

"Tell me what you think you saw."

"I think I saw the Scootman a'talkin' with good old Dave Walden. But that can't be, can it? He got sent up the river."

"Where did you see them?"

"The parking lot behind the center here."

"When was this?"

"A couple days back. No, three. It was late, ten or eleven p.m. They were shouting at each other. Mostly Dave was doing the shouting. Scooter was trying his damnedest to calm him down."

"Did they come to blows?"

"No. By the end Dave seemed to be grateful for something. He even slipped Scooter a few bills. Then I got a call. Alarm at the health center. People always think they keep drugs there overnight. I had 'em put a sign up, but it didn't do no good."

"Uh, what about Scooter and Dave?" Angela asked, knowing Keone wanted to get the man back on track.

"When I got back, they'd both hightailed it."

Lee paused when Max brought the burritos. "Want one, Lee? On the house?"

"No, but thanks for the offer. I better get back at it. I'm up to my ass in alligators, like always."

"See ya, Lee. Next time you see Sam, tell him I'm thinking about him. And let me know how he's doing, yeah?" Keone said and nodded at the older man.

Lee nodded back at Keone before he walked away.

After she finished her own mammoth burrito and put out some of the fire with the smoothie, Angela said, "I guess we get to talk to Scooter again."

"Yep. I'm guessing Walden didn't get blown up a week ago, despite what the FBI concluded. With Dave in the neighborhood, I can see why Scooter might feel safer on the inside right about now."

"Me, too." She doubted they'd need to talk to that therapist about Kāne.

7

Wednesday, October 30, 1:30 p.m. HST

The full name of the woman kneeling on the ruins of the heiau was Leilani Keahilani Kalehale Kalama, but the family just called her Tutu.

This heiau was special for her as it resided on a hidden patch of land at the highest point on the Boyd-Kalama Ranch. Here, high up on the slope of Haleakala Volcano, her favorite spirit communicated with her—when Pele was in the mood.

Tutu began, as always, with a prayer and the proper offering of salt crystals and luau made of the delicate unrolled taro root. Then she began the ancient *hula Pele*, which had little movement except at times sinking to a kneeling position. It began with the first words of *He Oli—O ka mele mua keia o ka hula Pele* (A Song—The first song of the hula Pele):

Mai Kahiki ka wahine, o Pele,(From Kahiki came the woman, Pele,)

Mai ka ʻaina i Pola-pola,(From the land of Pola-pola.)

Mai ka punohu ula a Kāne,(From the red cloud of Kāne,)

Mai ke ao lalapa i ka lani,(Cloud blazing in the heavens,)
Mai ka opua lapa i Kahiki.(Fiery cloud-pile in Kahiki.)

Kahiki, the Hawaiian word for Tahiti represents not only the home of the seafarers that first discovered the Hawaiian Islands, but also the birthplace of the goddess Pele, who legends say travelled from there to the site of the Hawaiian archipelago, where she created the islands from her fires in search of a place to live. She began in the north and worked her way from above Ni'ihau, where Tutu was born, all the way south and east to the Big Island of Hawaii, making her home in Halema'uma'u in the crater of Kilauea. Tutu knew that the geological record mirrored the travels of Pele preserved in her people's legends.

Tutu's faith was strong and had brought her into communion with a spirit of the 'aina she believed to be Pele multiple times in her long life. The vision that now infused her mind confirmed that Pele was once again willing to communicate with her. The hair on the back of her neck tingled. What she saw disturbed her.

8

Wednesday, October 30, 3:30 p.m. HST

Back at the station, Keone and Angela confronted Scooter with what they learned from Lee Marder.

"We have a highly credible witness that swears they saw you having tête-à-tête with Dave Walden in Lahaina three days ago. A discussion that ended with Dave passing you some cash. Let's see you wiggle your way out of that, Scoot." When he'd finished, Keone glared at the little man.

"Whoever told you that is a damn liar. I ain't seen that SOB Walden since I ratted on him to you. And I don't want to see him. I heard he got snuffed," Scooter shouted back.

"Where?" Keone asked.

"Wherever the hell they were hiding him."

"No. I mean where did you hear that?"

"'I heard it on the grapevine,'" Scooter sang, "'and I'm just about to lose my mind.'"

"Funny. What did you mean by hiding him?"

Scooter hesitated. "Holding him. I said holding him. He got convicted, didn't he?"

Serious slip, Scooter. You just told me you knew he was in witness protection and that he was supposedly killed. Only Walden or the FBI could have told him that, and Keone doubted Scooter was on speaking terms with the latter.

At a rap on the door of the interrogation room, Keone stepped out to find Tony Alcala in the hallway.

"I wanted to let you know. We should be able to keep Randy Opaka jumping through hoops 'til Friday. But he'll probably make bail then."

"I'd like a tail put on him whenever he gets out," Keone said.

"And I'd like ice cream sundaes for breakfast, but it's Halloween weekend and we're gonna be up to our asses in shit until Monday."

"I know, I know. Over eighty cops on duty on October thirty-first alone. I read the *Maui News*."

"Why don't you and Angela call it a week? You're both off tomorrow and Scooter's not going anywhere. Let him stew a little more."

Keone shifted his weight. Tony was right. He needed a day to sift through all the data. If Walden iced Hopper, he was probably long gone by now. Besides, Keone had plans for Halloween. That is, Julie had plans for him.

An officer entered the interrogation room to take Scooter back to his cell, and Angela joined them in the hallway.

"Hello, lieutenant. Mind if I join the discussion?"

"Not at all. Did you follow up on Hopper's attorney?"

"I did. He came from off-island and left as soon as the hearing was over. The only address I found for him is in New York City. He's licensed to practice in Hawaii, Nevada, and

California, as well as New York and New Jersey. No word yet on who paid his fee, but I've got a request in to NYPD on that."

"Good work, Angela. But I wouldn't expect to hear anything back from NYPD before Monday. Hey, I just told the big guy to go home and to tell you to go, too. Do you have plans for Halloween?"

When Angela hesitated, "Um . . ."

"We both do," Keone said. "Julie and Linda have us all going to Front Street. Best night of the year."

"Oh, well. Maybe I'll see you there. Goodnight." Alcala turned and disappeared back into his office.

"Ange?"

"What?" Her sharp response pinged his detective radar.

"You still haven't told him, have you?"

"I will. When the time is right." Angela crossed her arms over her chest. Keone knew that posture.

"I could tell him."

"You could also let it go, Keone. Please."

"Okay. But you need to tell him."

"How would you like to tell me everything that happened on your honeymoon?"

Time to change the subject.

"See you tomorrow night."

"We're looking forward to it."

Keone worried about Tony. His old friend might be setting himself up to get hurt. Still, he trusted Angela to do the right thing.

9

Thursday, October 31, 10:00 a.m.

Angela loved playing golf in Kāʻanapali with her new foursome. Each of the three women who joined her this Friday were special to her in different ways. Nancy Lister had been Angela's friend for years and her first golf partner. Nancy and her husband Rob were Angela's next-door neighbors before Angela moved in with Linda. From the moment Angela was assigned to Nancy's husband's shooting, she never forgot she was Nancy's friend first.

Mahealani Boyd was Keone's little sister, but they were already friends before Angela first met Keone in California. Angela learned to ride a horse from Lani's brothers when her family's ranch offered lessons. She always envied Mahealani's sleek body and accomplishments as a dancer. Though comfortable with her own compact body type and proficiency in sports, Angela secretly wished she could hula. Linda knew and goaded her to ask Lani about lessons.

Maybe someday.

The final member of their foursome was new to the game of golf. Julie Boyd had never played before they coerced her into golf lessons. Angela was happy to see that Julie was playing better and having more fun each week since they started playing together.

"Hi, Ange," Julie said as she stopped at the bag drop. Jack and Larry pretended to fight over who would put her bag on the cart. Jack and Larry were fixtures at the course. It wouldn't be the same without their warm greetings and friendly kidding. She hoped they never retired. Jack was the smaller and quicker of the two. He always seemed to be in motion. Larry, with his wavy white hair, exuded calm in the eye of the storm. They were the perfect pair.

When Nancy pulled up behind Julie's car, Larry went off to give her a kiss and grab her clubs.

"Howzit, sarge?" Jack waved to Angela as he put Julie's clubs next to hers on the cart. "You gonna break seventy today?"

"Maybe I bettah try break eighty first?"

"Aw, you do mo' bettah 'n dat every week. Don't you try sandbag me."

Julie returned after parking her car. "That husband of mine still making you do all his work for him, Ange?"

"Not all, just most. How're your hula lessons going?"

Mahealani walked over then. "She's doin' great. A natural."

I'm glad somebody is.

"I have a great teacher," Julie said.

Nancy joined them, and the foursome was complete. "Hey, Lani, you going to the Merrie Monarch again next year?"

The Merrie Monarch festival in Hilo on the Big Island was the premiere hula competition on the islands and Mahealani's *halau* had won many times when she was competing. "They asked me to perform an exhibition number during the final evening of the event and serve as a judge. I'm a little nervous. I'm getting older, you know."

"Don't even," Angela said. "We each have fifteen years on you, keiki."

"Fifteen? I wish," Nancy said.

They all laughed, before the starter, Eline, came over. "Ready to go?"

"Yeah. I paid upstairs already," Mahealani said. "June and Celeste gave me one hard time about losing last week. But Dale stood up for me."

Angela was happy with today's pairing. She needed private time to talk with Julie about a couple mysteries they shared.

AFTER SIX HOLES, THE TEAMS WERE EVEN. THEY CROSSED a surface street, drove across a bridge that spanned Honoapi'i-lani Highway, and arrived at the seventh tee. When they saw that the foursome ahead of them was still waiting to tee off, Nancy and Mahealani took the opportunity to visit the restroom. Finally, alone, Angela asked Julie the question she'd been avoiding. "Did Keone finally tell you something about what was still eating at him after the cruise?"

"Yeah. The chili worked. Thanks for the suggestion. He knows the man who killed the girl on the Acropolis wasn't Thanatos. He thinks that maniac is still out there somewhere. He's having his friend Tom at the DEA keep an eye out for any similar murders."

"What about his friend the Europol agent?"

"Andreos was reprimanded for his handling of the case. Keone's reached out to him but thinks the agent's emails are being scrutinized. Have you made any progress on the other thing that's bothering him?"

"Maybe a little. I heard Keone mutter something under his breath when he thought I couldn't hear. Something about Sam Loftus, a shave, and a haircut. Mean anything to you?"

"He had a nightmare on our flight from L.A. to Chicago. He screamed out, 'No beard,' before I woke him. He also followed up with my sister about something related to the Loftus case. I think you're onto something. Please keep probing. Uh oh, here come Nancy and Mahealani. They look like they're having a serious conversation, too."

"I think Mahealani finally read Rob Lister's book. I had a lot of questions for Nancy when I read it," Julie said as they drove the short distance to the next tee.

"Did you ever get Keone to read it?"

"No, but Tutu loved it. She's discussed it during our lessons."

"How's that going?"

"I'm working hard on my Hawaiian, but there are a lot of older words I still don't know. It helps that Tutu is incorporating Hawaiian culture and family history into my lessons. I feel a lot less awkward around her and the other senior members of the family."

They switched teams after the ninth hole, preventing Ange from following up any further with Julie regarding Keone's thoughts about Sam Loftus.

She was now paired with Mahealani, enjoying the views from the course on this sparkling, clear October day. When you had views like this on each hole, it was hard to get upset over a bad shot.

When they reached the sixteenth tee, Mahealani pointed to the ocean past Black Rock. "Look! My first humpback of the season," she called out. Angela followed her arm and saw a huge splash.

"A breech. Do it again, Tita," Angela shouted.

As if on command, the massive marine mammal rose completely out of the water. Its body completed a pirouette before splashing back onto the surface.

"Tita?" Mahealani gave Ange a look.

"I know. This early it's probably a young male, but I always like to imagine I'm one with the whale."

"You go, girl," Mahealani said.

———

Sitting in Roy's Restaurant inside the clubhouse after their round, Julie looked out floor-to-ceiling windows at the panorama of the eighteenth hole. They chattered like young girls over their nineteenth-hole beverages until Keone and Linda arrived. Linda turned the conversation to tonight's annual Halloween celebration in Lāhainā.

While her friends reminisced about earlier, wilder versions of the event, Julie's mind reflected on her costume for this year and the minor alterations she'd made to disguise the slight changes to her silhouette that had begun to appear. No one had noticed yet, and she wanted to keep it that way as long as possible.

10

Thursday, October 31, 5:00 p.m.

Keone knew he'd regret this. He'd rather have a root canal than face Ange and Linda right now.

Linda Carroll broke out in peals of deep, throaty laughter when he and Julie arrived outside the Cheeseburger in Paradise restaurant on Front Street.

If Julie hadn't held tight to his arm, Keone might have run back to their car.

Why did I let Julie talk me into this?

"I love it. The Scorpion King. How perfect," Linda gasped out when she was finally able to speak. "I always said you looked enough like The Rock to be his brother."

"He's Samoan. I only agreed to wear this thing so Julie could dress up like the evil sorceress," Keone growled. By, *this thing,* he meant the long braided black hair extensions that extended to his mid-back, a necklace of metal circlets in a chain around his neck with complementary bands around his biceps. Otherwise, he was naked above the waist.

Julie threatened to oil him up before he balked at the mess. She compromised by sprinkling some golden glitter over his body. The leather leggings were less embarrassing despite the gold scorpion clasp holding the belt together. He was actually grateful for the rest of his outfit, a vicious looking bronze scimitar in one hand and an ornate bronze shield in the other. They were clearly made of plastic, but if anyone got too close or too sarcastic, he was fully prepared to swing them.

"You do look sultry and dangerous, Julie. Especially in that exotic black wig and headpiece. Who made all this?" Angela said, defusing the moment.

"Janet, with a tiny bit of help from me. I found the original drawings online from the movie. The hardest part was making my neckpiece."

Keone found Julie's costume far more enjoyable. A wide necklace of small gold baubles and jewels extended from the base of Julie's neck, over her shoulders, and all the way down to the top of her breasts. Aside from a textured golden bikini, she wore little else, except nearly transparent golden slacks with embroidered hieroglyphs. Her red hair was hidden under a black wig surmounted by a golden tiara from which a segmented broach dangled over her forehead.

"And what about you two?" Julie replied. "You look appropriately raggedy."

"I didn't want to wear a costume, but Linda made me," Ange said, from under a curly red-yarn wig topped by white sailor hat with a blue puff on it.

"You look great, Ange. But I wanted to be Raggedy Andy," Linda said, pouting. Her, blue flowered pinafore and bright, white apron complemented Angela's red and blue sailor suit. Both wore black shoes and red-and-white striped socks and had their faces made up with rosy cheeks and bright-red triangle noses.

"You look cute as a button as Raggedy Ann," Angela replied.

"It's quite an experience to be laughed at by both Raggedy Ann and Andy. But I forgive you. Tonight's all about fun. Let's go see if Jennifer has our table ready." Keone guided them all up the stairs to the top level of the restaurant and its fabulous view of Front Street.

Once the tiny tornado that was their waitress saw them, hugs and kisses accompanied them to their table. The Keiki Parade was just starting with parents and kids dancing down the street in every costume imaginable. Keone knew Julie looked forward to it, especially this year. He, on the other hand, looked forward to cheddar-cheese-smothered fries and juicy burgers.

But watching the colorful mélange below, he thought of the gods of his Tutu's childhood stories and smiled.

"Why the smile, big guy?' Angela asked.

"Just some keiki memories."

"I can't imagine you marching in a keiki Halloween parade."

"Good. Because I never did." He hoped that would end this line of interrogation from his partner.

"You could tonight," Linda said. "Julie, you did a great job on his face and body makeup. With the smudges of mud and fake blood he looks like he just wrassled an alligator."

A distinguished-looking older gentleman from the adjacent table tapped Julie on her shoulder. "I'm sorry to bother you, but we're from Indiana. This is all new to us," he said softly, indicating the parade below.

Julie took charge. "Where in Indiana?"

"Carmel. It's just—"

"North of Indianapolis. I know. I grew up in Indiana."

"No kidding? Where?"

"I grew up near Wabash."

"Up by West Lafayette?"

"That's the one. Went to college at IUPUI in Indy and had a lot of friends there from Carmel."

"A true Hoosier," the man proclaimed loudly.

Keone never thought of Julie as a Hoosier. She'd worked so hard to become one with her adopted home.

"Enough about me." Julie extended her arm toward Front Street. "Let me tell you about Halloween in Lāhainā. It has quite a history. Beginning around 1989, it became the premier event on the islands this time of year. They used to call it the Mardi Gras of the Pacific."

"Used to?" the man's wife asked, glancing at Julie's bikini.

"By 2008 the name caused people to imagine that they were free to get a little too wild as the evening wore on. The mayor banned the sponsored event for two years, before the Lāhainā Town Action Committee and the Office of Economic Development arranged for a more supervised event."

Linda continued, "It's still great fun, but there's a significant police presence now. They do a great job of gently guiding those who might be a bit too lubricated or exhibitionist off Front Street."

"Oh my." The couple gulped in unison.

"Don't worry, the crazy stuff never starts until an hour after sunset. Enjoy yourself until then," Julie said with a knowing grin.

Keone enjoyed the way the women told the truth without dampening tourism.

They mirrored the efforts of Maui PD precisely.

Mirrored. There's that word again.

The word triggered another memory. Sam Loftus raising his right arm when told to raise his left.

Not tonight.

He ordered his subconscious to keep quiet and Jennifer to bring him another Longboard Lager. He wondered if anyone had picked up on the fact that Julie was sticking with non-alcoholic smoothies.

AFTER DINNER, THE FOUR FRIENDS WALKED UP AND DOWN Front Street taking and posing for pictures and soaking up the massive good spirit of the crowd. As Julie paused by someone dressed as Achmed the Dead Terrorist, Keone waved at a family dressed like the Flintstones. Angela snapped pictures of both tableaus.

Keone thought Julie's evil sorceress blended better with Achmed than his Scorpion King did with animated cave people but grinned and gave a shaka. Angela captured his rare public smile.

What the hell. It's Halloween.

"You feelin' your inner Hawaiian tonight, partner?" Angela asked.

"He sure is," boomed a voice behind them.

Lieutenant Tony Alcala wore his dress uniform.

"That's cheating," Linda hollered to him.

"No. Technically I'm on duty, so it's allowed. Angela, could I have a minute?"

Keone started to intercede, but Julie grabbed his hand and did a pretty good imitation of an arm lock.

"She can handle this," Julie whispered through her smile and gritted teeth.

"I'll meet you all at the shave ice before we leave," Angela called back as she walked off with Tony.

Keone reluctantly continued along Front Street with Julie and Linda. They walked up and down the street, taking in all the sights. Keone spotted Mick Fleetwood handing out candy to the kids in front of the entrance to his restaurant as they strolled past. Maui was so laid back that even local celebrities could relax and be themselves. He'd seen Oprah shopping, Clint Eastwood grabbing a cup at Starbuck's, and Willie Nelson multiple times in his restaurant and bar in Pāʻia.

"I'm about done in," Linda said as they returned to the shave-ice stand after a complete circuit of Front Street.

"Me, too. I need to sit down," Julie replied.

"I'll get in line for the shave ices. You and the big guy are each getting your usual, unless you say otherwise."

"Thanks, Lin. You're the best," Keone said and meant it.

Keone guided Julie to an empty bench to wait for Linda. His feet enjoyed the respite, and his eyes enjoyed the nimble, body-painted reveler who strolled by.

Julie saw her, too. "Okay. After the shave ice, we're heading home. The wilder part of the evening is about to begin. And I don't want you to start arresting people. I wonder if Angela—"

A ringtone from Julie's smartphone interrupted. Given all the noise on Front Street, Keone was surprised he recognized the song "Popular" from *Wicked*. That specific tone meant Janet, Julie's sister, was calling.

"I wondered where you were. What? When?" Julie stopped talking and worry-lines etched her face.

"Is Janet—"

Julie held up her palm, stopping him.

"Damn. Here, tell Keone." She passed him the phone with a flushed face.

Keone wondered if the rumor about Dave had proven true.

But why would they notify Janet before Julie? She was the one that married the jerk.

"Keone, it's Sam. He took him from the clinic. Why would he take him? Where—" Janet began.

"Slow down. Who took who from the clinic?" Keone was afraid of the answer.

"Dave. Dave Walden. He knocked out two of the attendants and grabbed Sam. Where would he take him? Why?"

"Janet, we'll get right on it. We'll start at the clinic." Translating Julie's hand signals, Keone added, "And Julie will come stay with you." Sensing both sisters were now calmer, he handed the phone back to Julie.

Hitting mute, she said to Keone, "You go get Angela. I'll tell Linda what's up and take her home on my way to Janet's. I just wish Mike wasn't on Oʻahu until Saturday." Then she switched off mute, and he heard her continuing to calm her sister as he walked off to find Angela.

After further consoling Janet, Julie caught up to Linda ordering the three shave ices at the colorful stand, just off Front Street.

Linda took one look at Julie and told the vendor to forget the order. "What happened?"

"Dave Walden just abducted Sam Loftus. Keone will go with Angela in their patrol unit. I can drop you at home, or—"

"Go to your sister. She needs you. I'll get home. Go. Now."

Her mention of Sam Loftus brought memories rushing back to Julie. The mild-mannered brother-in–law confusing right and left and thinking he was married to her and not Janet. Sam pretending to be cured and moving back in with Janet. Sam shoving a chloroform-soaked cloth over Julie's face before kidnapping her and taking her to a remote cabin. Sam trying to convince her that he wasn't from this Earth, but some parallel universe where they were married. Sam calmly describing their non-existent children and his plan to recreate them. Sam holding her down and trying to, to . . .

Julie shook off the memories when she reached their car. She needed to focus on getting to Janet's ASAP. But not so fast she'd fly off the steep cliffs overlooking the ocean on the Pali highway.

11

Keone scanned the frenetic crowd, people bumping into him right and left. *Angela where are you?*

Laughter over his left shoulder caused him to turn. Tony and Angela were heading his way.

"Did you see that auntie dressed like a show girl back there?" Tony asked.

"She wasn't dressed, Tony. She was painted," Angela said.

Their laughter stopped when they saw Keone's face.

"We have to go, Ange," he said with no preamble. "Dave Walden abducted Sam Loftus from the mental clinic."

"Shit," Angela and Tony said in unison.

"Ange and I will head over to Island Calm and see what actually happened. Then I'd like to swing by and press Scooter for more answers."

"Good plan. With Walden looking more and more like Hopper's killer, Loftus could be in mortal danger. I'll get a BOLO out on both of 'em."

"Thanks, Tony," Keone said as he and Angela ran to their unmarked squad car.

"Maybe I'll get some helos in the air," Tony called—to their backs.

ANGELA SPED THEM TOWARD SAM LOFTUS'S LAST KNOWN location, Island Calm. At her side, Keone brooded, remembering his last visit to the man who had caused them all so much pain.

Throughout Keone's visit on July fifth, Sam had huddled, catatonic, in the corner of his room at the Molokini Ward of Maui Memorial Hospital. Since returning from his honeymoon, Keone had called Sam's doctor, Drayton, to ask about the shaving mystery and if there had been any new developments in Sam's case. Drayton hadn't seen Sam on July fourth, as he was on Oahu celebrating the holiday, but when Drayton returned on the fifth, Sam had looked exactly as Keone had seen him with long hair and a beard. As for his condition, the psychiatrist said Sam was no longer catatonic but was obsessed with new delusions.

Angela intruded on his thoughts. "What's on your mind? The Loftus case or the Walden case?"

Keone looked at his partner as if surprised she was there. "Both. But especially Loftus. I never trusted Walden but had just about started to trust Sam Loftus—when he kidnapped Julie. There were always a lot of unanswered questions from both cases. Still are."

"Wasn't it a big Hawaiian that looked a lot like you who told me we never get all our questions answered in most investigations?" Angela asked.

"Thanks for reminding me. There's one thing about the Loftus case that I never shared with you. Something that I couldn't resolve." Keone paused. "I had conflicting eyewitness reports on Sam Loftus's hairiness. Please don't laugh."

Angela didn't, but he noticed she kept her eyes on the road and both hands tight on the wheel.

"Here are the deets. On July fifth, I visited Sam Loftus in the Molokini ward at Maui Memorial Hospital. He was catatonic and had a long beard and long disheveled hair. Dr. Drayton and Dr. Hasselbach were both there and saw what I saw. However, before he left, Hasselbach told me he'd seen Loftus the day before and the man had just had a shave and a haircut. The next day Julie and I left on our honeymoon."

"So, Hasselbach was mistaken. Witnesses make mistakes all the time. And you had three witnesses to hairy Loftus, including yourself," Angela said with a quick side-glance at Keone.

"That's what I thought, but decided I needed to find some other witnesses who saw Loftus on July fourth."

"Did you?"

"Yes, Ange, and that's the problem. I even called Janet while we were on our honeymoon because she gave Sam divorce papers on July fourth. She said Sam was clean-shaven, had neatly trimmed hair, and was wearing his best suit."

"Uh, oh."

"I then found out that Drayton was away on Oahu on July fourth and hadn't seen his patient, but a psychiatrist who subbed for him confirmed for me that Sam looked exactly as Janet described on July fourth. I even tracked down the orderly, a guy named Louie who cut Sam's hair and gave him a shave on Louie's last night working on the ward, July third."

"Shit," Angela said.

"You took the words right out of my mouth."

They pulled into the circular drive of Island Calm and spotted Dr. Evan Drayton pacing in front of the entrance.

When they exited the car, Dr. Drayton approached hesitantly. "That **is** you underneath all that makeup, isn't it Keone?" The doctor's voice was unnaturally high-pitched. He had a cut on his forehead and a bruise over his eye.

"Sorry about our Halloween costumes, Evan. We got here as fast as we could. Just tell us exactly what happened." Keone decided he'd alternate questions with Angela. That had worked well in the past. But they'd have to keep it brief. Drayton seemed close to losing it.

Drayton took a deep breath. "The timing couldn't have been worse. I was finally cracking through Sam's shell in our sessions. Then that maniac barged in and knocked me on my ass. He assaulted the two attendants who tried to stop him with the butt of his gun."

"Are you sure it was Dave Walden?" Angela asked.

"Yes. David Walden, Sam's best friend and former brother-in-law. I thought I knew him, but the man I saw tonight was totally out of control. Just kept yelling at Sam as he dragged him out the door, but Sam didn't respond."

"Did you say Walden was armed?" Keone asked.

"Yes. He had the biggest damn pistol I've ever seen. That's what he hit the attendants with."

"What was he yelling at Sam?" Angela asked.

"He was in a rage. Couldn't make out much. I did hear him say that Sam was faking and had ratted him out. He said he knew how to take care of rats. Then he said something strange. Something about a frog."

"Did he actually say the word frog?" Keone probed.

"No. He said 'that slimeball hopper,' but I assumed—" A patrol car pulled up with Tony inside.

"How did Sam react?" Angela asked.

"He didn't. He seemed to have reverted to complete catatonia."

"You said seemed," Keone noted.

"Well, if that maniac had come at me, I might have acted catatonic too. Sam had come so far this week. To lapse back that quickly . . . But it was quite a shock."

"Thank you, Doctor. You've been a great help." Keone caught a glimpse of Tony approaching out of the corner of his eye. "Lieutenant Alcala will ask you some more questions, but Angela and I need to get moving. Don't worry, we'll find them, and I'll call you when we do."

"I hope you're going by the station to change before you go anywhere else," Tony said as he rushed up.

"Definitely. We have a few questions for that bald-faced liar, Scooter Morales. It looks like Walden killed Hopper and thinks Loftus squealed on him, too."

12

Thursday, October 31, 8:00 p.m.

Keone knew that the key to finding Walden and Loftus was inside the twisted mind of the man being escorted from his cell to Interrogation Room One. They'd already received one disappointment on entering the station. Randy Opaka had made bail earlier than expected and left a few minutes before they arrived.

Not good.

A hand propelled Scooter into the room. A snotty grin spread on his face. "Hey, bradah, long time no see. You both look real cute in dem outfits. Wish I had some candy to give you kids."

Keone pushed away from the table, intent on punching the smug SOB. Angela grabbed his right hand, pulling him back down and taking over with Morales. "We haven't had time to change, smartass. Speaking of change, are you ready to tell us the truth?"

"Again with the questions, sarges? What, you tink I took

one college class while you been gone? You gonna get dah same answers you got last time. Always nice to see you smilin' faces, doh. Hey, why you ain't smilin'?"

"Dave Walden."

"I told you befoah. That Leroy's one crazy haole."

"Walden kidnapped Sam Loftus about an hour ago," Angela said.

"I don't know one ting 'bout dat."

"I want to believe you, Scoot, but . . ." Keone cocked his head and cracked his knuckles. "Since you lied to us about meeting Walden, looks like you're gonna go down as an accessory to both murder and kidnapping. And we can't help you with the feds." Keone saw Scooter begin to squirm. Point made.

Time for Angela to ask the questions.

"When you met Walden outside Lāhainā Coolers, we know he paid you to tell him where to find Hopper." Angela paused, watching him.

"He was crazy. Waldo threatened to kill me for what I told Keone that helped catch him last time, unless I told him where to find Hopper. Said he'd be back for me if I lied."

"So, you told him," Keone said.

Scooter nodded.

"What did Hopper ever do to Dave Walden?" Keone asked.

"Not one ting, 'til . . ."

"Until what?" Angela asked.

"Dis lawyer come to town asking everybody if dey knew where David Walden be hidin'. Nobody did, 'cluding Hopper. But Hopper's cousin work in dat federal building in Honolulu. She do some kine data entry. Hopper call her from prison, and she start snoopin' fo' him. I guess she found zumting, cause dat lawyer got Hopper sprung. Waldo knew 'bout dat lawyer and who paid him. He connect dem dots. Get me, Keone?"

"I get you. And you might be able to live with the charge that will come from that. But if you know how Walden got on the island and don't tell us, you'll go down for all of it." Keone put a dose of concern in his voice.

"Opaka."

"Good." Angela slapped the table. "Now, Scooter, my next question is very important. Think carefully before you answer. While Randy Opaka was in jail for his part in the Lister case, I watched the highway department work with Hawaiian Homelands to turn his airstrip in Hāna back into jungle. Where's he flying from now?"

Scooter did think, for a long time.

"Oh, fuck it!" Scooter finally said. "He got one strip up in Makawao, not far from dat ranch where you grow up, Keone. He fix it up like da uddah one."

"The old Marine strip from the war?" Keone asked.

"Dat's dah one."

"Meeting's over," Keone said pushing away from the table and knocking on the door.

"Wait," Scooter yelled, when the officer entered to take him away.

"What?" Keone asked.

"You be sure take care dat guy dis time, or he come see me next."

Keone smiled. "Officer, please see that our witness gets safely back to his cell."

After they changed into their uniforms, Angela rushed to their car, but Keone lagged behind. Pulling out his cell he thought, *I hope those kanaka are at the ranch this evening. I could really use their help.*

Janet hadn't stopped crying since Julie arrived. Janet once shared this house in Pukalani with Sam Loftus, but Julie saw nothing that reflected those days inside or out. Sam's bromeliad garden was gone, replaced with rose bushes, Janet's favorite. Every piece of furniture that held a memory of Sam was gone and the rooms repainted in pastel colors that Sam would have hated. The house was now bright and filled with avant-garde works of art that reflected Jan's new life with Mike Fowler. With Mike on Oahu until tomorrow evening, Julie needed to be here for her sister.

Julie's smartphone buzzed. She pulled it from her pocket and the caller ID confirmed it was Keone. She answered with a tap on the screen but kept her arm wrapped securely around her sister's shoulder. "Hi. Any news?"

She listened without interrupting as her husband provided a complete update. When he paused for breath, she asked, "Are you going after them at the airstrip?"

"Yeah, we're in the car now," Keone said. "You can tell Janet whatever you think will help. I called my brothers. Kimo and Lono are already riding up Haleakalā to the strip. Padraig will meet us at the ranch with rides. We'll stop Walden before they leave the island."

"Tell those big, lovable kanaka to be careful. And you and Ange stay safe, too."

"We will. Alcala put BOLOs out on Dave and Opaka, so they'll be taking back roads. They don't know we're onto their destination. That means they'll try to be invisible, not quick. We should have Dave in custody by morning, but it's gonna be a long night. Try to get Janet to rest."

"I will. Just keep us in the loop."

"Will do. Love you."

"Me, too. Go get 'em."

"What did he say?" Janet asked as soon as Julie ended the

call. "Have they found Sam? It's all my fault, you know. The divorce ruined him."

"No, Jan. Sam's problems started way before the divorce. Don't forget how he ended up in that mental hospital."

"I can never forget what he did to you, Jules . . . and what he tried to do. But I also remember Sam from before the car accident. What if he was telling the truth? What if that lunatic that kidnapped you was a different person from—"

"A parallel universe? Can you hear yourself?"

"I know it's too crazy. Still, the person who David took is the man I once loved. Keone has to get him back, even if he's sick."

"He will. They have a good idea where they're headed. Keone and Ange are on their way."

"But how can they know for certain, Jules?"

"He and Ange scared Scooter Morales into spilling the beans. A hood named Randy Opaka is going to try to take Dave and Sam off the island."

"From where?"

For the first time, Julie hesitated. "I'll tell you, but you have to promise not to leave my side, okay? Think it out."

"Well, the only ways off island are by boat or plane. I'm sure the police are watching the airports and docks. They're probably headed for a private airstrip or harbor."

"That's the sister I know and love. They're headed for an airstrip used by a drug transporter. But the good news is it's up by the Boyd-Kalama ranch. Keone and his brothers know every inch of that land better than anybody in the world."

"Is Keone sure?"

"He's so confident he sent two of his brothers ahead to keep an eye on the place until he can get there."

"But it's so far."

"Keone said he and Ange will get there before Dave. Dave

and Opaka will need to take back roads to avoid the police, while Keone and Angela can head straight to the ranch with lights and sirens." She didn't mention that they'd probably have to take horses from there to the strip like his brothers had.

"I'm so glad Keone's in charge. If anyone can stop David, he can," Janet said.

Julie saw the corners of her lips twitch upward for the first time that evening.

The teapot whistled, breaking the moment, but Julie gave Janet a big hug before heading to brew their tea.

Janet followed her sister into the kitchen and slipped her arm over her shoulder. "Say, didn't you go to the doctor today? What's the news?"

Janet was the only person other than Keone with whom she'd shared the ship's doctor's suspicions. Maybe the good news would help her sister get through this evening. "Okay, Jan. I do have news, but you can't tell anyone else."

13

Thursday, October 31, 8:15 p.m.

Angela deftly guided their unmarked squad car up the highway toward Makawao at top speed, with lights and siren opening a path. She'd heard the end of Keone's call to his brothers and the entire conversation with Julie. "How long will it take them to get to the airstrip?"

"In the dark, the ride up alone is twenty to thirty minutes. Based on when I called and the time to get saddled and ready, they won't arrive for another five minutes at the earliest. I just hope the plane's still—"

Keone's cell rang. The person on the other end of the line was whispering. Angela could only hear Keone's half of the conversation, but what she heard was encouraging.

"Thank God, it's still there," Keone said.

Whispers.

"Damn, I told you not to get that close."

More whispers.

"That's good to know but stay out of sight from now on. I mean it."

A suppressed laugh and more whispers.

"Yeah. That would help. I haven't been up that trail for a while and never in the dark. Listen, Lono, you two kanaka need be careful. See ya dere." Keone ended the call and turned to Angela.

"The plane's still there?" Angela asked.

"Yeah. But no sign of Walden or the pilot yet. The strip's deserted. My idiot brothers checked out the only building."

"They took a big risk."

"I know. They think they're too big to get hurt. But I know better. I'd told them to just get close enough to observe the strip."

"But they knew enough about police procedure to understand how important that information would be to us, despite the potential danger."

"I told you. They're lolo."

"What will they do now?"

"Kimo and Lono will stay out of sight and continue to watch the strip from the trees—or I'll kill them."

"And Padraig?"

"Padraig stayed back to help guide us out there. He'll have everything ready for us by the time we get there."

She could tell Keone was anxious and knew enough to keep quiet. But when he said, "Hey, good job with Tony, by the way. How did he handle rejection?" she broke out laughing.

"What?"

"Your brudahs aren't the only lolos."

"Huh?" Keone sounded completely confused.

"Tony's known I was gay, like fo' evah."

"So, what did he need to talk with you about privately?"

"His son." Angela glanced over at Keone.

"Tim? He moved over from Oʻahu a few months ago, yeah?"

"That's right, big guy. Tony's ex, Moani, got remarried and moved to the mainland with their daughter, but Tim wanted to stay in the islands. He and Tony have been spending more time together. And Tim decided it was time for him to open up to his dad about an important reality."

"Tim's gay?" Keone smiled.

"Ironic, yeah? Tony wanted my advice about how to let Tim know he's proud of him and supports him being who he truly is. Tony knows he can be a little reserved and doesn't want Tim to interpret that as disapproval."

"I'm sure you gave him good advice."

"I told him how I'd like my parents to react. That seemed to help. Tony's a good guy, you know?" Angela's words were upbeat, but her expression was not.

"Yeah, I know. So, you still haven't told your parents."

"You know how damn conservative my family can be. Mama might forgive me, someday, but Popi . . ."

"So, you've decided not to give them a chance to do the right thing?"

"Hey!"

"Ange, they love you. And I know you love them. They may have trouble with this, who knows? But you're strong enough to do what it takes for you and Linda to be together."

"I can't just spring something like this on them."

"You don't need to. Take your time but start. You think it was easy to bring one haole girl home to my Tutu? I was scared shitless. But she fell in love with Julie, just like I did. Your family likes Linda, don't they?"

"Sure, but they don't know . . . everything."

"Don't you think they might suspect?"

"Not Popi."

"Do you think they want to hurt Linda or you?"

"No, but—"

"Just spend more time with them. The two of you. And see what happens."

"I'll think about it."

"Good."

A grin crept over Angela's features. "As long as we're finally talking about personal stuff . . ."

"Uh, oh."

"Today at golf, Julie told me you'd finally shared your concerns about that mass murderer on your honeymoon cruise. I'm glad. I'm also glad you finally told me about that evidence that's been bugging you about Sam Loftus. As a detective, I agree you can't ignore it."

Keone hesitated. "You don't think I'm crazy?"

"Look, I told you everything about the Lister case. How I followed the leads from his impossible manuscript. How I came to believe he'd really found some way to talk to his family after he was killed. Even how I heard his spirit guide in my head before I woke up in the hospital. I've continued to have dreams with Calla in them. One since we started working on this case —about you and a baby. We're partners—and friends. I don't think either of us is crazy."

"You saw a baby?" Keone said. "Wow! I guess it wouldn't hurt to keep our minds open."

"That's what you told me when I called you on your honeymoon. Maybe, just maybe, 'There are more things in heaven and Earth, Horatio, than are dreamt of in your philosophy.' Like Mr. Shakespeare said," Angela replied.

"Oh, and Julie's pregnant. Don't tell a soul," Keone said and turned back to the window. As she watched him, she realized something. For the first time since she was shot, she was not embarrassed about what she'd experienced.

14

They arrived at the Boyd-Kalama ranch. But before they got out of the car, Angela needed to ask, "Have you talked to Sam since you got back?"

"To be honest, I was afraid to. Now I may never get the chance."

"What about Walden? I thought the FBI said he was dead."

"They found his severed finger at the site where he was in witness protection. A farm that had been blown to pieces when attacked by members of the Russian mob."

Angela knew there was more to the story, but that could wait. She was ready to tackle Walden and Opaka.

Angela caught sight of Keone's eldest brother on a huge horse over by the barn. Their grandmother, Tutu, held the reins to two other horses nearby. *If anyone expects me to go for a pony ride tonight, they're sadly mistaken.*

Padraig looked up as they approached. "You been in a fight, little Brah?"

Although Angela had cleaned off her makeup when they changed into their uniforms, Keone had forgotten he was wearing some, too. "It's from my damn Halloween costume. What's new at the airstrip?"

"Still no pilot or passengers when Kimo call five minutes ago. You sure dis da place, Brah?"

Angela felt a flicker of concern for the first time since Scooter had spilled his guts.

Keone patted his brother's horse and grinned. "We get it straight from da horse's mouf. Brah."

THE RAT TRAP WHERE DAVE HELD SAM LOFTUS WAS AT the furthest edge of Rose Ranch on Haleakalā Volcano. Dave once used the shack to store merchandise, in the early years of his crystal-meth operation. Abandoned for years, the splintery structure provided little shelter from the cool winds that whipped across the volcano at this altitude.

Dave realized the irony of keeping Sam here. He was just setting up this place when he and Sam went on that memorable kayaking trip. The trip where Sam refused to be his partner in the business that made his fortune.

Why did Sam have to be so finicky about the letter of the law? I'm the lawyer, after all.

Most right-thinking people considered a little chemical modification of their reality a victimless crime, like prostitution. Most hookers needed their mood elevators as much as everyone else. But perfect Sam was always faithful to his wife and drank in moderation.

Until he tried to rape my ex-wife, that is.

He knew Sam was still doing his crazy act but found it humorous to share aloud everything that happened since they last spoke in Sam's hospital room before Keone and that DEA agent arrested him on Molokaʻi.

No problem. Sam won't be sharing what I tell him—act or no act.

"Sure, I took witness protection when they offered it. What choice did I have? They nailed five of seven big guns in the Russian mob thanks to me. I even let that detective convince me to let Julie go. What a laugh. She'd been as good as gone for a long time by then. I heard they got married. I didn't give a shit."

Sam remained unresponsive, but Dave continued as though he could hear him.

"They put me in this tiny town in eastern Kansas. The place was such a Hicksville, I imagined myself as Oliver Wendell Douglas on *Green Acres*. Remember when we watched the re-runs at IU? Come to think of it, Douglas was a hot-shot lawyer like me."

If Sam remembered, he didn't show it.

"I learned to drive a tractor and even planted some crops on a few of the acres the government provided. A neighbor helped me and tried not to laugh too hard at my flubs. I was even looking forward to watching my first crop grow when they came."

Still no response from Sam. *What an actor.*

"The Russians knew I'd ratted on 'em, but not where to find me. At least not until they sent one of their attorneys to Maui. The shyster talked to everybody close to me but came up empty. Finally, he talked to all the guys in local prisons who ever worked for me, including one Hopper Alavezos. He had a cousin who hacked the DEA computers. Once the info passed from Hopper to the shyster to the Russians, I was a marked man."

How can Sam remain still so long? You'd think he'd get a cramp or something.

"Forgetting I was now clean and sober, the Russian mob

sent too few thugs. I'd planned for such a contingency and booby-trapped the farmhouse, the same way I wired the lab in our house in upcountry and a few other enterprises I've been associated with. My expert touch with explosives and electronics made a difference once again. All the authorities found were pieces. I made sure one of the pieces they found was mine. A pinky finger is a tiny price to pay for freedom. I learned that from *Harry Potter and the Prisoner of Azkaban*. I read all the Harry Potter books in Hicksville, not much else to do. Oh, Sam, try to guess my favorite character. I know you claim to hate fantasy stories. But give it a try anyway."

Sam continued to gaze into the depths of nowhere.

"No? Oh well. Then I'm sure as hell not going to tell you."

No reaction from Sam.

"Time to go, Sam. I don't suppose you'd be willing to drop the act and walk out to the van. No? All right. I'll carry you one last time. We've got a plane to catch."

ANGELA APPRECIATED KEONE'S CONFIDENCE THAT THEY were going to the right place but wasn't confident they'd make it in time. Opaka and Walden would want to leave well before sunrise.

"These are for you," Tutu said in Hawaiian, indicating the horses.

"I didn't sign up for this. I know you folks use ATVs on this ranch. Why can't I take one of those? More my style," Angela grumped.

"Quit complaining," Keone snapped back. "This is the only *quiet* way to get there before they do. I know you can ride a horse, Ange."

"Can doesn't equal will, especially in the middle of the night on a trail I've never seen before."

"Padraig will guide us all the way. It'll be fun. Like when my brothers taught you to ride." Keone grinned.

Like hell. "Keone, I hate this idea. But I'll do it on one condition," Angela said.

"What do you want?"

"The rest of Walden's story and the whole story about Thanatos."

"What story?" Padraig asked.

"You wouldn't be interested, Brah. You take the lead. Let's go."

Before they could leave, Tutu tugged on Keone's jacket and said something to him in Hawaiian that Angela couldn't understand. Keone nodded and they left,

But they'd only ridden a few feet up the hill when Angela said, "I believe the FBI discovered a piece of Mr. Walden on a farm."

Keone resigned himself to telling more of each story until they could get to the airstrip. "Okay, okay. The farm was in Kansas."

15

When they arrived at the edge of the airstrip, Keone left Angela with Padraig and the horses in the thick foliage and crawled over to his brother Kimo. Angela couldn't hear their whispered conversation but watched as Keone took up his brother's position and Kimo crawled back to her.

"Hey, Angela. Howzit?" he whispered as he took the reins from her. "I'll tie 'im up for you over here by mine. Keone wants you and Pad to 'quietly crawl up to him.' I'm gonna grab Lono and head back to the ranch."

"Thanks for all your help."

"No prob, Ange. I'll call Julie and give her one update on da ride back." Kimo quietly mounted his horse and rode off to get his brother.

Padraig and Angela got down on their hands and knees and crawled up the gentle slope to Keone. She understood why he preferred having Padraig stay with them and sent his younger brothers back to the ranch. Not only was Padraig a mountain of a man, even bigger than Keone, but he was also the levelheaded one—the one their parents had left the ranch to when they died.

Keone motioned for them to stay down when they reached his lookout point. She watched as he surveyed the entire landing strip with miniature low-light binoculars. He waved his hand toward the old cargo plane, then whispered, "That has to be the plane Opaka brought Dave in on."

"You got that right. He will have modified it, like the one we impounded in Hāna. A good bet it'll have extra fuel tanks, so he can make it to the mainland," Angela whispered back.

When Keone said nothing more, Angela added, "Until he gets here, you've got another story to finish."

"We need to keep quiet," Keone snapped back.

"You can whisper. Padraig can keep lookout."

Keone handed Padraig the binoculars and watched him crawl a little farther up the hill. Then he turned to Angela. "I've told you everything I know or suspect about Sam and Walden."

"Okay, and I believe you. But I want to know more about that crazy serial killer and the Europol agent who was conveniently present on all the cruises where murders occurred. You may have told Julie everything, but not me."

Keone sighed.

When Keone finished his whispered account through Thanatos's henchman's death at the theater on the Acropolis, Angela had a few questions.

"So, the authorities were willing to believe you killed a serial killer to get themselves off the hook. But you and Andreos had good reason to believe Thanatos wasn't the guy that died on the Acropolis."

"They just needed us to catch someone. But we knew that barely literate crewman, Pratt, hadn't written the notes we got from Thanatos."

"Was Pratt on all of the cruises where Olympians were murdered?"

"Yes. Those we know about. But so was Andreos."

"Since Andreos was pulled off the case, you haven't had a chance to speak to him directly, right?"

"Only through emails that I figure are being monitored."

Angela agreed that was likely. "What about the woman the killer tried to poison?"

"She died. The antidote Andreos carried couldn't reverse the toxin's effects."

"Hmm. How well did you get to know this Andreos, guy?"

Angela couldn't read her partner's face in the dark. And before either of them could say anything more, they caught the rumor of a motorcycle engine in the distance.

They both stopped whispering and crawled up to Padraig.

16

Julie thanked Kimo for the update, ended the call, and turned to share to newest information with her sister.

"Good news. Keone's at the airstrip, the plane is still there, and neither the pilot nor Dave have arrived yet."

Janet didn't appear comforted.

"Hey, I said it was good news."

"I know, Julie. I just worry about how Sam is taking all this and what Dave might do to him if he resists," Janet replied.

Julie was confused. "Dr. Drayton told Keone that Sam was catatonic after Dave confronted him."

"That's good. If it's real."

"What do you mean? Sam's been catatonic since he signed the divorce papers. Surely Drayton would tell you if there was any change."

Janet took a deep breath. "There was a change. This week Dr. Drayton called to say Sam was responsive again."

"What?" Julie couldn't believe what she was hearing.

"Sam's still delusional and believes he's travelled to a

parallel world, but he's talking again. I agreed to visit tomorrow to give the doctor my opinion."

"You were planning to meet with Sam?"

"No, Jules. Just watch through the one-way glass while Dr. Drayton questioned him. I can't be in the same room with him, after everything he's . . ." Janet's voice faded away.

"Look, I'm glad Sam seems to be making progress again. I am. But I can't forget the last time he appeared to get better."

"I know, I know. I'm not saying I believe anything he's saying. But if he's aware of what's going on, he might try to do something stupid if Dave provokes him. Dave never believed Sam was really sick."

Julie understood her sister's concern.

How would Dave treat Sam now that he had him totally under his control?

Could Dave trigger the violence Sam displayed once before with Julie?

How would Dave react?

"Julie, I couldn't forgive myself if anything happened to Sam. I should have tried harder to understand what Sam thought he'd experienced. The last time we spoke, in the psych ward, he asked me to give him one more chance and I refused. That Sam said he'd come to love and respect me. He even dressed up, got a haircut, and shaved his beard. But he was the Sam from after the accident, not my Sam."

That's right, he's not your Sam anymore. Julie needed to get Janet to stop beating herself up.

"The next time I saw Sam was later, through one-way glass with Dr. Drayton. What I saw wasn't a man but an empty husk. He'd been catatonic ever since the night he signed the divorce papers. The beard and wild hair were back. He just sat in the corner with a stupid grin on his face. But what if—"

"No, Janet. We can't worry about what might have been.

We can only deal with what is. Keone and Angela are risking their lives to get Sam away from Dave. We need to think about them."

Janet stared strangely at her, not speaking for some time.

Have I pushed too hard?

"You're right, Jules." Janet squeezed her arm. "I'm not doing anyone any good by obsessing over things I can't change. We need to keep faith with the people we love. And pray for their safety."

17

Thursday, October 31, 10:00 p.m.

Keone watched a motorcycle fishtail up the hill, spewing dirt. Randy Opaka headed directly for the parked plane and circled it before killing the engine and hurrying into the shack. After what Keone assumed to be a sufficient, bladder-emptying period, the pilot came out, zipped his fly, and began prepping the twin engine cargo plane for take-off. The pilot faced their way, and Keone caught a glimpse of a gun when the wind whipped Opaka's jacket open.

Maybe he learned something from his previous encounter with Ange.

Keone and Angela didn't move a muscle for the next fifteen minutes, knowing they were in Opaka's line of sight. Remaining motionless caused Keone's calves and inner thighs to tighten. When aching turned into sharp cramping, only willpower prevented him from shouting. Angela's face told him her legs were cramping, too.

A rusted out, rattletrap of a panel truck clattered into sight.

As the truck disappeared behind the shed holding the gas tanks, Keone handed the binoculars to Angela and rolled partway down the hill to Padraig. Once out of sight of Opaka, he stamped his feet to relieve the cramps.

Circulation restored, Keone whispered to Padraig, "You need to return to the ranch, but call Tony Alcala while you're riding. I saw Walden driving the truck, so it's a good bet Sam is inside." *If he's still alive.* "Now that we know both Walden and Opaka are here, I want Tony to send a chopper to pick you up at the ranch. You can direct them to the strip from there, yeah?"

Padraig flashed him a thumbs up and headed down to the horses.

Keone crawled back up to Angela and began vigorously rubbing her legs. When she signaled her pain had subsided, he crawled the rest of the way up the hill and took the binoculars back. Keone's action allowed Angela to keep eyes on the scene the entire time.

Teamwork.

Opaka still stood beside the plane, the van remained behind the shed, and no one had approached Opaka's position.

What are they waiting for? Did Dave have to pee, too?

As if in answer, two short honks sounded behind the shed. Keone pointed as Opaka jumped into the plane and started the engines. Both engines fired up with a cloud of exhaust, and Opaka began revving them. The van appeared from behind the cabin and pulled as close to the open door to the plane as possible without blocking the tail.

Okay, Keone thought. *Show time.* He pumped his fist twice and pointed at the plane.

He and Angela bolted from cover and rushed the plane. Keone, in the lead, shouted, "Freeze! Maui PD!"

They saw Walden jump from the driver's seat and run to the back of the van, keeping the vehicle between him and the advancing officers. Keone almost reached him before Walden dragged Sam Loftus's limp form out of the van and toward the cockpit door. Walden held a gun in his right hand—pointed at Sam's head. Keone hoped Angela saw it, too.

"Damn you, Boyd," Walden yelled. "You're not gonna screw me this time. Toss your gun away."

Keone dropped his weapon and saw Angela take cover behind the plane's tail.

"Time for you to die, Kanaka." Walden swung his gun toward Keone's chest.

Keone stood his ground. But Sam Loftus, who had been limp as a rag until this moment, came to life, grabbing Dave's arm and wrestling him for the gun.

Two gunshots exploded.

Angela's shot was a split second before Walden's but missed its target. Sam's desperate grab for the gun took them both out of her line of fire. Her shot struck the fuselage, but Walden's hit Sam.

Sam doubled over and fell to the ground.

Walden jumped into the plane and slammed the door shut before Keone could retrieve his weapon and rush to Sam's side.

"I kept hold of Dave's gun," Sam coughed, blood oozing from his chest.

"You did good." Keone jammed his finger into the wound to slow the bleeding and hefted Sam onto his shoulder with his free arm.

The plane, now inching forward, headed for the far end of the strip. Keone knew they would have to turn around to line up for takeoff. He carried Sam out the plane's path and laid him gently in the high grass, keeping pressure on the wound. By the time he looked back to the runway, Angela was standing directly in the plane's path. She took a firing stance and put three rounds into the plane's cockpit.

Keone watched the plane head straight toward his partner, until a blast of wind from the propellor blinded him. When he was able to look up, he saw the plane angle straight up out of the dust cloud that now covered the runway.

What the f . . .? Ange fired a perfect spread at the windshield. Oh shit, where is she?

Keone felt a tug on his sleeve and turned to see a smile on Angela's face. When he turned back, the plane had abruptly stopped its upward motion, hung a moment, then plummeted back to the runway.

Keone pulled Angela next to Sam and shielded both from the resulting explosion.

Sam struggled to speak. "Did we get him, Detective?"

"We sure did, Sam. Thanks to you." Keone tore off his jacket and jammed it against Sam's chest.

"I finally came to my senses this week, with the doc . . ."

"Don't try to talk," Keone said.

Angela stood up and headed over to check out the wreckage, but Keone knew there would be no survivors.

"Detective Boyd, I know who you are, but we've never actually met," Sam Loftus said. "I'm not who you think I am."

Keone kept pressure on the wound and said nothing.

"Doesn't matter," Sam gasped. "My memories started . . . coming back, during . . . sessions . . . with Dr. Drayton." Sam coughed up blood but struggled to continue. "You need to hear—"

"Keep quiet, Sam. Please." Keone continued to hold the pressure, and the bleeding slowed.

"Glad you . . . kept Dave away . . . from Julie. Always liked her. But only loved Janet. Other-Sam hurt them . . . not me."

"Sssh. Please." Keone felt tears in his eyes.

"Other-Sam . . . one you met . . . must have . . . gone back when I returned. I couldn't accept . . . other world . . . too wrong. Had kids. Janet with Dave. Left was right. But I didn't hurt anyone . . . just turned off."

"Sam, please." Keone could feel the man slipping away. "You need to hang on for Janet."

Sam seemed to rally at this. "Keone, don't tell her I came back. Let her think Other-Sam saved you . . . died. Drayton told me . . . she's happy. Deserves it. Promise me. Never tell . . ."

"I promise, Sam."

"And Keone," Sam raised his right hand slightly and grinned. "This is my right hand." Then his entire body fell limp.

Angela came up beside her partner, her face lit by the flames from the burning plane.

Keone turned and shook his head. "Sam's gone."

This one anyway.

18

Julie had finally calmed her sister down before the phone rang again. She glanced at the clock. Nearly eleven p.m.

She kept all expression from her face as Keone told her about Sam and Dave. She had no strong emotions left for Dave, except possibly revulsion. But the news about Sam made her sad. She would have never imagined this could happen. But, from what Keone said, Sam gave his life to save her husband's.

"Do you want me to tell Janet? I have a lot of experience talking with surviving family," Keone said.

Keeping her voice level, she said, "No. I'll do it. Thanks for the update."

"Julie, I'm so sorry it ended this way. I'll join you there as soon as I can. But it'll be late. I love you."

"I know. Love you, too."

Janet came over to Julie as she hung up the phone. "They're both dead, aren't they? Sam and Dave, I mean."

"I'm so sorry, Jan."

"Tell me Keone and Angela are safe?"

"They're fine. Keone wants you to know that, despite his delusions, Sam was alert enough at the end to fight with Dave to save Keone's life."

Now Janet allowed the tears to come, as Julie held her in her arms. They walked back to the couch, where Julie stroked the back of her sister's neck. She'd done this when they were girls. Julie cried, too. For her sister.

"Hey, partner. You okay?" Angela had never seen an expression on Keone's face like the one it bore now.

"Fine. I just called Julie."

"I'm so sorry for Janet. This has to be tough for her. What should we do now? Ride back to the ranch. Contact the LT?" Angela asked.

"No. I forgot to tell you. I had Padraig ride back to the ranch to call Tony and request a helicopter. They would have stopped by the ranch and picked him up to guide the chopper up to us but should be here in a few minutes. You can catch a ride with them. I'll ride my horse back."

Angela nodded.

"Oh, and have Pad ride yours back when they get here. I think you've done enough riding for one night." He tried to smile and failed.

"Keone, it wasn't your fault he died."

"Not today."

"What do you mean?"

"I was so certain Sam's story was crazy, that Sam was crazy, I never believed it was possible . . . even after Hasselbach and Carvell told me about the multiverse."

"You did your job."

"I never went back to visit him after that first time, if I had . . ."

Angela grabbed Keone's arm. "As you've told me many times, we're cops. We deal in facts, not theories."

"What about your friend Nancy? She believes her husband communicated to her—and you—from beyond death. What do you believe?"

He'd hit a sensitive spot with that question. Angela was still trying to make sense of what happened to her during that case. "I did experience something unusual. I can't explain everything. But I can reconcile it with my religious beliefs. Belief differs from person to person."

"I don't have a faith like you. My family kept to the old ways. I could never completely accept the primitive Hawaiian gods of nature or the Christian God the missionaries layered on top. Religion is fine, for other people."

"In Rob Lister's book, he decided all formal religions are a little bit right and a little bit wrong. Each person needs to find their own way to what they believe, in their own time. Nobody can tell you what to believe. But I think everybody has something inside. Something that comforts them."

"I don't know, Ange. That sounds a lot like religion to me."

"Not really. Religion isn't belief. Belief is completely internal. What you truly believe brings you comfort inside."

Keone stood completely still.

"I'm talking too much," Angela said. "Just take a look at Rob's book and think about it, okay?"

"I will." Keone squeezed her arm and walked back to the horses.

She watched him ride off, then heard a chopper approaching.

19

Keone took a round-about way back to the ranch. The trip earlier had refreshed his memory enough that he had no concern about getting lost. Besides the horse knew where they were headed, back to the barn and food. They'd find their way.

He spoke out loud as he rode. Given all the weird things he'd experienced, he hoped the horse wouldn't decide to answer.

"What do I believe? I guess I believe in my detective skills and my family. I know I believe in Julie's love. Those things give me comfort."

He continued to ride and looked at the ranch land that surrounded him. Riding on his family's land gave him comfort. Living on Maui did the same.

"This land. This ʻāina. Tutu always says Hawaiians are one with the ʻāina. I can feel that. But doesn't everyone take comfort from where they call home?"

He rode in silence for a while and watched a cattle egret sail overhead. The graceful white bird danced in the air currents and seemed to have no specific destination in mind. Odd to see him flying at night.

"I find comfort in having a mystery to solve. I feel complete when a case is solved to my satisfaction."

His thoughts went back to the Loftus and Thanatos cases. He finally realized what those cases had in common, why they both haunted him. There was nothing more he could do about the Loftus case. But he had a strong feeling that Thanatos wasn't done with him.

"I wonder what Andreos thinks. I could ask him. I have his cell number."

He looked at the horse and laughed. "Don't tell anybody about this, okay? They'd put me in Sam's old room if they found out."

A few minutes later, Padraig caught up to him, and they rode the rest of the way back to the ranch in silence.

Padraig took the horses to the stable. Keone knew he would unharness them, brush them out, and feed them. Those familiar chores always settled his mind. *Something else that gives me peace.*

On his way to the cruiser that he and Angela left behind, Keone noticed someone sitting on the porch that wrapped around the main house. Tutu was in her favorite rocking chair. Then he remembered. *She told me to be sure to talk with her when I got back when she tugged on my jacket as we were leaving.*

He slowly approached the porch and quietly climbed the steps, thinking Tutu might be asleep, as she often was in her favorite chair. When he saw her face, he knew she was some-place else.

Her lids were open but only the whites of her eyes were visible. Her entire body seemed to vibrate. He'd seen her this way many times before. She was having one of her visions.

When he was a keiki, his mother had taught him never to disturb Tutu when she was *with her gods*. As an adult, he'd worried about these episodes and wondered if she might be epileptic or something. But a complete physical from a trusted local doctor ruled that out.

When Keone asked him what it was, if it wasn't a physical illness, the doctor smiled and said, "After treating people on this island for dozens of years, I've finally accepted that I will treat what I understand and leave the rest to the gods."

As Keone looked back toward the stables, Tutu's voice said in Hawaiian, "I'm here, Keone. I have a message for you. From Pele."

Could this day get any weirder?

"I know you don't believe yet, keiki. But I need to tell you this."

"Okay, Tutu."

"I saw something today I have never seen before. I saw Pele awaken."

Keone remembered enough from the fables his Tutu told him growing up to understand this was important. "Did she speak to you?"

"That is not Pele's way. I peered into her flames with her and saw the future."

Sure, Tutu.

"I know your thoughts. But you must hear this. Pele's *pa'oa* shows many things when it stirs her fires. The past. The future. Other places. I saw another land, far away. A dark shape was killing women with his touch. All his killings were near an ocean, and waves of evil went forth from these places. Pele felt them in her home in Kīlauea. There was a brief threat to one of her children, but it passed so she continued to slumber."

Keone felt that tingle at the base of his skull.

"She has awakened now because that threat is coming to

her islands. The dark shape comes for you. She wants you to know that she will guide you and help you. This threat must be defeated. You must feel the truth of the fires of Pele from her home in Halemaʻumaʻu crater, my keiki."

Tutu rose from her chair and walked into the house, leaving Keone in a daze.

When he finally walked to the car and drove off, the comfort he'd felt earlier was fading.

20

Friday, November 1, 1:30 a.m.

Keone fought the urge to hang up the phone when he heard the voice on the other end of the line.

"Dr. Drayton, this is Keone Boyd. I'm sorry to call so late, but I wanted to tell you about Sam."

"I'm still awake. Sleep was impossible tonight. Did you find him? Do you need me to come to the police station and collect him?"

"We found him. But I'm afraid he's dead." Keone gave the psychiatrist a moment to digest the information.

After a long pause, Drayton cleared his throat and asked, "What happened?"

Drayton sounded more disappointed than sad when Keone detailed what transpired at the airstrip. "Poor man. At least he died saving someone. Was he able to say anything after he was shot?"

Keone had recorded everything Sam said at the end on his

notepad. He read the words verbatim to Drayton. "Was Sam back, Dr. Drayton?"

"He believed he was. I believe he regained his ability to communicate and move beyond everything that he'd done through one final delusion. The delusion that he was somewhere else when all the bad things happened and couldn't have been responsible."

"But the Other-Sam was convinced, too."

"There was only one Sam, despite what his physicist friend Carvell came to believe. After treatment, Dr. Carvell realized his personal obsession with parallel universes influenced his interpretation of data."

"What about Sam being clean-shaven and alert one day and heavily bearded and catatonic a couple days later?"

"Did you see that?"

"No, but Carvell's boss, Dr. Hasselbach, did." *And two other independent witnesses*, Keone thought.

"He probably believes he did," Drayton replied.

"Hasselbach also independently confirmed two energy surges at the times when Sam claimed he crossed between the different universes. Are you saying Dr. Hasselbach is crazy, too?"

"No. The good doctor is quite sane. But he's seventy years old and not immune to failing eyesight and inaccurate memories. Look, I know he's Director of the Hawaiian Observatories, but he's still a scientist. Scientists look for physical explanations of physical events. His field is astrophysics and his colleague, Carvell, studied the theoretical possibility of a multiverse. Sam represented a potential validation of those theories. As a courtesy to Carvell, he reviewed the data to find anything that corresponded with the timing of Sam's experience. He found what he was looking for."

"You think he lied?"

"I think he viewed events from his own perspective. We all do."

Keone thought about this before responding. "Thank you, Doctor. I'll let you get some sleep," he said and hung up his office phone.

Keone's mind went over the events of the last year. A sense of disconnection infused many of Keone's memories since Sam's car hit his and started him down this rabbit hole. But he had to admit Sam's explanations were more consistent with the data than Drayton's.

Drayton said that he thought Hasselbach viewed events from his own perspective. *We all do.*

Keone supposed the theory held true for psychiatrists, too. He considered calling Hasselbach. As an astronomer, he often kept late hours up at the observatory on Haleakalā.

No, not tonight. I have what I need.

There was a lot of paperwork to do regarding the events that transpired at the air strip. When Angela offered to help, he sent her home and insisted on doing it himself. The Loftus case was his and so was the Walden case. He'd be very careful about how he wrote this up. He didn't need Tony questioning his sanity. Drayton's explanation provided a viable solution.

But what do I believe?

He tore the last used page out of his notebook and stuffed it in his pocket.

A glow in the east announced sunrise when Keone finally parked in the driveway of the home Janet now shared with Mike Fowler. He hoped Julie and Janet were asleep, after what he knew was an emotional night. Those hopes evaporated at the open front door, but the kiss Julie gave him made up for it.

They reluctantly ended their embrace and stared into each other's eyes. Finally, Keone asked, "Where's Janet?"

"Asleep, at last. She let me give her a sedative that Dr. Drayton prescribed."

"How did she take the news?"

"Not as badly as I feared, but . . . I'll tell you all about it, after we get some sleep. Janet made up the guest room for us before the capsule kicked in."

"Fine. I'm beat."

"There is one thing I you need to tell me before we go to bed, though."

"What?" Keone said, hoping she didn't want to continue their conversation about the murders on the ship.

"On the phone, you said Sam came out of his trance long enough to keep Dave from shooting you and took a bullet. When I told Janet that, it seemed to help her deal with all of this."

"Good."

"But you didn't tell me if Sam said anything before he died."

"No, I didn't."

"I understand if you didn't want to share any grisly details. But I got the sense you were also being careful, so I wouldn't share something with Janet that might upset her."

Keone thought for a long time before he said, almost to himself, "No secrets." He continued in a more normal voice. "I'll tell you. But I really hope you won't tell Janet."

"I promise."

"Sam was a completely different person tonight. He told me he had crossed over to the other Sam's world and returned. He knew who I was but said we'd never met. He said he loved

Janet and was not the person that harmed you. Then he made me promise to tell Janet that the man who died tonight was the crazy Sam, so Janet could move on with her life."

"Did he sound crazy?"

"No."

"Do you believe him?"

That question again. "I believe that he believed what he told me."

Julie stared at him. He sensed that she saw something in his eyes.

"Okay, maybe . . . I'm still working on it. Give me a little time, okay?" Keone gave her a hug.

Julie hugged back and gave him a kiss, before leading him to the bedroom. Stripped down to his shorts, Keone fell asleep as soon as his head touched the pillow. Exhaustion trumped confusion at last.

Part Two
Investigation

"Supposing is good, but finding out is better."

— Mark Twain

21

Monday, November 4, 6:00 a.m.

The calm voice on the line provided Keone a sense of normalcy. "Andreos Calliopoulos. How may I help you?"

"Aloha, Andreos. Keone Boyd calling."

"*Geia sou file mou.* How are you and your lovely wife, whom I must someday meet?"

"We're fine." Keone said, pleased that Andreos remembered he'd studied Greek and Latin and would understand the agent's greeting—and that he'd called him "friend." "Julie's back to writing her books."

"Oh, yes, the ones about the little Hawaiian girl, Anna. My daughter loves them. Her name too is Anna."

"You must think I'm very rude. I just realized that I never asked about your family when we worked together on the *Argonaut.*"

"Not at all. We were quite occupied when we were last

together. Anna is seven years and our only child, so far. I say so far because my wife Marie, is starting to get . . . How do you say it?"

"Maternal."

"Ah yes, maternal. So, who knows?"

"Good luck with that. Hey, the reason I called concerns our last . . . uh . . . collaboration."

"The Thanatos case." Andreos's voice turned serious.

"Yes. I was never completely satisfied with the outcome."

"Nor was I."

"After we parted, was there ever any follow-up?"

"Officially, I was not permitted to continue my investigation. I was limited to desk duty for a month and given unrelated assignments thereafter."

"Officially the investigation stopped after Athens. What about unofficially?" Keone chose his words carefully.

Andreos hesitated. "You called on my personal cell phone. I am away from the office, en route to a pleasant meal with my family. So, I can speak *anoichta* . . . uh . . . speak freely."

"I'd appreciate that."

"Thanatos is not dead. I hope this does not shock you."

"It doesn't, but how do you know?"

"Officially, I do not. But he has been sending me cards at work and at my home address. The first message came to my home on September tenth, my daughter's birthday. The second arrived at the office on October thirtieth. I took images of them with this phone. May I send them to you?"

"Definitely. I'm calling on my personal cell as well. This will remain between us."

"Thank you, Keone. Do you still have the scans of his earlier notes? The ones I gave you on the ship?"

"Yes, I do. Have there been any more murders? Any hints as to where he might be?" Keone feared the answer.

"Since we do not know who Thanatos is, I have no effective way of tracking him. I followed up on the post marks, but they were dead ends. He probably had someone repost them for him. As for more murders, none in European waters."

"What about suspects?"

"Handwriting analysis of the earlier notes ruled out the Olympians and their family members on board. It also ruled out the barely legible scrawl of the crewman, Jonas Pratt. Both of the new notes are written in Thanatos's unique script. You will note that, as with the earlier notes, they are in English and not Greek although addressed to me."

"Interesting. What about the Canadian guy with the phony name, Veronica Napoleoni's husband?" Keone had a strange feeling about that guy.

"Yes, John Ferrino. The name was not real, but he was not our killer either. He truly is a high-ranking member of the Canadian Government, who was travelling incognito for security reasons."

"That's why he avoided our shore excursions. I'd still bet his job involves some aspect of intelligence gathering."

"Quite insightful. However, if that were the case, I would not be at liberty to say. I can say that he left the ship on his own in each port, which is why I had to be sure he wasn't our man."

"If you're sure, that's enough for me. Is there anything I can do?"

Again, Andreos hesitated. "Since you called, I would like to request a favor."

"You'd like me to check with my government, right?"

"If it would not be a severe imposition."

"No problem. I have a friend in Honolulu with the Federal Drug Enforcement Agency that I can call. He has multiple contacts in the FBI. How are you holding up?"

"I am frustrated. I passed all the messages on to my superiors, but as far as I can tell, they took no action, beyond the handwriting analysis. I fear it will take another murder to motivate them."

"No one wants that. I'll see what I can find out from the FBI."

"Thank you for believing me, Keone."

There was that word again, *believing*.

"Keep me posted on what you discover, Andreos, and I will do likewise. *Antío fíle mou.*"

"Aloha, Keone."

KEONE BROUGHT THE SCAN OF THE POSTCARD FROM Singapore up first on his phone. The note on the card was handwritten like the message Andreos received on the Argonaut. He recognized Thanatos's handwriting immediately. The final sentences caught his attention:

> . . . But leave that heathen at home this time.
> For him and his puny gods, I have no respect.

Thanatos must not be familiar with Pele, Keone thought. She was anything but puny and could really burn his ass. Tutu's vision about Pele awakening and danger coming to her islands tugged at Keone's thoughts, but he wouldn't exaggerate its significance.

The other message was an actual birthday card, but the words he read chilled him.

Saturday, September 10

My dear Andreos,

I trust you do not mind my use of your given name. Congratulations on your daughter's seventh birthday. I hope I do not surprise or frighten you by knowing this fact. I am a god, after all.

I write in peace. I shall never harm you or any member of your family. You are my worthy opponent.

I cannot say as much for your Hawaiian colleague. When I next encounter him, he will die. Unlike my children, the glorious Olympians, he will not reach Elysium after our encounter. I shall transfer him to my abode, the underworld, where my brother Charon will ferry him across the river to Hades.

I sense he might produce offspring before I catch up with him. Have no fear, I will take them, too. Even if I must rip them from their mother's womb.

You may warn him to avoid me. No matter. When I desire it, he will fall.

Oh, and wish your daughter a very happy birthday from her Uncle Thanatos.

He and Julie had told no one, including Andreos, about the baby she was carrying, the cause of the morning sickness that kept her away from the Acropolis that awful morning.

Was Thanatos just guessing? Had he asked the ship's

doctor? Had Andreos? And what about Angela's dream about protecting him and a baby?

He knew that Angela had suspicions about the Greek agent, but did he? He reflected again on Andreos's words. *Thank you for believing me.*

22

Angela noticed Keone laying his phone face-down on his desk when she tapped on his cubicle wall. She also spotted the word *Thanatos* on the screen before he did. "Good morning, big guy. You feel like a little ride up Haleakalā?"

"What's up?"

"A very strange break-in and shots fired at the observatory. Your old friend Hasselbach called it in. Did you ever call him about Loftus?"

"No. I . . . uh . . . I wanted to tell him in person."

"Here's your chance."

"Let's go."

The drive up Haleakalā combined beautiful views with hairpin turns. Angela let Keone enjoy the former while she navigated the latter. The view must have gotten him thinking.

"Ange, I have to admit something to you."

"Okay."

"I think I subconsciously blocked myself from calling Dr. Hasselbach about Sam."

"Why?"

"Because I was afraid he might undo what my call to Dr. Drayton accomplished."

"What call?"

"After I sent you home Halloween night, I called Sam's psychiatrist . . . to tell him . . . you know . . . about Sam."

"Makes sense. He was pretty concerned when we left him that evening."

"I felt I owed it to him. I even told him . . . what Sam said to me before he died."

"You didn't tell me."

"I know. I've only told Drayton and Julie."

Angela decided this was the point where she needed to be quiet.

After a long pause, Keone continued. "He said he was the other Sam."

"Which Sam is that?"

"The one who started here, went into another dimension, then came back later."

She noticed Keone was still looking out the window.

It must be my turn, Angela thought and said, "Not the one that tried to rape Julie, right?"

"Right."

"What did Drayton say?"

"He said it was all a new delusion Sam devised to avoid accepting what he'd done."

"What do you think?"

"I think Drayton believes what he said." Keone finally turned away from the window.

Angela looked at her partner, understanding his quandary. "I think Sam's deathbed confession rang truer to you than Drayton's psychobabble."

"I relied heavily on Drayton's explanation in my report to

Tony. I needed to stick with believable facts. Tony couldn't have handled my crazy musings."

"You did the right thing."

"Do you think I'm crazy?"

"No. I think you're a detective."

"Since you shared all that stuff about Lister with me, I wanted to be straight with you."

Now Angela hesitated. "In the same spirit, I need to tell you I saw Thanatos's name on your computer before you cleared your screen. Any news?"

"Well, I finally talked with Andreos. He's heard from Thanatos since the crewman was killed—probably twice. Here's what he told me . . ."

23

While his partner pulled up to the entry gate for the first of three concentric fences surrounding the Hawaiian Observatories facility on Haleakalā volcano, Keone gazed out at the people swarming around with homemade signs about two-hundred feet away. A police cordon held the protestors back.

"What the hell, Ange?"

"I don't know. They can't be here because of the shooting. Too soon."

The gate guard approached their squad car and Angela showed her badge. "You here about that nutcase that tried to blow us up?"

"Uh, probably. Why are all these people here?" Angela asked.

"They've been here all night. They're protesting that big, new telescope. I don't know if the bomber was one of them, but we're lucky your folks were here keeping things orderly. It still got pretty dicey when they heard the shots."

She turned to Keone. "Want me to go check with our guys, so you can head on up?"

"Yeah. Get an officer to bring you up once you get a handle on things."

With that, Angela got out. Keone slid over into the driver's seat and showed the guard his badge. Keone was glad Angela remembered to scoot the seat all the way back before she exited. The guard printed out a time-sensitive badge for Keone, so he could drive on to the second gate.

As he drove through the first gate, Keone glanced in the side-view mirror and saw his partner authoritatively approach the uniforms holding the cordon.

Go get 'em, Tita.

ANGELA WALKED UP TO THE NEAREST UNIFORM AND tapped him on the shoulder. "What happened here, Patrolman?"

"We were keeping the protestors in line when we heard some shots, Sergeant. Our sarge tore off for the next guard shack and told us to maintain order."

Angela noticed the officer was very young and bet this was his first assignment. "The guard said the guy tried to blow you up. Why would he say that? Was there an explosion?"

"No. Just the shots. But the guard had to let the bomb squad and an ambulance through the gate before you got here."

How did they get here before us? Angela wondered.

They walked over to the other two uniforms restraining the crowd.

"I'm Sergeant Beyers of CID. I want each of these protestors ID'd and interviewed about this morning before you send them home. You can tell them it's for their own safety if they're resistant to abandoning their protest."

"Yes, Sergeant." Finally having a defined task, the officers jumped into action and arranged the protestors in three lines.

"I'll take this guy." She walked deliberately toward a protestor she recognized, her cousin Billy Kalama Barnes.

"Okay, Billy," Angela began. "What's a fine upstanding citizen like you doing here this lovely morning?"

"Oh, Ange. You know I'm in dat HHPS ting. We just doin' a little protestin'. Dat new observatory bein' built too close to sacred land."

"The other observatories never bothered you." Angela knew HHPS stood for Hawaiian Homeland Protection Society. The group worked to protect ancient sites from defacement.

"Da ting is, dey keep building new ones and never take down da old ones dey no use no moah. Dat's why this new one so close to sacred sites."

"We can talk politics later. Did you see the guy that went through the gate right before the shots were fired?"

"Yeah, and he not wid our group. I don' think he wid da Sovereign State of Hawai'i group neither. You bettah check wid dem 'bout dat."

"I thought I saw Keone's uncle Kimo when I drove up."

"He was here but bugged out when he saw you two. Dat one careful kanaka."

"Go home, cuz. There's still a chance that guy has a bomb. And stay outta trouble, yeah?"

Billy shrugged and wandered back down the road to his pickup.

Angela checked with the uniforms and found they got a similar story from the people they interviewed. The guy who went through the gate wasn't with either group.

"So, one of your guys went up to the second gate after the shots?" Angela asked one of the older uniforms.

"Yeah, our sarge," the man replied. "He radioed back that

the bomber was dead. He wouldn't risk going any closer until the bomb squad got here."

"Smart move."

The older officer motioned Angela aside. "Sarge, a couple of folks told us Kimo Kalama was here from Moloka'i. Do you want us to put out a *detain and question?*"

"Can we hold on that until I talk with Keone?"

The man nodded. He knew they were dealing with *'ohana.*

24

Three layers of security protected the scientific complex on Haleakalā. The protest below at the first gate represented the nearest unauthorized individuals could get to the conglomeration of academic, government, and commercial observatories and related research facilities on the crest of Haleakalā volcano. To get through that first gate, visitors required an authorized invitation and their name on a checklist to receive their time sensitive badge.

Keone now approached the second layer of protection and saw Hawaiian Observatories Director Martin Hasselbach on the other side. This second gate was higher, stronger, and thicker than the one a couple of miles lower on the volcano. Private cars were not allowed through this one. But at the moment, an ambulance was parked midway through the open gate.

Keone parked their cruiser and walked to the gate. Next to the ambulance, a team of EMTs were working diligently on a man in a security guard uniform. The *top* of a security guard uniform, to be exact. Below the waist his clothing had been cut off to expose his thighs. What remained was soaked in blood. Keone was not surprised the man was unconscious and knew the EMTs needed to transport the wounded guard immediately. He hoped the man would make it.

He walked past the ambulance with his badge displayed on his hip and approached Hasselbach, who was standing next to the open gate and physically shaking.

"The man they're taking away in that ambulance, he saved us all," Hasselbach said in a quivering voice.

"What's the guard's name?"

"Kono . . . something. He worked with another guard called Frank."

Keone surveyed the scene. "Where's Frank? I'd like to talk to him."

"So would I. He shot Kono. He shot them both."

"Who else was shot? Another guard?"

"Yes, Duke. He gave his life for us."

"What about the visitor?"

Hasselbach pointed to a spot about five hundred yards away. "You mean the shooter and attempted bomber?"

"Okay. What happened to that person?"

"He's dead, too. Thank God he didn't make it through the third gate."

He walked toward where Hasselbach pointed, but a uniformed sergeant he knew, Steve Hahn, blocked his path. "Sorry, Keone, but nobody gets any closer until the bomb squad finishes."

How'd they get here so fast? he wondered, but to Hahn he said, "I understand, Steve. Were you able to interview the guard?"

"No. He pointed me to the other two casualties. I didn't realize how badly he was hit until I got back. He was unconscious by then." Hahn gestured to Hasselbach. "This guy was tending his wound. I called for an ambulance, but the dispatcher said one was already on the way. That guard kept the bomber from completing his mission."

"You said two casualties, but I only see one body from here."

"The dog is on the other side of the perp."

"Dog?"

"Guard dog. His name was Duke."

With no choice, Keone returned to Hasselbach to continue his questioning and noticed the director was wearing an under-shirt over light slacks and still shaking all over. He decided to approach him as a friend. "Martin, here. Take my jacket."

He draped his jacket around the man's shoulders, but Hasselbach kept staring off into space. Keone gently turned the director to face him.

"It's all right, Martin. You remember me, Keone Boyd?"

"Sure, Keone. You helped with Brad and Sam Loftus." His voice seemed distant.

"That's right. How is Dr. Carvell?"

Keep him talking.

"Great. Brad loves teaching kids."

Keone decided he couldn't avoid one subject any longer. "About Sam Loftus—"

"Evan Drayton told me about Sam on Saturday morning. I'd stopped by Island Calm to visit."

"I'm sorry you had to find out that way. I should have called." Keone watched Hasselbach closely. He hoped the unrelated conversation would allow the director to slowly regain his composure.

"I heard you had a pretty busy Halloween weekend."

"Sam Loftus saved my life."

"I'm glad his death mattered." Hasselbach patted Keone on the shoulder. A good sign.

"Do you feel up to answering a few questions about what happened here?"

"Of course. Kono told me everything on the phone before he passed out."

Keone flipped open his notebook. "Start at the beginning and try not to leave anything out."

"An authorized guest arrived at the second gate. Kono and Frank met him there. The visitor told them he was here to see me. Frank went back to the guard shack to check the guest list. That's procedure."

"Yes, I know from when I visited before." *During the Loftus case.* "What happened next?" Keone asked, trying to keep the sequence of events in chronological order.

"Frank hollered up from the shack that the man was on the list. He said there was a note by his name to call me when he arrived. A lie. That must have been when he tied up Duke."

"Let's just stick to what Kono told you happened, in order."

"That's what Kono said, when he called me. *That must have been when Frank tied up Duke.* Well, he said *musta been.* I'm paraphrasing."

Keone took a deep breath. "Fine, fine. Frank and Duke are in the guard shack and Kono is by the gate with the guest. What happened next?"

"Frank came out and told Kono I was in the middle of an experiment. Another lie."

Keone gave Hasselbach a look that encouraged him to hurry on with his story.

"Frank said he'd take the guest up in the golf cart they had parked by the shack. Frank opened the gate to let the man through and Kono walked back to the shack. That's when he realized Duke hadn't come to the gate. When the gate is opened, Duke always comes to the gate. Standard procedure."

"Did Kono find Duke in the shack?"

"No, not yet. He turned around to ask Frank where Duke was, but he was already heading up the hill in the golf cart and the guest was turned around pointing a gun at him."

"What kind of gun?"

"Kono didn't say. Anyway, Kono jumped into the guard shack and hit the floor as the man fired. That's when he saw Duke. He had duct tape around his muzzle and was hooked to the shack with a leash. Duke that is, not Kono."

Before he could react to the odd phrasing, Keone heard a loud crunch on the gravel behind them. He spun, reaching for his hip.

Angela showed Keone her open hands. "Sorry. I should have walked louder."

Keone grinned at his partner's discomfort but turned back to Hasselbach.

"Okay, we have two guards in the shack, one restrained and gagged. The other guard is with a guest. And that guest is taking potshots at the shack. Is that when Kono was hit?"

"No, he slipped out his pistol and crawled back to the door. The visitor was out of the cart and kept shooting."

"What about the other guard, the one with the visitor?"

"Frank? He just stood there. Anyway, Kono was about to roll out and take a shot when something brushed past him."

"A bullet?" Angela asked.

"No. Duke. He'd chewed through the duct tape, broken the leash in half, and run out to do his job. Duke lunged at the visitor and immobilized his gun arm. Just as he was trained."

"Good work." Angela sounded impressed.

Keone's look silenced her. He turned back to Hasselbach. "Go on, director."

"Kono aimed and fired at the guest. Kono said he scored a clean hit and the man fell with Duke still gnawing on his arm."

At Angela's shocked look, Keone said. "Duke was a guard dog. Go on, Martin."

"When Kono started back up the hill, Frank stood over the man's body with his own gun drawn. Kono knew the man was dead, but Frank was following procedure. Then everything went crazy."

"What happened?"

"Frank waited until Kono got closer, then shot him. While Kono fell, he saw Frank shoot Duke, too. Why did he have to . . ." Hasselbach looked about to cry.

Keone softened his voice. "Did Kono see anything else, Martin?"

"Yes. Yes. Um . . ."

"Take your time."

"Kono told me that he forced himself up onto his hands and knees in time to see Frank jump into the golf cart and drive downhill through the still open gate. Kono fired at him but missed."

"Let me guess. While Kono dragged himself back to the guard shack, Frank made it past the lower gate."

"I have no idea. About the lower gate, that is. Kono did crawl back to the shack. That's when he called me. I could tell he was in a lot of pain." Hasselbach stared at the guard shack.

Keone was losing the man's attention. "Martin. Look at me."

The physicist turned his face back to Keone.

"Did Kono tell you anything else after you got down here?"

"No. I saw your sergeant running up the hill and went to Kono. He had a large hole in his thigh. I held my shirt on it until an ambulance arrived. The ambulance and the bomb squad arrived together. Then, you came. Keone, I think I need to . . ."

Hasselbach's pallid face looked skyward before the noted astrophysicist fell into Keone's arms.

25

Angela checked in with the station from their cruiser and provided an update. Keone had taken the unconscious Hasselbach back up to his lab in the director's cart. She signed off quickly and headed back through the gate to find the senior officer on the bomb disposal unit walking toward her, a large, helmet/face-shield apparatus in his hand. The man's face and hair were drenched in sweat. "Site's clear. That guy was packing a wallop, though. He had enough C-4 to take out the new construction and a few of the facilities around it."

"Hey, how'd you guys get here so fast?" Angela asked.

"We were following up on a telephone tip. Exploding drug lab on the Haleakalā Highway. Turned out to be a red herring."

Interesting, Angela thought. She was wondering if she should start up to the cleared site when a cart pulled up and her partner jumped out.

"They just cleared the shooting site, Keone."

"Good. Let's go."

Angela led Keone up the narrow trail. "Hasselbach okay?"

"He'll be fine. Did you get the gist of what he told me?"

"Yeah. Looks like that guard, Frank, was in on the bombing."

"It gets better. While I was in Hasselbach's office, after he came to, he showed me the personnel files of the two security guards. Frank used to be a detective with MPD, until he screwed up. His last name is Kulima."

"Isn't that the detective who worked for Dave Walden and tried to get you kicked off the force?"

"Uh-huh. I called the station and had them put out an APB on former Detective Sergeant Frank Kulima. Did you report in?"

"Yeah. We've got the case for now. So, who hosts a bomber at an observatory?" Angela asked.

"Supposedly Hasselbach, but Kulima faked everything. The good doctor had no clue. Now it's your turn."

"My cousin Billy Kalama Barnes and your Uncle Kimo were among the protestors. Billy was there with HPPS."

"And Kimo was there with the Sovereignty people."

"Right."

"Did you talk to Kimo?"

"No. Billy said Kimo bugged out when he saw us pull up."

"Damn."

They reached the site where the bodies of a dog and a man with a backpack lay entwined on a bed of lava cinders.

"At least the dog didn't suffer," Angela said.

"Yeah, shot in the head. The man's covered in blood. Wonder if it's his or the dog's?"

Angela rolled the body slightly to get a better look. "I think most of the blood belonged to the shooter. The guard's shot caught him right in the heart."

Keone pointed to the bomber's gnawed wrist still in the dead dog's jaws. "Good boy, Duke."

"COD is a no-brainer, but why the explosives?"

"I wonder if Uncle Kimo knows?" Keone said, staring back down the hill.

Angela pointed to an approaching van. "Looks like CSI's here."

Keone's smartphone rang. "Boyd. Yeah." He pointed to the van.

Angela took the hint and jogged back to the guard shack to help direct CSI to the site. She spotted *Sergeant* Ed Jenkins in the group. When they worked together on the Lister case, she'd outranked him. Ange wondered if her praise of his work to Lieutenant Alcala might have played a part in his promotion.

Jenkins approached and offered his hand. "Good to see you again, Sarge. Oh, I guess it's Detective Sergeant now, congratulations. What have you got for us this time?"

"Shooter and would-be bomber, and it's Angela from now on. Bomb squad's cleared the site. I'd be very interested in who this guy is and where he's been recently. Good bet the name on his visitor pass is fictitious."

"I'll scan his prints. Should have an ID for you directly if he's in the system." When they reached the site, Jenkins and his team got right to work.

Angela walked back down to the guard shack to find Keone with a troubled look on his face. "What is it?"

"I've got a lead on my uncle, Kimo Kalama. Let's hold off on the *detain and question*, okay?"

"Sure."

"And, Ange—"

"Let me guess. You might have better luck talking with him if you go alone, yeah?"

"You're truly growing as a detective. Can you catch a ride back with CSI?"

"No problem. Give your uncle my best."

26

Monday, November 4, 11:00 a.m.

Arriving at the Boyd/Kalama Ranch, Keone saw his grandmother waiting for him on the porch that circled the main house.

"Where is he?" Keone asked, in Hawaiian.

"I know you are upset, keiki. But Kimo stayed to talk to you," Tutu replied in Hawaiian as well. "He could easily be on Moloka'i by now."

Staying in Hawaiian out of respect for his tutu, Keone said, "I'm not upset with you. I know you had nothing to do with this."

"He told me that he had nothing to do with that bombing, either. I believe him."

"And I believe you, Tutu."

Tutu led Keone into the woods behind the ranch house.

"While you wait for him, you might reflect on the importance of 'ohana." With that, Tutu left him alone deep in the woods.

*'Ohana. Family. One of the things that gives me comfort—
most of the time.*

Ten minutes later, his uncle appeared, without a sound.

"Tell me about the bomber," Keone said in Hawaiian,
without preamble.

"Not one of our group or HHPS," Kimo replied in
Hawaiian.

"I already know that."

"I thought you might not believe it." Uncle Kimo smiled.

Keone couldn't help himself and smiled back.

"Okay, here's what I know, Keone. My sources tell me the
name on the visitor pass was a fake."

"I'm still waiting for you to tell me something I don't
know."

"The guy works for a hush-hush group of drug dealers and
developers. There may be a connection to that bastard that I
helped you catch on my island, but I'm not sure. What was his
name?"

"Dave Walden."

"Right. I do know they want to embarrass the sovereignty
and homelands groups. Maybe they figure to open up some
land for development somewhere."

"And?"

"Keone, I swear on my Kalama blood. That's all I know."
Kimo walked back toward the dense foliage. "If I learn
anything else, I'll get word to you. If you need me, I'll be on
Moloka'i."

By the time he spoke the last words, Kimo had disappeared
into the woods. Keone could have followed but didn't. His
uncle almost always told him the truth.

On the walk back to the ranch, Keone considered his words to his tutu.

And I believe you, Tutu.

He'd discovered something else he believed.

Maybe this was what Angela was getting at Halloween night. He'd think about that.

Returning to the house, Keone found Tutu waiting by his cruiser. "Pele sent another message for you."

"I'm following up on the evil from overseas," Keone said. "I do take what you tell me seriously."

"I'm glad. She communicated again about the evil coming to her islands. This time I also saw another island, far away. That vision was hazy, but I saw a cruise ship and a large white mountain. And, Keone, I saw blood."

"Mahalo, Tutu. I will follow up with my friends on this." Keone needed to get going.

"And keep your mind open to Pele on this. Please, keiki?"

"Sure. But right now, I've got another case to solve."

"You will have time for both, and for the birth of your son. Just keep an open mind about any unusual evidence you may encounter."

"I will. After I take care of this one, we can set aside time to open our minds together. Aloha, Tutu."

Tutu smiled and nodded.

Back in his unmarked cruiser, it hit Keone that he'd never mentioned Julie's pregnancy to Tutu or any of the family. He drove through the main part of Makawao on Baldwin Avenue and pulled into the parking lot of Polli's Mexican Restaurant. After his years in California, he appreciated the authenticity of Polli's Mexican food, and their enormous serving sizes. His stomach reminded him it was almost lunch time, but he wanted to contact someone before he went inside.

"Agent Tom Freeman, Drug Enforcement Agency. How may I help you?"

"Tom, you have no idea."

"I think I might, Keone. I'll meet you at Kahului Airport in fifteen minutes. I'm already in the air."

There went lunch.

27

Monday, November 4, 12:30 p.m.

Angela arrived at the station to find Karen Matsuyama waiting for her at the front door. *Am I in trouble?*

"Lieutenant Alcala needs to see you, now, Detective Sergeant Beyers," Karen said.

Not *Ange? I'm in trouble.*

Karen was Tony Alcala's administrative assistant, but she and Angela had been friends since high school. Although anxious to get started on her paperwork, Angela took Karen's unusual behavior to mean Alcala wanted a first-hand account of the observatory investigation, ASAP.

Something bigger is going on.

While Angela waited outside Alcala's office reviewing her notes, she watched Karen immerse herself in routine paperwork, never looking up. Angela reviewed not only her notes but also Keone's, which he'd given her to type up, as usual.

She heard the door open and turned to see her friend

Detective Lindsay Kalani emerge from Alcala's office. Lindsay avoided eye-contact as she rushed by.

What the hell?

Angela felt very close to Lindsay. She was the first person in CID to make Ange feel at home here. They weren't just both female detectives, they were friends.

But one friend was avoiding eye-contact. *What's going on?*

Before Angela could ponder this further, Lt. Alcala's voice boomed from the office. "Come in, Detective Sergeant Beyers."

When Karen closed the door behind her, Alcala continued, "Tell me all about the call you and Keone went on to the observatory. Don't leave anything out."

Prepared, Angela pulled out her notepad and started her report.

During her entire report, Alcala only interrupted twice with clarifying questions. One final interruption came as Angela finished her report—a buzz from Alcala's desk phone.

"Send them in, Karen. And go collect the other one." Alcala didn't seem surprised by the interruption.

Angela heard the door open and was about to turn around, when Alcala smiled and said, "Take a seat, big guy. You too, Agent Freeman. Nice to see you again."

Keone sat down beside Angela, laying a calming hand on her shoulder. The man next to him wore a DEA windbreaker over his shirt and tie. This was her first look at the agent Keone and Lindsay had told her about. Although her preferences went in another direction, she could see why Keone suspected more than a professional relationship between Lindsay and Tom Freeman. The guy was tall with blond wavy hair and a handsome unlined face—a bona fide chick magnet. Lindsay had carefully evaded Angela's questions about her relationship with the Fed.

She knew Keone had asked Tom to investigate that nutcase from the cruise ship. *Is this about Thanatos?*

"Tony, what's going on?" Keone broke the silence. "Tom told me he couldn't share anything about his case until we were all together." Turning to his partner he added, "Ange, this is Agent Tom Freeman from the DEA. He helped me catch Walden the first time, on Moloka'i."

Angela nodded and shook Tom's warm hand.

"If the introductions are over, I'd like to get started. One other member of this team needs to join us, though." Punching the speaker on his phone Alcala said, "Send her in."

28

Keone watched a visibly uncomfortable Detective Lindsay Kalani enter the office. He was surprised to see her and not a fan of surprises.

Although Tom refused to discuss *this* case on the drive over, he had shared information about the Thanatos investigation. His contact in the FBI told him they weren't any more satisfied Janos Platt was Thanatos than Keone and Andreos were. He also gave him the name of an agent assigned to the case, who was currently following up on an East Asian cruise that matched Thanatos's M.O.

Keone had asked Tom before they reached the station if the cruise had any stops in Japan. The agent told him the cruise docked in Shimizu Port. Keone knew from friends who'd visited Japan that, on a clear day, Shimizu port had a panoramic view of Mt. Fuji. *Damn it, Tutu!*

Alcala's voice brought Keone's attention back to the case at hand. "Agent Freeman, since this is your show, maybe you can bring everyone up to speed on the case you and Detective Kalani have been working," Alcala said. "I would appreciate it if you two would all let Agent Freeman and Detective Kalani provide their information without interruption."

Tony and Tom have both kept this from me. Not to mention Lindsay. Keone was officially pissed off.

Tom Freeman addressed the elephant in the room. "First, let me apologize for all the secrecy. As you all know, a few months ago your department was compromised by some men working for a drug dealer here on Maui. Detective Sergeant Frank Kulima, from CID, and Sergeant Roger Walker, from Lāhainā Division were both ejected from the force for their actions, as was a lieutenant from the vice squad."

Hearing his friend Tom Freeman speak so officiously, Keone couldn't restrain himself. "I seem to recall their old boss is no longer around. Fellow named Walden, I believe. Isn't that right, Detective Sergeant Beyers?"

"I believe it is, Detective Sergeant Boyd."

Alcala glared at both. But before he could chastise them, Freeman rushed on.

"One month ago, Walker and Kulima were both released from incarceration on Oʻahu and began new jobs. The lieutenant was not so lucky. He ran into a shiv in prison and died from his wounds.

"We suspect someone in a position of power helped get the other two reduced sentences. Kulima got the security guard job at Haleakalā, which you know. Walker stayed on Oʻahu and began working security for a land development company. But they both have another job. They work for a clandestine group that has recently come to our attention."

Keone knew Alcala wanted Freeman to finish his report but decided to risk Alcala's wrath by interrupting again. "Tom, given you work for the DEA, I'll take a stab and say some of the members of this group are in the illegal drug trade."

"A logical deduction," Tom replied evenly.

"My uncle Kimo Kalama told me the observatory bomber was working for some secret group combining big shot land developers and drug dealers. He thinks they're trying to embarrass the homeland and sovereignty groups. He also swore neither he nor anyone else in the sovereignty or homeland movements were involved."

Freeman waved off a red-faced Alcala. "What he told you is true. We've confirmed the existence of the group he mentioned to you. They draw their members from both professions your uncle named. What we don't know is what they call themselves or their ultimate goal. They've been linked to some efforts to embarrass the HHPS and various sovereignty movements, but we don't have a firm handle on why."

Keone was hesitant to interrupt further.

"I appreciate you getting Kalama's take on this, Keone," Freeman offered. "Did he have any idea what their deeper motives are?"

Keone appreciated Tom keeping Tony at bay, for now. "Kimo thought it might be protected land."

"That's our guess, too. But, so far, it's only a guess. That's why we've been keeping track of Kulima and Walker. Detective Kalani, I think you should pick up the story here."

"Thank you, Agent Freeman. Keone, Ange, you need to know. I hated keeping this secret from my best friends." Lindsay looked relieved to be allowed to apologize.

When Angela nodded to Kalani, Keone followed her lead.

We understand about secrets.

"When Lieutenant Alcala asked me to assist Agent Freeman in a special investigation about a week ago, he told me I couldn't discuss it with anyone, even in the department. I was assigned to shadow Frank Kulima to find out if he made any contacts with members of the MPD. Agent Freeman told me he had no evidence of another mole in our shop. But he said we needed to be extra careful, because of the major investigation he was heading. He had a detective he trusted on the Honolulu PD watch Walker."

"I swore Detective Sloane and his commander in the Honolulu PD to secrecy, too," Freeman added.

Angela shifted in her seat, no longer able to remain silent. "So, Frank Kulima's actions at the observatory are somehow related to all of this?"

Alcala exploded. "Damn it, the only reason you two are here is because Hasselbach called you before we could get Detective Kalani back up there. When I told Agent Freeman you'd discovered Kulima's role in the attempted bombing, he agreed to fly here and loop you two in. We never suspected either of you of being a mole. At the time I assigned Detective Kalani, you were tied up with the Alavezos murder."

"Understood. Do you plan to tell us what the hell is going on now, Agent Freeman?" Keone decided to mimic Alcala's impatience.

"Hell yes, Keone," Freeman echoed. "Given what Lindsay discovered, we needed to expand the team anyway. Go ahead . . . uh . . . Detective Kalani."

Was Tom looking a little embarrassed now?

Keone wondered how closely Tom had been working with *Lindsay.*

"I managed to follow Frank Kulima without much problem. Frank was never the sharpest nail in the box. He stayed in an 'ohana, studio-apartment, behind his uncle's house in Kula. Mostly, he just went back and forth between there and his job at the observatory. But yesterday, Frank tried to leave his little house over the garage without being seen. I spotted him and followed on foot.

"After about an hour, he met up with a middle-aged Caucasian in a hoodie and slipped him an envelope. I wanted to follow the envelope, so I called the Lieutenant and asked if he could have someone take over the tail on Frank. I never guessed he'd do it himself."

"Let's focus on your suspect, Detective Kalani," Tony said. "We all know I'm capable of tailing someone."

Keone also knew his boss enjoyed getting personally involved in investigations.

"Sorry, sir," Lindsay said. "The man I followed went on a little hike. After two hours, I wasn't sure I'd made a good choice."

Tony squirmed in his seat.

"I'm sorry." Lindsay knew what she'd done. "I'll stick to what I observed."

Tony nodded.

"After a long trek up the side of Haleakalā, we arrived at a large barn deep in the heavy brush between Kula and Ulapalakua. The building must have been over fifty feet high, but the outside looked like it was about to collapse. I spotted several guards arrayed around the place and decided to wait outside their perimeter and keep watch. Through my binoculars, I observed the suspect enter the building and emerge about a half-hour later wearing a brown, leather backpack. I reported all this to the Lieutenant."

Keone had seen a brown leather backpack just a few hours earlier on Haleakalā. *Not a coincidence.*

Alcala chimed in. "Agent Freeman asked me to have Detective Kalani keep the unnamed subject in sight, but not approach."

"Did you know who the guy was, Tom?" Keone asked.

"No. He wasn't from the group. We figured he was hired for a specific job."

Lindsay paused to take a sip from a bottle of water, which left everyone looking at Freeman.

Tom took the hint. "I guess I should tell you what we've been doing all this time on O'ahu. Former sergeant Walker led us to a meeting of the leaders of the group Kimo Kalama told Keone about. The developers were mostly headquartered in O'ahu and the dealers on Maui, but there was some overlap. We used long-distance auditory surveillance and discovered two facts. First, they have three key facilities on Maui, and one is protected with explosives, installed by your old friend Walden. Second, their next meeting is scheduled on Maui, at one of the three facilities, immediately after they complete something called, *Stooge Poke*. Detective Kalani can take it from here."

Keone understood Freeman was trying to give Lindsay fair credit, but someone had to state the obvious. "Let's cut to the chase. Lindsay found one of the facilities. And the guy she followed was the one who tried to blow up the observatory, right?"

Tom looked surprised, but Tony flashed a quick smile at Keone.

"Look I'm a detective, okay? *Stooge Poke* clearly refers to fingers to the eyes, ala Moe to Larry and Curley. And telescopes are damn big eyes. Angela and I also saw the backpack you described on the bomber at Haleakalā. Now, when did you lose the bomber, Lindsay?"

"I tracked him back to his car in Kula but had to rush back to mine to continue the tail. I did lose him for a while but caught up to him on the back road to Hāna. I guessed he was heading home, but he wasn't. He went off-road to another hidden warehouse and must have switched cars because I lost him. After a couple of hours another guy drove off in the un— uh . . . bomber's car, stopped, and pushed it off the Hāna highway. I drove back to Kula and took over Kulima's surveillance from Lieutenant Alcala. He confirmed that Kulima hadn't left his house since returning from his walk."

"Detective Kalani relieved me at eight p.m.," Alcala confirmed.

"I followed Frank to work this morning and should have been there to see the guy arrive at the first gate." Lindsay looked at her hands.

"Should have been?" Angela asked.

"Detective Kalani answered an emergency call just down the Haleakalā Highway," Tony said.

"An exploding drug lab?" Angela asked.

Lindsay nodded.

"That's the call the bomb squad and ambulance were answering when they were re-directed to the observatory. This group is well connected. Maybe they do still have someone inside?" Angela said.

"Unlikely, but we can't take any chances." Tony looked at Freeman.

"I'm worried about our shop, too. The woman who leaked Dave Walden's location to Alavezos is no longer in the Federal Building, but we have reason to believe there's another compromised federal employee in Honolulu, either with DEA or FBI."

"That's why you're bringing us in," Angela said. "If you can hit all the warehouses at the same time, you stand a good chance of catching the leaders from Maui and O'ahu."

"But, if I'm counting correctly, you only know the location of two of the warehouses. And you don't know precisely when they're meeting, just sometime after the bombing attempt, yeah?" Keone said.

Tom Freeman smiled at Keone. "Actually, we know a bit more."

29

Tuesday, November 5, 9:00 a.m.

Keone was concerned about the size of the team assembled in the main conference room at CID Headquarters in Wailuku. Including Keone and Angela, only ten individuals were preparing to initiate the operation.

Angela nudged Keone. "Your buddy Freeman is quite an optimist."

"He's also lucky. Roger Walker could have led them to any of the three warehouses."

"Good thing it was the one we had yet to locate. Good thing Freeman had the HPD detective follow the jerk from Oʻahu. Good thing—"

"Luck." Keone rolled his eyes.

Tom Freeman opened a binder in front of him and tapped a pen on the conference table to start the briefing. "I want to thank you all for arriving on time. We have a lot to cover in this organizational meeting for what we are calling Operation Two-

W. This operation is aimed at shutting down a criminal organization we're now calling, for lack of a better name, the Big Shits."

Smiles around the table confirmed the name was popular with the law enforcement professionals involved.

Tom continued. "We believe a meeting of all the leaders of the Big Shits will begin around one p.m. today at one of three possible locations. I'd like to have Detective Sheldon Sloane of Honolulu PD tell the team what we know about the members from Oahu."

"Thank you, Agent Freeman. Most of the Oʻahu people left yesterday. Major real estate developers plus a few who occupy senior positions in the illicit drug trade on our island. None have been spotted on Maui, except Roger Walker, who I tailed here on a commercial jet two days ago. We suspect the, uh, biggest shits used private helicopters, yachts, or both. We chose not to inform the coast guard for the same reason only those in this room are aware of the operation. One leak, and we're screwed."

"Thank you, Detective. Now for the details of the operation. There will be two helicopter teams and two ATV teams. I'll lead Helicopter Team One. Detective Lindsay Kalani from Maui PD, Agent Allen Frederking from DEA, and pilot Ho Yung from the DEA will comprise my team. We'll investigate a large wooden barn between Kula and Ulapalakua. Detective Kalani discovered this site during her surveillance of Sergei Plotkin. Plotkin is the person who later tried, unsuccessfully, to place explosives at the Hawaiian Observatories on Haleakalā. We've designated the barn as warehouse one on the maps in front of each of you.

"Helicopter team two will be led by Detective Lieutenant Alcala, Head of CID here on Maui. Maui PD pilot Nguyen

Tran Nu will fly him to a location near Hāna where they will be met by MPD officers William Mahoe and Nathan Sapiandante in a four-wheel ATV. Would you like to add anything Lieutenant?"

"One brief update for those of you involved in the observatory investigation, Security Guard Kono Matsuda, who stopped the bomber and was shot by Frank Kulima is going to pull through and will be receiving a citation from the Governor for his brave acts, as will the guard dog Duke, posthumously."

This news brought a rare smile to Keone's face. He noticed Angela was smiling, too. Angela's two colleagues from Hāna division had no idea of their mission with Tony, but Billy and Nate were masters of the rugged terrain beyond Hāna. They could guide Alcala quickly and quietly through the bush to his target.

"Helo Team Two will join ATV Team One and investigate an abandoned cinder-block structure off the back roads beyond Hāna. This warehouse was also discovered during Detective Kalani's surveillance of Plotkin. It is designated warehouse two on your maps."

"My, these feds are certainly imaginative in their designations," Angela whispered.

Keone smiled and briefly closed his eyes.

"Detective Sergeant Keone Boyd of Maui PD will lead ATV Team Two. His partner, Detective Sergeant Beyers, Detective Sheldon Sloane of the Honolulu PD, and CSI Sergeant Edward Jenkins of Maui PD will round out the team. Sergeant Jenkins discovered the identity of Sergei Plotkin and the scheduled time of the meeting from his examination of the corpse of the bomber. Thank you for agreeing to join our team, Sergeant."

"My pleasure, Special Agent Freeman." Ed Jenkins formal tone suggested he was a little uncomfortable.

Keone was one of the few who completely understood the significance of this exchange. He whispered in Angela's ear, "Tom didn't have a lot of options. He could either use Ed or lock him up. I'm glad Tony vouched for him."

"He'll be fine," Angela assured her partner.

Keone thought so, too. The friendly CSI had risked his own life to save Keone's during the original Loftus and Walden cases. But he still wondered how he discovered the time of the meeting from a corpse.

Freeman continued, "Sergeant Jenkins, what else do we know about Plotkin?"

"He lived in Newark, New Jersey and worked as an explosives contractor, mostly for the Russian mafia."

Probably how Dave met him.

"Detective Sergeant Boyd's team will travel by four-wheeled ATV from this station to the abandoned pineapple-processing facility discovered by Detective Sloane." Freeman glanced again at Sloane.

"Oh, me again? I followed suspect Roger Walker to a remote location between Wailuku and Kapalua on the back roads of West Maui. From photographs, Sergeant Beyers recognized the site on the cliffs and offered to take us up there."

"Our departures will be coordinated so that each team arrives at their designated site at least one hour before the meeting is set to begin. No one is to approach their target until we have confirmation of arrival of the participants. Let's say we move in at thirteen thirty hours unless something changes. Ground team one will depart immediately." Freeman closed his binder and stood. "Good hunting, everyone."

They'd been on the road for fifteen minutes in total silence.

Angela shared the front seat with Keone. Jenkins and Sloane occupied the back. Ange didn't know Sloane, but she knew Ed Jenkins was dying to talk but wouldn't speak until someone else broke the silence.

"'Thirteen thirty hours.' Couldn't he have just said one thirty p.m.? I'm not used to all this cloak and dagger crap," Angela said.

"Neither am I, Ange," Keone said and twisted around in his seat to face the rear. "Ed, I'm glad to see you you've been promoted since we last worked together."

"Thank you, sir."

"Cut the *sir* crap. We're both sergeants. Ange tells me you helped her on her last case, too. How the hell did you find out the time of the meeting from the bomber's body?"

"He had the bad habit of writing notes to himself on his wrist," Jenkins replied.

"Really?" Angela said. "I'm surprised a pro would be so sloppy."

"Well, he wrote in an obscure Georgian dialect. I know most eastern European languages, but not this puppy. I spent almost an hour online translating what he wrote."

"What did the note say in English?" Angela noticed Keone gave Jenkins his full attention.

"In effect, Big Shits—Warehouse—Thirteen hundred hours —Tomorrow. We were lucky he used military terminology for the time."

"Quite a difference between the early afternoon and the middle of the night. Now I understand why Tom's calling the group of developers and drug lords the Big Shits." Keone could tell his smile surprised Sloane. "Say, did your IT guys figure out who sent the false tip that sent Detective Kalani to a non-existent meth lab?"

"The call came from the security gate at the observatory from a burner phone, before the bomber arrived," Sloane answered.

Good old Frank Kulima, Angela surmised.

Detective Sloane continued. "You've got me wondering. Given the three targets are all warehouses, why didn't Agent Freeman call this Operation Three-W?"

"That's a good question and you're part of the answer, Sloane." Keone looked at his partner. "You'll appreciate this, Ange."

"I'm all ears," Angela replied, keeping her eyes on the winding road.

"Remember that unknown subject you found back in October, Sloane?" Keone asked.

"Sure. I was following Roger Walker while he provided security for a developer. They met with the unsub at Punchbowl. I couldn't get too close but had a directional mic and tried to catch some of what they said."

"You had no idea who the unsub was?" Jenkins asked.

"They never used names, and I'd never seen him before. Anyway, this guy was apparently responsible for getting the drug dealers to join the developers' little scheme a couple of years ago. He needed a wad of cash to disappear, and the developer owed him. He'd designed and built their explosives facility shortly before he was nailed by DEA."

"DEA and Maui PD to be specific," Keone added.

"Dave Walden?" Angela was somehow not surprised. "Of course. Walden made a stop on his way to Maui. He needed things. Like the gun he used to shoot Hopper Alavezos."

Jenkins nodded. "We confirmed that the gun Walden used

to kill Alavezos and Loftus was also used to kill a woman on O'ahu on October twenty-seventh."

Nice to have a CSI along. Angela remembered Sam proudly clutching the gun Walden used to shoot him as he fell to the ground.

"Wait. October twenty-seventh was the day of the Punchbowl meeting," Sloane said.

"Do you know the woman's name, Ed?" Angela asked.

"Mrs. Carrie Ann Shaw. She used to work—"

"At the Federal Building in Honolulu, until she was fired. Do you happen to know her maiden name?" Keone asked.

"Alavezos." Jenkins clearly was surprised by the connection.

"Let's get back to Walden," Keone suggested. "Tom Freeman knows Walden by sight. He helped me catch him on Moloka'i. Why didn't he give us a heads-up before Walden got to Maui?"

Sloane looked embarrassed. "I recorded the meeting and took a few pictures with my smartphone. I saw the man's face but couldn't get a clear picture of it."

"What about the tape?" Keone asked.

"I was far away. They were whispering to each other. The fragments I caught had to be enhanced by experts before we could even make out words. Agent Freeman and I reviewed the enhanced recordings. I couldn't have recognized my own voice. No one could have." Sloane moved uncomfortably in his seat.

"I understand," Angela said. "The ones I've heard sounded like robots talking."

"When your LT called Freeman to tell him about your final encounter with Walden at the airstrip on Haleakalā, Freeman had a hunch and sent a picture of Walden to my smartphone. That's when I confirmed Walden was the unsub I saw."

When Sloane finished, Jenkins risked a question. "Did Walden know about the bombing?"

"He recommended Plotkin on the tape," Sloane replied.

"Walden probably met Sergei when they both worked for the Russian mob," Keone added.

After a period of silence, Jenkins said, "Sorry, but I still don't understand Operation Two-W."

"Let's see." Angela glanced at Keone. "Dave Walden, also known as the Great Waldo. Keone, you didn't?"

"I always liked those books." Keone chuckled.

"You've lost me. What books?" Jenkins asked.

"A series of children's books called *Where's Waldo?* Operation Two-W," Angela explained.

"Good work, partner," Keone said. "What else would you call finding a needle in three haystacks?"

"With one of those haystacks wired to explode by none other than Dave Walden." Angela couldn't believe Keone convinced Freeman to name the operation after children's books, then it hit her. Writing children's books was Julie's occupation. "Let me get this straight. We're talking about Dave Walden. The guy who cheated on and abused Julie, had a meth conversion operation in his basement, and almost blew you to bits."

"Who's Julie?" Sloane asked.

"She's my wife," Keone answered calmly. "But she was Walden's wife at the time."

"Don't interrupt." Her irritated voice reflected the fact that Angela was still navigating the narrow, winding tracks to their destination. "Walden? Really? The same guy who hired people to discredit you in the Maui PD, ratted on the Russian mafia, and blew up some of those same Russians, when they found him in witness protection. The guy who faked his own death, killed Hopper Alavezos and Sam Loftus, and flew a plane at you and me. That guy, right Keone?"

"Uh huh."

"That same guy helped start the Big Shits, killed Alavezos's cousin, and suggested the bomber that hit the observatory?"

"Quite the bad penny, yeah?"

"Yeah. And you were griping to me about Freeman's luck?"

"We all have luck, Angela. His just happens to be good."

A thought gnawed at Angela's mind. *Frank Kulima and Roger Walker both worked for Dave Walden. I wonder? No way.*

30

Tuesday, November 5, 11:30 a.m.

Detective Lindsay Kalani gazed out the helicopter's window upon the rich green hillside that approached. Their pilot prepared to land far enough away from the warehouse to avoid being seen or heard. The remainder of the journey involved a long, uphill hike. A trek she was familiar with.

Freeman turned to the pilot. "Agent Yung, you'll remain in the chopper and keep in touch with the other teams by radio and by walkie with me."

"Yes, sir. I'll be ready if we need to bug out."

"Roger that." Tom Freeman's face displayed confidence and his excitement at being on the chase. Lindsay liked that face.

"Detective Kalani and I will take point. Frederking will cover our six. Check your walkies. All good? Let's move out."

When Lindsay and Freeman reached an appropriate

distance from the other agent, Tom adopted a gentler tone. "Sorry about the orders back there, Lindsay."

"I understand, sir. This is your operation."

They continued walking up the volcano in silence, Frederking five or six paces behind.

"Here's the thing, Lindsay. I'd like to see you after the operation. Outside of work."

Lindsay's heart jumped. She'd sensed Tom might have feelings for her, like she had for him, but—

Freeman held up a hand and pointed ahead. "The warehouse. We'll talk later. Stay here."

The agent circled to Lindsay's right and soon disappeared into the heavy brush.

When Tom Freeman reappeared ten minutes later, he walked Frederking up to Lindsay's position. "We need to keep low," he said and crouched.

Lindsay and Frederking followed suit.

With whispers and hand signals, Tom described the layout. "Six guards are scattered around the outer perimeter, about a hundred yards out from the barn. Two more guards are posted directly outside each of the two entrances to the barn, one entrance in front and the other in the rear. I've located a position where I can watch both the two peripheral guards who flank the front entrance and the two directly in front of the door. Now, let's get you in position." He duck-waddled forward, and they followed, staying low.

Freeman led them to the left of their current position and slightly forward. Tom pointed to his right. "Lindsay, do you see the top of the guard's head?"

She nodded.

"He's at the left center of the barn. If you follow an arc sixty degrees to his left and raise up slightly, you should be able to glimpse the head of the guard at the left rear of the building." Tom rose slightly and pointed.

"I see him," Lindsay whispered.

Before he and Frederking moved on, Tom whispered, "I'm going to take Frederking around behind that guy and continue around the circle until he can see the guards at the right rear and right center. Then I'll circle around to cover the left and right front. "My gut tells me the meeting will be here. If the Big Shits start arriving, I'll contact Ho Yung by walkie to have the other teams converge on our chopper. If they reach one of you first, disperse them to the other team members' positions so that we end up with at least one person per guard when we move in. If I'm wrong and the meeting is at one of the other two sites, Yung will inform me by walkie, we'll disengage and meet the other teams at one of the other sites. I'm not sure about connectivity up here. So, if you hear nothing more from me and the other teams arrive, we move in as scheduled at thirteen thirty hours. Got it?"

Lindsay and Frederking nodded.

Tom took Frederking to a position where he could watch the guard at the right rear and right middle of the barn then headed to the site he'd picked out for himself.

Once in position, Tom surveyed the area in all directions with his binoculars. At forty-five degrees southwest of his position, he spotted a small puff of dust. A few minutes later, a black SUV with tinted windows so dark he couldn't see inside pulled up to the front entrance.

Over the next fifteen minutes, five more vehicles pulled up and discharged their passengers. Tom recognized the Big Shits from Oahu as they exited. The meeting would be here.

Tom spoke to the pilot by walkie with a detailed message for Tony Alcala.

Meeting at warehouse one. Eyes on six perimeter guards. Two more at each entrance and rest inside. Leave one team member at each of the other warehouses and fly here. Pick up ground team one on the way. Will try to wait to approach until you arrive. But I'd still like us to move in by thirteen thirty hours, so make haste.

Tom Freeman watched as the Big Shits continued to arrive. If this meeting followed the pattern of others he'd observed on Oʻahu, it would begin a few minutes after the last arrival and continue for a couple of hours.

The other teams should have plenty of time to get here before anyone left.

But you can never rely on what should happen, Tom thought.

A message arrived from Tony via Ho Yung.

Picked up ground team. Heading your way. Neither of our warehouses had explosives or evidence of an impending meeting. Mahoe and Sapiandante guarding other two sites and won't request back-up until Big Shits in our custody.

Freeman was uneasy. Why would they schedule the meeting in a warehouse wired to explode? The place was wired to self-destruct on unauthorized entry or exit. Who would willingly walk into a potential bomb? Unless . . .

"Shit!"

Tom's grabbed his walkie. He had an urgent message for his pilot.

31

Tuesday, November 5, 12:15 p.m.

Aboard Alcala's chopper, Keone compared notes with Tony on the two warehouses. They both had disobeyed Freeman's orders and done recon.

"My target had light security, so we just wove around them and snuck into the warehouse. It was a simple cinderblock cube. The only things inside were a few small arms and a huge stash of drugs. No explosives, no wires. No Big Shits. When I got the message from Freeman's pilot, I left Mahoe there and hightailed it over to pick you folks up," Tony said.

"Our warehouse was the same. Thanks for leaving Sapiandante there so we could all be in on the capture." Keone wished the chopper could go faster. His friends were in danger.

Tony received a text update from Freeman's pilot, sent a reply, then turned to Keone. "If Tom's right about the meeting being at his warehouse, it also has to be the one that's wired with explosives."

"Wasn't that the barn where Plotnik picked up his explosives for the observatory?" Keone asked.

"That's what Lindsay said," Angela answered. "Why would they store all their explosives in a place wired to blow and then invite their leadership there for a meeting?"

"They wouldn't. Not on purpose." Keone didn't like where this was leading.

The pilot began their descent near Kula and landed a few minutes later next to the DEA chopper.

Angela jumped out first and ran to the other chopper. She returned, with her weapon drawn. "Pilot's missing. No sign of a struggle."

"Damn. He was supposed to stay here," Keone said.

Tony turned to his pilot. "Keep our chopper hot and watch the other one, Nu."

Turning back to the rest of the team, Alcala pulled his own weapon and said, "Let's go."

The others followed the lieutenant's lead, weapons drawn. Keone took up the rear, sweeping his eyes and his weapon back and forth across their flank.

Great plan. If one of those guards finds us before we find one of Freeman's team, the operation's toast.

"Over here, Ange." A whisper from the brush became the hidden form of Lindsay Kalani.

Angela, Keone, Tony, Jenkins, and Sloane crouched low next to the detective.

"Glad you could make it," Lindsay said in a low voice. "We're supposed to advance on the barn in just under an hour if we don't hear otherwise from Agent Freeman. There are six guards on the perimeter and two more by each door. We each have two perimeter guards in sight."

"Where's your pilot?" Tony whispered.

"We left him with the chopper."

"He's not there now," Keone said and watched Lindsay stiffen.

"Lieutenant, you need to go to Agent Freeman's position. Better take Jenkins with you. Freeman may know what's going on with the pilot. You'll find him on an arc about one hundred and twenty degrees to my right. Try to maintain your distance from the perimeter guards."

"Did he give you instructions for everyone else?" Tony asked.

"Yes, sir."

"Follow his orders until you hear from him or me, Detective." Tony and Jenkins disappeared into the brush.

"Where do you want me, Detective Kalani?" Sloane asked.

"I need you to find Frederking. He's on an arc one hundred and twenty degrees to my left. He'll give you further instructions there. Like me, Frederking got specific orders directly from Agent Freeman."

Keone watched Sloane move away and saw Lindsay turn to Angela.

"See the top of the guard's head over there?"

Angela nodded.

"Creep up to about twenty yards from him and, at one thirty p.m., take him out. I'll be doing the same to the guy over here, on my right. After you take him out, meet me near the back door and we'll deal with the remaining guards."

Keone remained silent through all of this. When Angela and Lindsay reached their new positions, he tapped Lindsay's shoulder. "And me?"

"Sorry, Keone, I'm a little wired about the missing pilot. I'm also not used to relaying orders to people who outrank me."

"You're fine. Just fill me in on Tom's plan."

"He wants at least one of us on each periphery guard. You and Tony are supposed to be back-up and meet us at the entrances after we secure the perimeter. Tony will join Frederking, Jenkins, and Freeman at the front and help take out the two guards. Angela, Sloane, and I will meet you at the rear and do the same there."

"Then what?"

"Then we go in." Lindsay pointed to an explosive-charged battering ram in the foliage at her feet. "Unless something changes."

"It already has," Keone said. "I consider the missing pilot a change."

"I know. Tom said he trusts your instincts and that you and the Lieutenant should feel free to improvise."

As if on cue, Lindsay's walkie buzzed.

Alcala [static] Boyd to my positionnnn, Freeman's already ennnnnnnnn . . . Stiiiiiii [static] move in at thirteen thirty hours . . .

"Reception on this part of the mountain sucks," Lindsay said and asked Alcala to repeat the message.

"No response. Shit, shit, shit." She pounded the walkie against her knee.

Keone tried to reassure his colleague. "Tony and I will keep Tom safe, Lindsay. You need to stay with the plan. Can you do that, Detective?"

Lindsay nodded.

"Tony will let you know if anything changes." Keone checked his Glock and the machete on his hip before moving off.

"Keep safe, big guy," he heard Lindsay whisper to his receding back.

Keone tried to visualize a one-hundred-twenty-degree arc.

Damned egg-head feds and their complicated plans.

32

Keone arrived near the spot where he'd calculated his boss should be and whispered, "Tony."

"Over here." Tony's whispered response came from a few yards away.

"What the hell is going on?"

"Shut up and listen, Keone. This is Freeman's missing pilot. Yung, tell Keone what you told me."

"Agent Freeman's worried this whole thing could be a trap," Yung began. "Do you remember Freeman telling us during the briefing that the explosives facility is wired and can be armed to blow if anyone enters without the proper code?"

"Of course. But they wouldn't arm the explosives with the Big Shits inside," Keone said, stating the obvious.

Yung continued. "After he texted me to join him, Freeman saw a guy in camouflage fatigues walk up to the two guards at the front entrance. The guards greeted him like an old friend and opened the door—"

"Was he another guard?" Keone asked.

"No, the guards wear green jumpsuits," Tony interjected.

Keone realized his questions and Tony's interjections were just prolonging the pilot's story. The clock was ticking. "So, the guy in camo went inside."

"Yep. Right after he put two slugs into the guards with a silenced handgun. This all happened right before I got here. Once Freeman debriefed me, he snuck down to the entrance and went inside." The pilot paused.

"How? Did Freeman know the code?" Keone asked.

"No idea. But I swear, he walked right over the two bodies and went inside. If that's all, I'd liked to get back to my chopper, sir." At a nod from Tony, Yung took off.

"You don't think he knew the code, do you Tony?"

"He would have told us."

"Did he say anything else about the codes? Think, Tony." Keone couldn't keep his impatience out of his tone.

"Just before we left in our chopper, Freeman said there were two different entry/exit codes. One set worked like a home alarm system, unlatching the doors and nothing more."

"And the other armed the building for when no one was inside. Could they arm it remotely?"

"Tom said it was too dangerous, electronic signals bounce around with all the peaks and valleys on this side of the volcano. That's why we've had so much static and gibberish over our walkies."

"So, how *do* you arm it?"

"From the inside, with some sort of time-delay to allow you to get out. Once it's set, it can only be disarmed from the outside with the same code used to arm it. Keone, the guy in camo—"

"Wants the Big Shits to set off the explosives when they try to leave the meeting, unless our team storms the place first."

"But who would want—"

"Walden. Don't let anyone approach the building," Keone said, then ran towards the front of the barn.

"But Walden's dead," Tony whispered at Keone's back.

Prone on an I-beam, thirty feet above the concrete floor of the converted barn, Tom Freeman listened to the Big Shits from Maui and Oʻahu discuss their plans.

His journey to this point had been eventful, but his luck held, so far. The two dead guards at the rear entrance made his job easier. One had been so kind as to fall next to the entrance, blocking the door open. As he sprinted through the door, the shooter must not have seen the guard's boot prevent the door from closing completely.

From his perch in a tree above his two periphery guards, Tom had.

He'd climbed down the tree and back to the spot he hoped to meet his pilot. A moment later Yung arrived.

After briefing the pilot, Tom ran to the entrance and eased the door open just enough to slip inside. A silenced shot hit the wooden shell of the barn, inches from his face. He dove to the floor and the door slammed shut.

Damn.

Tom must have moved the guard's boot either when he opened the door or when he hit the floor. A keypad glowed on his side of the door. Tom was locked inside. He didn't know if it was the regular code or the disarm code, but it didn't matter. He didn't know either one.

A dim light illuminated the space around him. He saw no one on his level and an open metal stairway leading up. The shot must have come from up there.

Tom belly-crawled under the open stairway. From his vantage point, he saw the shadow of a man holding a gun. From the sound Tom heard, the man was two flights up the stairway and slowly moving down.

Tom waited until the man's left boot appeared around the corner of the first landing. The agent leapt for the top step from underneath and grabbed an ankle. The man shrieked as his ankle snapped against the metal step. When Tom let go, the guard tumbled down the remaining steps and landed in a heap, his head at an unnatural angle. Tom leaned out far enough from under the stairway to feel the man's twisted neck. No pulse.

Gazing at the dead guard's face, Tom recognized Roger Walker, formerly of the Maui PD. But Walker was wearing a security jumpsuit like the two dead guards outside. The shooter from outside was dressed in camouflage, six inches shorter, and bigger around the waist.

Walker let the man in camouflage pass his position, but not me. He was in on the plot. That's why the silencers. Neither the shooter nor Walker could afford to alert anyone inside.

Tom wondered when Walker was moved here from the place Sloane tailed him to. *Maybe they sent him there first to misdirect us.*

If Walker was in on the plot, could the shooter be—?

Tom heard quiet footsteps coming from above where Walker had fired.

It's him.

Tom moved silently up the stairway, eyes alert and weapon pointed ahead. Two flights up, he found an unguarded door with a small window. He peered inside. A long corridor led to the center of the building where it opened onto a much larger room. He heard echoed conversations but couldn't explore further. The door had a keypad, and Tom had a shooter to catch.

Continuing his climb, Tom examined the interior walls of the structure. The stairway was made of steel and bolted to huge concrete walls on his left and the shabby wooden structure of the barn on his right. The steel and concrete core made certain the older wooden shell outside stayed in place, while housing an open topped concrete box. When Tom climbed above the concrete walls of the inner structure, he saw it was a box within a box, neither of which had any windows. Climbing from the stairway to the lattice of steel girders, everything made sense. The inner box was the conference room reached by a hallway from the front entrance. The outer box held an extensive collection of explosive devices.

Initially, Tom couldn't understand why they would take such a terrible risk, convening so many important people in such a dangerous place. Now he realized it had always been the plan. Walden's plan.

***

When Keone reached the entrance to the barn, the metal door was closed. The keypad on the right glowed ominously back at him.

Think, Keone. If Tony can't stop our team, they'll storm this place in a few minutes.

The bodies at his feet belonged to two sorry specimens often used as hired muscle on Maui. Combined they had the IQ of a worm.

Wait a minute.

Keone rifled through the first thug's pockets and came up lucky. A slip of paper with five numbers.

What if the guy in camo has already changed the code?

Keone pressed in the numbers and heard the door unlock.

No boom? Hasn't changed the code—yet.

Keone leapt through the door, leading with his weapon, and—tripped.

33

From his perch on the rafter, Tom could clearly make out the meeting room in the precise center of the building. The walls had no windows. Neither did the single corridor which led from the front entrance. The rear door led into the outer box, with two small offices and a kitchen dining area along the rear wall. The remaining U-shaped warehouse contained the explosives cache, neatly arrayed on shelves. The warehouse was far from full but contained dozens of small devices on the shelves surrounding the embedded conference room.

Interesting placement, Tom thought. *Reminds me of a demolition site.*

Tom turned his attention to the discussion below.

"So, we've got the lieutenant governor, the leaders of upper house, and three of the five mayors on our side. Did you lock down the heads of the agriculture and environmental protection groups, Les?" The man who spoke from the head of the table was a well-known developer on Oʻahu. Creighton Blythe ran flamboyant ads on TV all the time but had no criminal record. Tom had checked.

"Yep. They're solid. How about the police, Red?" Les was a tall, bulky Caucasian. Probably played football in college.

Tom fished his smartphone from his pocket and used its camera to capture the features of each person at the table. Slipping his phone back in the pocket without losing his balance was a challenge. Tom somehow succeeded and returned his attention to the conversation below.

"No luck on Maui. They've been extra careful since Walden. But we've got Captain Grimm in Honolulu and Lieutenant Frawley on the Big Island. Only managed a couple of sergeants on Lanai, but they should be enough." Red must have been a nickname from youth as the frail man's hair was completely white.

"They better be. The grumbling will be historic when we open fifty thousand acres to new development," Blythe snapped. "How about the justification?"

"The seven acts of terrorism to be carried out this week will destroy the reputations of the Hawaiian Homelands Protection Society and the various Sovereignty groups completely." This voice had a Slavic accent. "Our teams will head to the other two warehouses to collect their explosive devices when we adjourn."

What the hell? The explosives are here.

The Big Shits don't know.

If the code is changed, they'd trip the explosives if they tried to leave. Even if they didn't, when his team broke in . . .

Tom moved his arm back toward his pocket but remembered he had no signal once he entered the structure. *Besides a stray signal might—*

Tom surveyed the steel framework and spotted packages at each of the major junctions—Dave Walden's detonators.

Following the wiring, Tom noticed a large circuit box where everything converged.

Tom walked the maze of girders to the box, having to balance on one leg three terrifying times.

The arming code had been entered but not yet triggered.

Did I interrupt someone?

Tom studied the tangled wiring. He had to make sure the explosives couldn't be brought online.

He followed a suspicious green wire to a digital display flashing three-zero-zero about ten feet away.

The timer. Three hundred what?

Tom moved slowly toward the glowing numbers. Something fell over his head and landed on his shoulders. Thinking fast, Tom shoved his fingers between a noose and his throat before it tightened, yanked him off his feet, and slammed his head hard into the metal floor.

Keone was surprised to discover that he'd been tripped by a dead body. The body of Former MPD Sergeant Roger Walker. Bending down to examine the corpse, Keone retrieved his Glock.

A crash from high above made Keone crouch. He surveyed his immediate surroundings. The steel staircase beyond Walker's body angled around the central cement structure, making it impossible to see more than one flight ahead. The entry door had sealed behind him. There was only one way to go—up.

Keone tried to make no sound as he climbed but heard footsteps that seemed to come from the roof.

Freeman? Did he make the crash or the shooter? Either way it didn't bode well.

Continuing his silent ascent, Keone heard an engine turn over.

34

Tom opened his eyes and watched the corrugated metal ceiling of the storage building slowly come into focus. His arms ached. An attempt to move sent a piercing pain through his shoulders.

How long was I out?

Tom's fingers remained stuck between his throat and the noose. Sliding around on his ass, Tom turned his face back to the junction box. A chubby figure in camouflage worked with the wires.

He's arming the explosives. Starting the timer.

Wait, if the shooter's there, who's holding the noose?

Tom used his legs to crawl backward toward the ledge. This loosened the noose enough for him to roll onto his stomach. Until he could assess his true predicament, Tom kept his fingers between the noose and his neck. Once he had enough slack, he'd whip it over his head.

The rope went to a pulley attached to a huge beam directly across from where he lay. Tom estimated he'd have twenty feet before he reached the edge of the ledge. Plenty of slack to remove the noose.

Now that he was on his stomach, he belly-crawled forward until he could get to his knees. The added slack and leverage would allow him to remove the noose.

The loud growl of a motor engaging was accompanied by intense pressure around his neck. The backs of Tom's fingers cut off his airway.

The motor was to his left and belonged to a winch. The winch's tow wire was connected to the rope around his neck. The man in camouflage stood next to the winch and smiled. A gun in one hand and the winch control box in his other, the shooter said, "Good try, Agent Asshole."

To avoid strangulation, Tom had to crawl slowly forward on his knees toward the edge of the ledge that held the junction box. Beyond the ledge, the drop. But what worried him more was the twenty feet of rope between the end of the ledge and the first pulley.

THE ENGINE'S LOUD CHUGGING ALLOWED KEONE TO RUN up the remaining steps without worrying about the noise he made. He wondered what the Big Shits made of the sound. When he reached the top of the metal stairway, a bizarre tableau greeted his eyes. Tom Freeman was on his knees, fighting with a rope near the edge of a beam.

Keone's eyes followed the rope to a pulley attached to a cross beam. From that pulley, a cable went to his and Tom's left toward the noise of the engine. The sound came from around a metal barrier in front of Keone's position. Silently, Keone eased his machete from its leather sheath and grabbed the edge of the barrier with his free hand. In one movement, Keone swung around the metal barrier and sliced his machete through the air, noting it also passed cleanly through the forearm of a man holding a Glock in one hand and a control box in the other.

A gun clattered on the metal flooring as Frank Kulima whipped his remaining hand over the blood spewing from his stump.

Kulima. With Walden and Walker dead, it had to be him.

Tom Freeman gasped out something unintelligible.

Keone snatched the control box from Kulima's severed hand and hit reverse.

The rope went slack. Tom flipped the noose over his head and immediately fell over backward.

The Big Shits below were yelling at each other about some detail of their plan. It was a miracle they hadn't noticed the engine or the struggle unfolding far above their heads.

Keone felt no remorse about leaving Frank and climbed from girder to girder to reach Freeman. "Tom. It's Keone."

The agent's eyes snapped open, and he struggled to stand up.

"Take it easy. You need a few deep breaths before you're going anywhere."

"No time." Tom gasped, pointing to the junction box. "Changed code. Set timer."

Keone had to walk on girders again to reach the timer.

"What does it say?" Tom rasped.

"Two, one, one. Now, two, one, zero.

This can't be good.

Tom joined him. "Only that guy you took out can disarm it now. Is he still alive?"

Keone retraced his steps along the girders and felt for a femoral pulse.

Nothing.

Keone made his way back to Freeman and shook his head.

Freeman looked down, all around them, and finally up. "That could work."

Keone followed Tom's outstretched finger. Ten feet above them held up by the steel girders was the roof of the old barn. On the back wall, behind the girders, a faint light glowed through a window. "Do you think it's wired?"

"Maybe only to the alarm, given its location. Breaking through it shouldn't trigger the explosion. I hope." Tom glanced at the digital display. "Keone, we have three minutes to get out of here and chase our friends away from the barn. Unless, of course, one of the Big Shits tries to step out for a breath of fresh air."

Keone looked at his watch.

It was 1:29 p.m.

35

Tuesday, November 5, 1:30 p.m.

Lindsay and Angela neutralized their guards and approached the rear of the barn. Their last message from Tony was garbled. Since it came at almost their arranged jump-off time, both assumed it was just a confirmation to move out.

Angela pointed out the two guards at the rear entrance to the barn.

Both women knew what to do. They hoped Tony, Frederking, and Jenkins were doing their jobs at the front entrance.

The guards were facing each other, smoking, and talking. Probably figured no one could get through the perimeter guards. Lindsay and Angela surprised their targets from behind. Lindsay knocked hers out with the portable battering ram she'd retrieved from the brush. Angela looped her right arm around the other guard's windpipe and squeezed until he dropped like a rock.

"Where's Sloane?" Angela asked.

Lindsay shrugged her shoulders. She was more concerned about where Tom was.

Lindsay pointed the ram at the door and braced herself to absorb the explosive charge that would break the latch.

A sound of breaking glass from above made her hesitate and look up. She heard a voice, Keone's voice.

Keone leaned out the broken window and shouted something.

"What did he say?" Angela asked.

Keone threw a rope through the broken window and started to belay down, yelling again.

Lindsay heard him this time. "He said, 'Run. Run like hell. It's gonna blow.'"

She and Angela didn't hesitate. Glancing back, Lindsay saw Keone hit the ground at the bottom of the rope and start to run. Her eyes followed the rope up to a window at the very top of the barn. Someone else was climbing down the rope from a window.

Tom.

The explosion knocked Lindsay over. But her eyes remained focused on the small form hanging from the remnant of the now burning rope. Tom Freeman's body flew in a gentle arc towards the trees. She wondered how that must feel, then lost consciousness.

36

Wednesday, November 6, 9:30 a.m.

Keone looked from Angela's hand on Lindsay's shoulder to his own hands. The rope burns were covered with salve and wrapped in gauze. His hands and his concussed brain would heal, but his guilt . . .

Tom was right, of course. Only Keone's bulk could break the window. Tom promised to be right behind him. But right behind him wasn't good enough.

Keone couldn't sit any longer. He circled the waiting room at Maui Memorial Hospital. After his fifth circuit, Angela put her arm in front of him, like a barrier. Forced to stop pacing, Keone wanted—needed—to say something comforting to Lindsay Kalani. Words failed him. He couldn't even put his hand on her shoulder, with all the gauze.

Lindsay turned her head and looked up at Keone through glistening eyes. "I love Tom, you know."

He could only nod.

"I'm glad." Angela hugged her friend. "You'll make a lovely couple."

Tony Alcala leaned against the wall at the other end of the surgical waiting room. "He was conscious in the helicopter. That's positive, right?"

"Of course, it is. And Tom wouldn't let them sedate him until he'd given you his cellphone and a full report," Angela added.

"That's right, Beyers. We have a dozen people in custody now because of him. Politicians, dirty cops, federal employees, even a few Big Shits who missed the meeting." The developers and drug pushers had never given their organization a name, so Tony continued using the one the bomber coined. "I'm just glad Keone warned you and Lindsay off. I reached the others by walkie or in person to tell them to stand down but couldn't reach you two in time."

Keone was glad Angela and Tony had themselves together enough to say what Lindsay needed to hear. *Where are my words of comfort?*

A wave of warmth infused Keone's body. He felt a surge of confidence. "Tom's gonna make it, Lindsay. I know it."

Lindsay smiled up at him through her tears.

Tony pushed himself off the wall and nearly collided with a doctor in scrubs who barreled through the door.

Suddenly realizing his surgical mask was still in place, the doctor tugged it down under his chin. "Are you here for Agent Freeman?"

"Yes," Tony answered.

Keone and Angela helped Lindsay to her feet.

"I had little hope when we began the surgery. So many bones were broken. But that was what saved him. When he hit the tree and the ground, the massive force was distributed almost evenly across a large surface area. He looks terrible and his rehabilitation will take time. But he'll recover."

"Nerve damage?" Keone asked.

"Surprisingly little. The real trick was removing all the bone fragments and repairing injured vessels. He should be able to return to limited duty in a few months—with extensive physical therapy. Someone's looking out for that young man."

"When can we see him?" Lindsay asked.

"Are you Lindsay?"

She nodded.

"Before we administered anesthesia, I asked if he needed anything. He was woozy but grasped my scrub top and pulled me close so I could hear what he was about to say: 'Doc, you make sure that when I wake up Lindsay is holding my hand, and I'll promise not to die on you.'"

Keone watched the doctor lead Lindsay back through the double doors. Keone then wrapped his bandaged arms around Tony and Angela and didn't bother to hide his tears.

Tom struggled to break the surface and open his eyes, but the pain fought him every inch of the way. Every surface on his body stung from the burns. But the pain deep inside was far greater. He concentrated on one small ring around his wrist that felt different.

Using this tiny ring as a lifeline, he swam through his unconsciousness. He heard a voice say, "Hi."

Tom opened his eyes. "Lindsay? What time?"

"Ten a.m., Wednesday. You've been out more than twelve hours."

"You're here. I don't . . ."

"Don't try to talk. I need you to suck on these." Lindsay brought some ice chips to his lips.

"So . . . damn . . . thirsty."

"I said don't try to talk. Let me." Lindsay was firm.

"But I have . . . so many . . . questions."

"I know. During the mission, you asked me about going out."

"Huh?" Tom was caught off guard.

"I've been thinking about it, and I guess I'll take a chance."

Tom looked at her through glistening eyes. "I'll be . . . a p-p-plurfect gentleman."

"The hell you will." Lindsay gave him the softest of kisses on the lips.

"Is everyone else okay?"

"Better than you. When did you decide you could fly, Peter Pan?"

"How far did I go?" Tom's last memory before his painful helicopter ride was staring at the burning rope in his hands and seeing the ground far below.

"You were about twenty-five feet up when the rope burned through. The blast sent you about a hundred feet in a north-easterly direction. You then encountered a stand of Cook pines."

"The branches cushioned my impact."

Lindsay glanced at the tip of a steel rod protruding through Tom's left femur. "Yes, that's true—until you fell the remaining fifteen feet to the ground. Nice arc, though."

"I must have broken a few bones."

"Pretty much all of them."

"Nerve damage?"

"Left leg took the worst of the impact."

Now Tom was scared. "Will I walk?"

"Doc says yes, eventually. Probably with a cane."

"Lindsay, I . . ." Tom's eyes closed.

"Me, too," Tom heard Lindsay say, before sinking back below the surface.

———

THEY MUST HAVE STAYED IN THIS POSITION, LINDSAY'S fingers on Tom's unburned wrist, him flat on his back, until Tom resurfaced from the heavy sedation sometime later.

"I need to talk to Keone."

His voice made Lindsay jump. She must have dozed off, too. "You gave Tony a comprehensive report before you let them sedate you."

"I know. But there's something else. Something for Keone."

"I'll let him know you're awake. He'll come in after his shift, if you're up to it." Lindsay emphasized the last part.

"No. I need to talk to Keone now. Please call him for me, Lindsay." Tom's eyes made his case.

Lindsay hit speed-dial on her phone. "Five minutes, max," she said to Tom before Keone answered.

Tom heard a click, then Keone's voice. "How's our boy, Lindsay?"

"I'll let him tell you. You have five minutes." She put the phone up to Tom's right ear, one of the few open spaces between his various casts.

"Keone?"

"It's great to hear your voice, brah. You did a hell of a job up at the—"

"Thanks. Now shut up and listen."

Keone went silent.

"I planned to tell you this as soon as the mission was finished but didn't get the chance. While we were flying to the warehouse, I got a call from a guy at the FBI. He was on that cruise of East Asia that I told you about."

"Can't this wait?"

"No. I'm not sure how long I can stay conscious with all the drugs I have on board. The guy, I forget his name, asked me for your contact in Europol. Two more female Olympic medalists from the Greek games were killed during that Asian cruise."

"Where?" Keone's voice became serious.

"Japan."

"When?"

"Yesterday, no day before. The day you picked me up at the airport." Tom was having trouble forming sentences, again.

"Get well, quick. And thanks for everything."

"Anytime, brah." Tom was feeling the lure of his medication.

"I'll stop by tomorrow with Angela."

Tom surrendered to the warmth and comfort of the sedation.

37

Thursday, November 7, 5:30 p.m.

Keone and Angela arrived at Maui Memorial in separate cars but at nearly the same time. As they waited for the elevator, Keone sensed something bothering his partner. "What is it, Ange?"

"Why did Kulima do it? How did Kulima do it?"

"Just following orders, as they say."

"Whose orders?"

"Walden's. Frank Kulima and Roger Walker were always Dave's men. Walden got the Big Shits to shorten their sentences and hire them."

"Why? They screwed up before. Why would Walden give a shit about them?"

The elevator doors opened, and Keone let Angela enter first. "He didn't," Keone said as the doors closed. "Kulima and Walker had the advantage that they were expendable. Dave never really trusted the Big Shits. The drug dealers' history with the Russian mob made Walden nervous. You may recall Dave's last encounter with the Russians produced casualties."

"Tom said somebody at the meeting in the barn spoke with a Russian accent."

"Not surprising. Anyway, Dave made Kulima and Walker promise that if anything happened to him, they'd spring Dave's trap. All they had to do was make sure the Big Shits held their next meeting in that little barn he'd wired and change the code while they were inside. Tony found detailed instructions in Kulima's place."

"I knew those two weren't smart enough to set that up. What about the explosion almost killing us, too? How could Dave have known?"

"He couldn't. We were just collateral damage. But he wouldn't have minded. Neither would Kulima and Walker."

"That luck of yours. Still mostly bad, brah?" Angela punched Keone's shoulder.

"But not all. I got you fo' one pahtnah, Tita."

"Agreed," Ange said when the elevator reached their floor.

Keone opened the hospital room door to find Tom Freeman holding Lindsay Kalani's right hand in his bandaged left. Keone guessed it hurt. He also guessed Tom couldn't care less.

"You look like a beached monk seal."

"Great to see you, too, Ange."

"I think you just insulted monk seals, Ange." Keone smiled.

Tom glanced at Lindsay. "Friends, what a comfort."

Angela walked over and gave Lindsay a big hug. "That's for both of you, Tom."

"Thanks, Ange," Tom said. "If you hugged me like that right now, you'd hear a loud cracking sound and embarrassingly high-pitched screams. But I appreciate the thought."

"You saved my life and Lindsay's."

"What about the rest of the team, Angela? Everything after the explosion is still pretty fuzzy."

Lindsay rolled her eyes, suggesting to Angela that Tom had asked her the same question before and didn't remember the answer.

"Everyone is fine. You know how Keone got out of the barn. Tony sent a message by walkie to the rest of the team to take out the perimeter guards and hold there, but only Sloane and Jenkins confirmed. After taking out his own guard, Tony hurried around the circle to check on the remaining team members. He reached Frederking after he took his guard out and had him stay put. He didn't reach Lindsay and I until we were running back from the barn."

"Then we all got knocked on our asses," Lindsay concluded for Angela. "I never saw Tony. I was looking back at the barn when the impact hit us. I did get a good view of your flight, though, Peter."

"Lindsay, I truly love you, but if you call me Peter Pan one more time . . ."

"What are you gonna do? Gauze me to death?"

Tom started to laugh, grimaced, and settled for a chuckle. Keone could tell that even chuckling hurt.

"Ange, thank you. For your help on the mission and for stopping by—"

"But you need to talk to my partner alone, yeah? I understand, Tom. Get well soon." Ange glanced at Lindsay, who stood.

"We'll give you all the time it takes to get a cup of lousy hospital coffee." Lindsay kissed Tom on the lips and grabbed Angela by the arm. "Not a second more."

Once they were gone, Keone walked over to the bed.

"Did you call Andreos?" Tom asked.

"Yep. He said an FBI guy contacted him. Andreos found him mildly annoying, which is saying something. The FBI agent felt comfortable grilling him about everything that happened on the Greek cruise but was less forthcoming when Andreos asked him about the new murders. He gave him the basic facts. Nothing more."

"Were the women killed in port, like before?"

"They're not sure, or about the cause of death. The two are officially listed as missing at sea."

"Damn."

"Andreos contacted the Japanese himself. When he told them about the murders on the Greek cruise and the two others, the local authorities agreed to search the ports where the women went ashore. Andreos thinks someone is covering the cruise line's ass."

"Not surprising. What else did he tell you about the FBI guy?" Tom asked.

"The guy flew all the way to The Netherlands from Japan to meet with Andreos."

"I thought Andreos was Greek?"

"He is, but Europol headquarters is in The Hague."

"I knew that. Anyway, was it the guy who called me?"

"Well, he showed Andreos his badge, then asked him not to share his name with anyone as a professional courtesy. When Andreos shared what he had on Thanatos, the guy treated him like he was lolo."

"Sounds typical for an FBI agent."

"That's a little harsh, Tom. I've seen FBI agents who can deal with abstract concepts."

"Where?" Tom asked.

"*The X-Files.*"

"The ones I know are more like Scully than Mulder. So, you don't know if it was the same guy that called me."

"I told you the guy *asked* not to share his name, but Andreos never actually agreed."

"I see."

"On a completely unrelated matter," Keone said with a wink, "I would be grateful if you could share any information you might run across regarding a Special Agent William Gurney."

"You've got it. Come to think of it, I may already have that gentleman's phone number. I believe he recently took a cruise."

Part Three
Faith

"Prejudice, a dirty word, and faith, a clean one, have something in common: they both begin where reason ends."

— Harper Lee

38

Thursday, November 28, 5:30 p.m.

Julie surveyed the activity swirling around them and told Mahealani, "Thanksgiving on the ranch is my new favorite day of the year."

"It's always been mine. The one day a year we all come together. Even when Keone was on the mainland, he always came home for Thanksgiving."

"Where is he anyway?"

"Don't worry, Julie. He's with Tutu. He's been spending a lot of time with her ever since . . ."

"Since Sam Loftus died. Has he ever said anything to you about that?"

"Not really. He asked me what I believed once, a couple weeks after the kidnapping. I tried to hide my surprise. You know how Keone is about religion. But he wasn't talking about Sam. He wanted to know about God and stuff. He seemed to listen very carefully to what I had to say. I was completely open with him. We'd never talked about faith before."

"He always gives people the impression it's irrelevant to him. But, since Sam died and his friend Tom Freeman got seriously injured, he's been a bit more open."

"Did you ever get him to read Nancy's book, *Something More*?"

"No, but Angela is giving him a copy for Christmas. She told me he's promised to read it. Did you read it?"

"I did. Most of the story was way out there. But, you know, I do believe in God. I guess I found it comforting. The way Nancy's husband described the afterlife would be pretty cool." Mahealani's eyes stared up the hillside toward Haleakalā.

Julie followed her sister-in-law's gaze.

KEONE SAT QUIETLY NEAR THE HEIAU. AS TUTU PRAYED TO the old gods, his mind struggled with concepts he'd never allowed himself to consider before: philosophy and faith.

"Keiki, my gods and ancestors have finished communicating. Ask the questions that are troubling you," Tutu said in Hawaiian.

Keone's response was also in Hawaiian. "I am grateful for our sessions, Tutu, and have asked others about their faith as you suggested. It's frustrating. So much belief and so little evidence. I've finished the Jewish Bible and am over halfway through the New Testament. I'll read the Koran, next."

"Good. They all hold good words. They also tell stories of imperfect people. Even their deities do a lot of things that are difficult to understand. Those words can be gateways to belief. But your question isn't about those books, is it?"

"No, another book. While Julie and I were on our honeymoon, Angela worked on a case. She said she talked to you about it."

"She did. I believe she had a special experience, as did Dr. Lister."

"Do you believe in an afterlife?"

"I believe our spirits go on."

"But you don't practice his religion."

"I have faith. Have you read his book?"

"You mean the one his wife published. The one with stuff he was supposed to have written *after* he died. Uh, not yet."

"I am not surprised, keiki. And you may not be surprised that I *have* read it." Tutu switched to English for this part of their discussion, a language in which she was fluent but used sparingly. "By the end of the story, Rob Lister decided all religions are a little right and a little wrong. But faith is something more. The same is true with science and experience. I spoke with Dr. Hasselbach about this."

"You've talked with Hasselbach?"

"He came to the ranch the week before Halloween looking for you. He thought you could help him understand what he was experiencing with Sam Loftus. He is an atheist and saw and heard things he could not explain. While we talked, he said something I found interesting. He spoke about the questions science should and should not try to answer."

"He once told me science tries to answer the questions what, when, and how, while assuming there is no why or who," Keone said.

"He leaves the other two to philosophy and religion. Which questions do you need to answer in a police investigation?"

"All of them. Motive and the identity of the criminal are as important as the what, when, and how of the crime."

"Correct." She switched back to Hawaiian. "I believe both Dr. Hasselbach and Dr. Lister are right. Just as there is a difference between science and criminal investigation, there is a difference between religion and faith. Religion is a collection of teachings that attempts to explain the purpose of our existence. Although based on faith, it isn't faith. Faith is what every individual truly believes, inside. People identify with certain organized religions and do things together in keeping with their beliefs. When these things are good, religions serve a valuable role. Comforting the tired, the hungry, the sick, and the lost is a worthwhile undertaking. But every religion, including that of your ancestors, has spawned evil things. Wars, torture, ostracism, and hatred have all flourished in the name of religion."

"Do you believe in God, Tutu?"

"I believe in a power beyond ours. I approach that power through a spirit I call Pele. Christians approach it through a spirit they call Jesus. Muslims approach it through the teachings of their prophet Mohammed. Buddhists, Hindus, Confucians, Ancient Greeks and Romans all approach it through one or many spirits. In most cases, the spirit was first described by a human, a person who shared important concepts. In a sense, those ideas are the spirit. Do you know what I mean?"

"In one of the books in the New Testament, one of the stories about Jesus, the writer said something about word becoming flesh. And later, after Jesus died, his spirit came to his followers and told them he would be with them forever."

"Good. This is what I'm talking about. I believe the vessel is less important than its contents. For the Hebrews, was the ark more important or the covenant inside? Is faith the description, what is described, or what is understood and believed?"

Keone was surprised by the theological knowledge Tutu displayed in her answers. "That's why you asked me to read all these documents of faith."

"Yes. They are all a part of your journey—including the one Angela's going to give you. Through them a spirit may speak to you."

"Which spirit? There are so many."

"Your spirit, keiki. The one that matters most."

Keone considered this for some time in silence.

Tutu held out a hand to her grandson. "Let's go join your lovely wife and the rest of our family. Thanksgiving is a holiday I understand and respect. We must give thanks to whoever we believe in."

Belief again, he thought and helped Tutu down.

"And I believe it is time for you to announce the child that Julie is carrying. She is starting to show."

Keone agreed it was time.

39

Linda's emotions were jumbled as they arrived at Angela's parents' Wailuku Hills home for a family Thanksgiving. After the events on Halloween, Angela promised Linda she'd tell her parents about their true relationship tonight.

"Aloha, ladies." Angela's father, called Popi by the family, embraced each of them at the front door. Then Mama Rosa and Angela's oldest sister Marissa took a turn.

Marissa, the only one in the family who knows our secret.

"Aloha, Beyer's 'ohana," Linda said and gave right-armed hugs to everyone she met on the way from the door to the kitchen, holding tight with her left to the casserole she brought.

Linda guessed Angela would wait until after dinner to make their announcement, after most of the relatives had gone home. She suspected it would happen while they were doing the dishes, a task traditionally carried out by Angela's mother and the two oldest daughters. Angela would make an excuse to bring Popi into the kitchen when the time was right.

Before dinner there were games and refreshments but, thankfully little serious conversation.

Once they sat at the dinner table, Angela's second oldest brother said the blessing. Michael was studying to be a priest and his blessings were always long and heavy on sin and punishment. Linda breathed a sigh of relief when he said, "Amen."

With the blessing over, several conversations began at once around the table. At their end, Angela's oldest brother Elgin bragged about the upcoming betrothal of his daughter.

"Thomas is a wonderful boy. You'll all love him," Elgin's wife said with a huge smile.

"I'm just glad he's a male. So many of Tina's friends have gone to the dark side," Elgin added.

"Well, what do you expect in California," Popi said. "I was so glad when Angela got out of that place."

"She was in Orange County, Popi. They have far less queers there than in the Bay Area." Angela's youngest sister, Jessica, dropped this bomb.

Linda tensed, but managed to say, "It takes all kinds. On Thanksgiving, I'm always grateful God loves us all."

"You are so right, Linda." Angela's mother, Rosa, cast a stern look at her youngest. "Jessica will leave us now and go upstairs to pray about her use of language."

"I didn't mean anything. It's what the other kids call 'em."

"You are not the other kids. And we live in America, where people are free to make their own choices." Mama Rosa apparently had strict rules about what should and shouldn't be said at the dinner table.

Linda watched Jessica trudge up the stairs and realized how hard this was going to be, if even Angela's mother saw being gay as a choice and not a biological reality.

Thankfully the topic shifted to the new mayor of Maui County and how badly he was destroying the island's central valley. When the growers decided to stop growing sugar cane, a lot of promises were made about keeping the land agricultural.

"They say they're going to plant crops that are less costly to grow, use less water, and are better for the environment," Michael said.

"And we know what those crops are going to be don't we?" Elgin paused. "Condominiums and strip malls. Just like everywhere else."

"No. They wouldn't do that. The people won't let them. Maui's a special place," Mama Rosa said.

"So was the San Fernando Valley in California. It was loaded with orchards and truck farms. But now, all houses. Tell them you agree with me, Angie."

"I'm concerned, Elgin. But so far only one small plot has been approved for homes and they're required to grow crops on that land. A lot depends on the next county election. The green party has grown since the county announced that development. They could win more seats."

"My sister, the optimist. What do you think Linda? You're in real estate."

"The builders are strong, Elgin. They struggled under the former mayor and are looking to rebound. I'm sure Kihei will grow farther up the mountain. The Wailuku and Waikapū hillsides will be getting more homes and townhouses. But the valley is still a big question mark. I think everyone was surprised how quickly the cane disappeared. But that recent scandal about the developers partnering with drug-dealers and politicians should generate more oversight. We can thank Angela and her partner, Keone, for catching those crooks."

A lot of nods around the table reflected the respect Angela's family had for Linda's opinion.

"Don't forget the folks from DEA and Honolulu PD. It was

a team effort." Angela took this moment to tap Linda's shoulder and begin clearing the table.

Linda wasn't happy about the missed opportunity but held back to allow Ange to find the right moment to talk with her parents. She realized it was probably better to have *the talk* after Elgin's family went home.

40

Friday, November 29, 6:30 a.m.

Keone never felt constrained by his assigned working hours. He was off today, but the two-day Thanksgiving holiday was too long for him to stay disconnected. When he strolled into the detective division, he was surprised to find his partner in her cubicle. From her awkward, hunched posture, he realized she'd fallen asleep over some reports. He bent down to look at Angela's face. Moisture on her checks beneath her reddened eyelids suggested she'd been crying before sleep overtook her. Something was wrong.

Quietly exiting her cubicle, Keone went to his own and pulled up his newest email from Andreos.

Keone – As we predicted, two bodies found in ports. Tokyo (point of departure) and Kyoto. Victim in Tokyo killed pre-boarding. Two small holes in each woman's neck. Same toxin as in Greece. I wonder if that FBI agent will bother to let me know. Happy Thanksgiving. – Andreos

The attached report had little more except background on

the two athletes. They were both female and medaled for the Philippines in the Athens Olympic games. Keone knew from Andreos that Thanatos hadn't just targeted Canadian Olympians. The victim on the Scandinavian cruise was a Greek female Olympian, but again from the Athens games.

These are not crimes of opportunity. They match Thanatos's MO too perfectly.

At a rap on his cubicle entrance, Keone closed the file and turned to face Angela.

She must have wiped away the tears.

"Hey, Keone."

"Hi, Ange. I . . . uh . . . didn't know you were here. Did two days off bore you as much as they did me?"

Her expression told him she'd seen through his fib. "I look like crap, don't I?"

"Now that you mention it . . ."

"Did Linda call you?"

"No. What's wrong?"

"I blew it, Keone. I think I've lost her." The tears returned.

Keone stood up to comfort his partner and friend.

After a long hug, he guided her to a small conference room and shut the door. He knew others would be arriving at the division soon and didn't want them to see her like this. He made her sit in the stuffed chair at the head of the conference table and went to grab them coffee from the break room. He'd never seen Angela break down even in the roughest situations.

Back in the conference room, Keone assumed the concerned, controlled demeanor he adopted so often when interviewing crime victims. "Take a nice long sip and tell me what's going on. From the beginning."

Angela took the cup and seemed calmer after a sip of the brown stuff. Calling it coffee was a bit too generous.

"We went to my folks for Thanksgiving. The whole clan was there, and things were going okay until dinner. My asshole brother praised his daughter for choosing to marry a male."

"Did you or Linda react?"

"No. I was proud of Lin's restraint and thought we'd dodged a bullet. You see, I promised her after Halloween that I'd tell my parents the truth about us on Thanksgiving. I was waiting for the right moment and knew this wasn't it. I hoped she did, too."

"What happened next?"

"Well, my father and little sister reinforced my brother's point of view. Jessica even used the Q-word. Thankfully, Mom chastised them. But she also said what many people who are trying to understand something they don't understand say about homosexuality."

"She talked about the right to make your own choices, yeah?"

"How did you know?"

"I used to walk into that trap when I first went to Irvine. I was lucky enough to have a gay roommate who educated me on the difference between who you are and what you choose."

Angela nodded.

"What happened next? Did Linda stay calm?"

"She did. Someone changed the subject and we managed to finish the meal and clear the table. When we brought in dessert, everything seemed to be going well. Linda chatted with Popi, and the others had their own discussions. After dessert, the older siblings and their families left, and the younger ones went to the game room. I fortified myself with wine and prepared to breach the subject with my devoutly Catholic mother as we did the dishes."

Keone had met Angela's sister and her mother. "Marissa is the only one in the family who knows, right?"

"Yes. I asked her to help with the wedding. I knew she'd have my back."

"Sounds like you had a plan," Keone said.

"I did. I thought about what you said about doing things gradually. I wanted my mother and sister on my side before I approached Popi."

"Had you shared that part of the plan with Linda?"

"Not exactly. That was my first mistake."

Keone sensed he was about to hear about the second.

"Just as I opened my mouth to tell Mama Rosa about Linda and me, Lin and Popi came into the kitchen. She poured two glasses of red wine, handed Popi a glass, and hugged onto his free arm. When she opened her mouth, I knew my plan was dead."

"What did she say?"

"She said Popi had touched her heart with what he'd said in the sitting room and asked him to share it with us."

"Popi looked surprised but explained that he'd apologized to Linda for what Elgin said. Popi said he was tired of having to pretend he didn't know Linda was gay. He was glad I had a good friend like her. Our friendship had proven to him that homosexuality wasn't contagious."

Uh oh.

"Then he laughed." Angela's eyes glistened.

"You felt backed into a corner, didn't you?"

"I dropped the dessert plate I was drying and was surprised to see it bounce and not break. I saw Linda giving me a look that told me it was my turn to speak. For a long time, I just stared at the plate on the floor. Everything seemed to move in slow motion. Instead of saying something, I just picked up the plate, gave it a wipe, stacked it in the cupboard, and reached for the next plate. I'd finished drying three more plates before my family told me Linda was gone."

"You haven't spoken to her since then?" Keone asked.

"No. I was too ashamed."

"Did you ever tell your mother?"

"We were never separated from Popi after that. Marissa finally walked me to the car. Linda must have taken a cab back to Lāhainā. I couldn't face her at home, so I just drove here and tried to concentrate on work."

"What are you going to do?"

"What do you think I should do?"

Keone thought long and hard before he answered. He felt his friend's future was in his hands. A strange confidence came over him. His Tutu might have called it faith.

41

Wednesday, December 25, 6:30 p.m.

At the ranch for yet another holiday, Keone was pleased to be surrounded by his family. The buzz from his cell couldn't even disrupt his happy mood.

"*Mele Kalikimaka*, Keone."

"Same to you, Tom. How's the DEA treating you these days?" Keone was pleased to hear Agent Freeman's normal voice again.

"Same old, same old. I can hear you're celebrating, so I won't be long. I just called to tell you I might have something new for you."

"About?"

"I can't discuss this on an unsecured line. Let's just say the guy in D.C. looking into your thing wants to talk to you sometime about something. We'll talk more after the first of the year."

"Okay, but call me if you confirm anything."

"Will do. Take care. Aloha."

"Aloha." Keone felt that tingle again.

"Who was that?" Julie asked. She looked so lovely in the maternity clothes she was now wearing.

"Tom Freeman. He said he didn't want to interrupt and wished us a Merry Christmas."

"That's nice. I hope you asked him to visit. I'd finally like to meet the guy who saved your life."

"He said he'll call me after New Year's."

"But—"

"I refuse to talk further about criminal matters, Mrs. Boyd. It's Christmas."

Too bad his mind wasn't listening. He knew there was only one something the FBI might want to talk to him about.

Julie was thrilled to see Angela and Linda at the party. When she'd asked Keone why she hadn't heard from either of them since Thanksgiving, his answer was too vague for her liking.

Tonight, both women had a glow about them. Julie thought something more than the holiday was responsible.

"Mele Kalikimaka, ladies."

"Same to you, Julie. Thanks for the invite," Linda said and gave her a hug., then stood back to observe Julie's new shape. "How special this Christmas must be for you and Keone. Next Christmas . . . everything will be different."

"This is a very special Christmas for us, too," Angela added.

"I thought you two looked unusually happy tonight."

"This lovely woman has agreed to be my wife," Angela said.

"And she's agreed to be mine," Linda added.

A group hug followed, with an appropriate flow of tears from all concerned. "Have you told Keone?"

"He's next on our list, but I'm sure he's figured it out," Angela said. "He's a detective you know."

"Who else knows?"

"Just our families." Angela's expression suggested issues.

"How did that go?"

"Linda's mom was ecstatic."

"Your sister was thrilled you asked her to be maid of honor," Linda added.

"And your parents?" Julie asked.

"Well, that almost didn't go at all."

"I put Angela on the spot during Thanksgiving at her folks. We almost broke up," Linda said.

"No." Julie managed to sound shocked.

"Actually, we have your husband to thank for making up," Linda said.

"Keone?" Julie couldn't imagine Keone getting involved in something so personal and emotional.

"He gave me the courage to follow through on my original plan and tell my parents before I went home to apologize to Linda." Angela smiled. "I never felt closer to my mother."

"And your father?"

Angela exchanged a pained glance with Linda. "Popi didn't forbid Marissa and Mama Rosa from participating in the wedding. But he made it clear that he did not approve."

"I'm so sorry. But your Popi is a good man. Give him time," Julie said.

"We both hope you're right. Keone said, 'Ange, dig down deep and decide. Are you going to be ruled by what you're afraid your parents might say? Or will you trust in what you believe they will do, in the end, based on their love for you?'"

"My Keone said that?" Julie was pleased but surprised. *His talks with Tutu must be having a positive effect on him.*

"On a happier note, would you help us plan the wedding and reception? Mahealani already offered us the ranch." Linda clearly wanted to redirect the conversation.

"Of course. I'd love to help," Julie said.

Keone's arm slipped around his wife's shoulder. "Help with what? Ange, are you finally gonna spill what's going on? Or do I have to continue my investigation?"

"We confess, Detective. No enhanced interrogation techniques will be required." Linda raised her arms in mock surrender.

Angela poked Linda in the ribs with one hand and displayed the ring on the other to Keone.

"'Bout damn time," Keone said. "Bring it in."

This time the group hug included all four of them. But the tears were Keone's.

"Hey, Julie. You got a minute?" Mahealani tapped Julie's shoulder.

"Wow, you're not wasting any time. They just asked me about the reception."

"Oh, yeah. We'll need to talk about that." Mahealani looked distracted.

Julie moved Mahealani away from Keone and the happy couple. "What's wrong, honey?"

"It's Tutu. She's spending a lot of time by herself. Says she and Pele have a lot to talk about. I hope she's not getting senile."

"Sweetheart, your Tutu's always been committed to her faith. Is it a special feast time?"

"Not all Hawaiian holy days are annual. It could be something like that. But . . ."

"Don't you and I have one of our hula lessons planned for

January? Who knows, we might accidentally run into her." Julie smiled.

Mahealani gave Julie a hug.

42

Friday, January 17, 12:30 p.m.

Angela was busy doing paperwork at her desk, when she felt a presence behind her. She turned to see Keone standing quietly, watching her work.

"Hey, big guy. What can I do you for?"

"Nothing. I was just thinking maybe you've had enough practice on paperwork. I'll do my own from now on. Okay?"

"Hell yes." She handed him half of the pile she was working on. Before he could leave, she asked, "What brought this on?"

"I finished that book you gave me for Christmas, the one Nancy Lister wrote. I don't know if it was the holiday season or having too much time off . . . Anyway, that book got me thinking about things."

"You read *Something More?* I'm glad. Reading it certainly opened my mind. I think Rob Lister was a great writer."

"I'm not saying I buy all that stuff about the afterlife. But, you know, I'd kind of like to."

"Nothing wrong with imagining."

Keone nodded a few times then wandered off.

BACK AT HIS DESK, KEONE DECIDED IT WAS TIME TO CALL Tom Freeman. He'd waited long enough for Tom to call him.

"Department of Justice, Drug Enforcement Administration. Special Agent Freeman. How may I help you?"

"*Special* Agent? Do I sense a promotion?"

"A new title anyway. How are you?"

"Great, Tom. And you?"

"Sorry I didn't call you back. This promotion business was a huge distraction on top of all the other work that needs to get done at the first of the year."

"You've got enough on your plate for four guys. But you did make me curious with your Christmas call."

"I'm glad you called, Detective Sergeant Boyd."

Keone straightened in his chair. *Something is off. Tom is controlling his side of the conversation.*

"A special agent from D.C. is here in Honolulu and has requested a meeting with you the first of next month."

Keone's mind made the connection. Keone sensed someone was in Tom's office with him, possibly Special Agent Gurney himself. He needed to let Tom know that he understood his friend couldn't talk freely.

"Special Agent Freeman, you know I'm always anxious to help a fellow law enforcement officer. Could you tell me the man's name and what he wants to discuss?"

Freeman paused.

Keone wondered if Tom was asking permission.

"Special Agent Will Gurney wants to talk to you about something that took place during a cruise," Tom said at last.

"I understand, Tom."

"You do? Well, that is encouraging. Let's get together when you come to Honolulu, okay?"

"I'd like that. One thing though—I'll need to run this by my boss before I can promise anything."

"I believe Special Agent Gurney is speaking with Lieutenant Alcala on his cell right now."

*Gurney **is** in Tom's office.*

"Thank you for the information, Tom. All of it."

"You're quite welcome, Detective Sergeant Boyd. Aloha."

"Aloha."

Alcala was in his office when Keone barreled through the door. "You been talking with the FBI, Tony?"

Karen Matsuyama had jumped up from behind her desk when Keone rushed by.

"It's okay, Karen," Alcala said to his assistant. "Close the door, Keone."

"So, did Gurney tell you about Thanatos?"

"He doesn't think it's the same guy. FBI and Europol don't think so either, but this Europol guy Calliopoulos is obsessed."

"Another killing on a cruise ship?"

"Just one. Africa this time."

"Olympic medalist?"

"Yeah. Chinese acrobat."

"Female?"

"Yes."

"Same M.O."

"Same injection mark on the neck. But they haven't identified the poison mixture yet."

Keone just smiled.

"Could be a copycat."

"Right. Thousands of miles away from the other killings, the details of which were kept out of the press."

"Okay, it's unlikely. But he seems to think you and Calliopoulos got the guy in Athens."

"He wasn't there. Andreos and I were."

"I can get you off the case."

"No way. I need to finish this."

"That's what I thought you'd say. I'll arrange for your flight to Honolulu. The meeting's scheduled for February third. That's a Monday, at nine a.m. The agency's paying for everything."

"How kind of them."

"At least you'll be on home turf this time."

Keone felt that tingle at the back of his neck again. His grandmother's words came flowing back.

She has awakened now because that threat is coming to her islands. It's coming to you. She wants you to know that she will guide you and help you. This threat must be defeated.

43

Sunday, January 19, 12:30 p.m.

After their hula lesson, Mahealani asked Julie if she was still up for a ride out to see Tutu at the heiau.

"I'd love to, Lani," Julie replied. "I asked my doctor during my appointment yesterday, and he said I could still ride for a few more weeks if I'm careful."

After half an hour, Mahealani hoped the doctor was right. "We'll walk from here," she said as they dismounted.

"How much farther to the heiau?" Julie asked.

"About a half mile, but I didn't want her to hear the horses."

They walked a few hundred yards before Mahealani waved Julie to a halt and pulled out her binoculars. After a couple minutes, she handed them to Julie.

Two figures sat on their knees with their heads bowed low. Tutu wasn't alone. Praying beside her on the overgrown platform built from huge lava blocks, Mahealani saw her brother.

"Did you know Keone would be at the ranch today, Julie?"

"I knew they were having discussions about faith, but he didn't tell me he'd be here today."

"We better wait until they're finished."

FOR THE FIRST TIME IN THEIR SESSIONS, KEONE WAS having an experience of his own. He was seeing what he could only describe as a vision, behind his closed eyelids.

He found himself in a small meadow on the side of a mountain, but it wasn't Haleakalā. On one side of the meadow was a heiau with a brightly lit silhouette standing on it, shooting flames from its extremities. Was he seeing Pele?

Across the meadow, a man stood pressing his arms outward toward the heiau, but nothing was emerging from his hands. Suddenly a crack appeared behind the man and Keone could feel heat coming from the crack. Was the mountain Kilauea? Mauna Loa?

The vision was hazy and ended as quickly as it appeared.

He opened his eyes and saw Tutu staring at him. Then she began to speak in Hawaiian. "Did she speak to you, keiki? Did you have a vision?"

"I . . . I saw something. It was hazy. But I definitely saw something."

"Good. Good. Keep what you saw in your heart. It will make sense to you some day."

"Thank you, Tutu. Thank you for sharing your faith with me. I'll come again after I finish my next case. Aloha."

"Aloha."

It was Julie's turn with the binoculars. She saw Keone rise from the heiau, climb down from the stones, put on his boots, mount a three-wheeled ATV, and ride away.

Turning the binoculars back to Tutu, Julie noted the serene expression on her face.

"Keone's gone, Lani."

Lani took the offered binoculars from her and followed the cloud of dust that marked Keone's path. "He's heading back to the ranch. It's our turn," Lani said.

As they slowly approached the heiau, Tutu gave no indication that she'd heard them, until she asked in Hawaiian, "Did you come to pray, Mahealani? Do not try to tell me you just happened to ride by."

Staying in Hawaiian, Mahealani said, "Julie and I came to talk with you."

"I knew you would come."

"How, Tutu?" Mahealani asked.

"Pele told me."

"I'm worried about you."

"I know, keiki, but you need not be. I am not lolo. I have something I must do, and you cannot help me, yet. But our Julie can."

After this brief exchange in Hawaiian, Mahealani and Tutu both looked at Julie.

Julie was proud that she'd understood their conversation in Hawaiian. With ankle-length silver hair blowing in the trade winds, Tutu motioned Mahealani away. What she had to say was for Julie alone.

"Pray with me, *kaikamahine*."

Julie smiled from ear to ear. For the first time, the old woman had called her daughter. And she did so in Hawaiian. It sounded as though Tutu sang the words.

Julie removed her boots and socks and she climbed onto the

heiau. She knew Tutu's invitation was an incredible honor for a haole woman. She kneeled beside Tutu, glad she'd worn a classic Hawaiian tapa print top with her jeans. She'd never felt closer to her adopted home.

"Close your eyes," Tutu said in Hawaiian, using words she knew Julie understood. "Now, listen for a lovely voice, my child. She has something to tell you."

She? Julie thought. *Pele?*

For many minutes, she heard nothing. Then there was something. The sound was very gentle, like trade winds through the nearby trees.

But the trees are still. And I feel no breeze on this holy place.

If there were words, she didn't understand them. It sounded more like a voice singing in tones. Along with the voice, Julie saw a picture in her mind. Keone was holding his Tutu in his arms. They were walking away from a glowing lava flow. Then she felt her baby kick, and the sound stopped. In the silence that followed, Tutu touched Julie's shoulder.

"Pele wanted you to know that Keone will be away from you soon, in great danger. But she will be with him. Do not be afraid. He will return to you alive and well—before your baby is born."

Julie was surprised to find that she wasn't afraid. "Mahalo, Tutu."

Tutu pressed her nose aside Julie's and inhaled.

The honi.

Julie inhaled also, acknowledging the sharing of *Ka*, the breath of life.

Tutu led Julie to the edge of the heiau. "You go now, daughter. I have more to hear."

Julie realized, tugging on her boots, that everything Tutu had said to her was in Hawaiian.

Julie would never view these islands in the same way again.

She had truly experienced being one with the ʻāina. Keone had tried to describe the feeling to her, but she never fully understood, until now. Her experience with Tutu reminded her of a feeling she used to get in church, back in Indiana when she'd just received a sacrament.

As she and Mahealani walked back to their horses, neither spoke, but she sensed Mahealani had been comforted by the experience, too.

Part Four
Trust

"In God we trust: all others pay cash."

— Jean Shepherd

44

Monday, February 3, 8:30 a.m.

The taxi from Honolulu International made good time in rush hour traffic. The driver knew how to avoid the worst congestion on the crowded interstate.

Keone always thought interstate was an odd thing to call a highway in a state made up entirely of islands, thousands of miles away from any other state in the union.

They arrived at the federal building fifteen minutes before Keone's nine a.m. appointment. Keone headed straight to Tom's office. Although his first visit to the DEA, the precise directions Tom provided led him straight to his friend. Just what Keone expected from the organized agent.

"Come on in, Keone," Tom's voice boomed from the office. Keone found a chair beside his friend's painfully neat desk.

"Where's Gurney?"

"Conference room down the hall, thank God. I'm glad we can speak privately for a few minutes. Gurney's been very tight-lipped about everything since he arrived. As a courtesy, I took him to a luau last night to discover if he has any personality. He was friendly enough, but I couldn't get him to say anything about the assignment."

"Not a huge surprise though, yeah?"

"Not really. By the way, thanks for picking up on the fact that Gurney was in my office when you called. You really are an amazing detective."

"I wish I could tell you more about the case, Tom. But all I know beyond what you relayed over the phone is that there was another Olympian killed on a cruise. And it was Thanatos's MO."

"When this is over, I expect a full report from you. Or I won't show you where the conference room is." Tom chuckled.

"I'm pretty sure when it's over the story will come out. If not, I'll tell you everything I know."

"Not great, but good enough."

"Oh, I almost forgot. Julie will kill me if I don't invite you to visit us on Maui."

"Tell her," Tom said and pointed to his cane, "when I no longer need this thing, Lindsay and I will show up on your front doorstep. Lindsay misses all her friends on Maui terribly."

"I can understand that."

"You know, I've been here six years and I've never visited any of the outer islands, except on business. One was that trip to Moloka'i when you and I captured Walden the first time. The other was Operation Two-W. Both involved you and resulted in me flying through the air. Do you think we can get together with neither of us getting hurt next time?"

"I think so, if we can agree not to rappel down any steep cliffs or get blown up."

"I'm just lucky you attached that safety line and arrested my plummet on Moloka'i. If I'd splatted onto the jungle floor, I'd have missed the next trip to Maui."

"Speaking of your visit to Maui, howzit being an engaged man?"

"Lindsay has the patience of a saint. Rehab was rough. I lost heart more times than you could count. But she never did. She expects me to throw away this cane in another month. The doctors suggest it will be two."

"My money's on her. Anyway, don't let Julie down. Come see us before you get married."

"I promise."

"I guess we've kept him waiting long enough, Tom."

"Yeah. But before we go in there . . . something about Gurney rubs me the wrong way."

"Does he have a history?" Keone asked.

"No, nothing like that. You've seen his file. He's clean as a whistle. He comes across a little formal and domineering. Maybe it's just this case. He doesn't seem to trust your friend Andreos's instincts."

"Thanks for the heads up. I'll wear my professional face."

Tom grabbed his cane and headed for the door. "Let's get on with it."

Gurney was sitting at the conference table, typing on a laptop when they entered. He looked up but didn't get up.

"Special Agent Gurney, this is my good friend Detective Sergeant Keone Boyd of the Maui Police Department," Tom said.

Gurney slowly rose and walked over to them. "Thank you, Freeman."

Keone extended his hand.

"I'm Will Gurney. Freeman says you know your stuff," Gurney said and shook Keone's hand. They both had firm grips, but neither tried to pull the other toward him.

Tom turned around, using his cane like an expert, but hesitated at the door.

Keone knew Tom was hoping to be asked to sit in. They were, after all, in his shop.

After an awkward silence, Tom left them alone.

Keone assessed Special Agent William Gurney of the FBI. The agent was a tall, slim man, probably mid-thirties with neatly trimmed blond hair. No extraneous fat, Keone could tell the man kept his body tuned. Gurney returned to his position behind the desk, so Keone took a seat.

"Let's get right into it, okay, Sergeant Boyd?"

Not Detective Sergeant, Keone thought but said, "What can I help you with, Special Agent Gurney?"

"The Bureau is responding to Europol's request for security support on a cruise scheduled for April. We do not share their opinion of the threat level. Nor do we acknowledge that the serial killer known as Thanatos is still at large. That being said, some Canadian Olympic medalists will be on board, and we are obligated to take all threats in American waters seriously. I have asked an Agent Calliopoulos to join me on the cruise. I believe you know him."

"I do. I helped him catch a murderer in Athens."

"Yes. Your assistance on that case was noted in reports from Europol and the Greek cruise line. Unlike Agent Calliopoulos, you have their complete confidence."

Keone did his best not to react to Gurney's dig at Andreos. *Tom was right. I'll have to be careful what I say about Andreos around this guy.* "In addition to Agent Calliopoulos, how many agents will you have on the cruise?"

"The bureau believes the presence of Agent Calliopoulos and myself will be sufficient."

"So, why am I here?"

"As a courtesy to Europol, I agreed to contact you through agent Freeman. I'm authorized to offer you a cruise of these lovely islands at the Bureau's expense—if you're willing to assist in our security detail."

There's always a catch. "You do realize that there are six remaining Canadian medalists. Are they all coming?"

"Yes. But no husbands this time," Gurney noted.

"Are they sharing state rooms?"

"No. But—" Gurney began.

"Then you're undermanned," Keone interrupted but didn't raise his voice.

"You're entitled to your opinion, Sergeant."

Still not detective sergeant. Your testosterone is showing, bud.

"Special Agent Gurney, I would like to come along, but there is a chance I won't be available to. My wife is expecting our first child in late April or early May. If the cruise is in April, I could have a conflict."

"I understand. The cruise is currently scheduled to leave on April twenty-fourth. In any case, I've set it up so you can join the cruise when it gets to Maui. You can join us or not. It's up to you." Gurney stood, collected his laptop, and left the room.

Keone spent a few minutes in thought before retracing his steps to Tom's office. There was no sign of Gurney.

"Need a lift?" Tom asked.

"I sure need something. Where's your car?"

Once they left the federal building parking lot, Tom turned to Keone. "Quite a piece of work, yeah?"

Keone winced. "He's not taking the threat to these women seriously enough."

"He may be reflecting the opinion of the bureau. The FBI and Europol seemed very anxious that the specter of Thanatos end after Athens."

"Of course, *they* would want that. As for me, I've always

worried that the crewman was a henchman at best. But I knew it wasn't my call."

"Have you heard anything new from Andreos?"

"Nothing since that last email. Something is off about this."

"Are you going on the cruise?"

"Gurney told you about that?"

"Yes. But that's all he told me. FBI here will have responsibility for the Canadians until they board."

"Tom, I know Thanatos is alive. In here." Keone pointed to his gut.

"I'm not sure Gurney disagrees."

"What?"

"Okay, I could get fired for telling you this. But when he was here before, just before you called me, I heard him talking to Europol."

"He was setting this up back then?"

"Seems likely. I only heard his side of the conversation. Gurney was talking softly most of the time, and I didn't hear everything. But at one point, Gurney raised his voice. He sounded pissed off."

"What did you hear?"

"He said, 'If you really believe that, let me have him. I'll prove who Thanatos really is.'"

"You think he was talking about Andreos?" Keone frowned.

"I don't know. But, whoever he meant, he believes Thanatos is still out there."

"I feel responsible for these women, Tom. And if Gurney suspects Calliopoulos, I'll need to watch Andreos's back, too. I just wish it wasn't so close to Julie's due date."

THE SOUND OF A RINGTONE IS A RARE OCCURRENCE FOR ME.

Listening through borrowed ears, I discover my plan is coalescing.

A cruise of the Hawaiian Islands. How perfect.

I have some unfinished business to complete. I look forward to reconnecting with a resident of one of those pagan, Pacific pearls.

They even have their own gods. Wouldn't it be fun to meet one—then kill it.

45

Friday, March 7, 5:00 p.m.

This wasn't just Aloha Friday. Tonight, all their friends would be on hand to celebrate Julie and Keone's new home in Waikapū. One of the tinier towns in the middle of the Valley Isle, Waikapū was the site of some lovely new homes. In the islands, many newly built homes were first offered to members of the native population and folks with a limited income for an affordable price. Keone not only qualified, but he and Julie drew the first lot offered. The months of construction were finally over.

"Thanks for loaning us all the folding chairs and tables, Jan. This place would have looked like an empty warehouse without them."

"Don't be silly, Keone. Not much new furniture graces the shops right now. That tsunami played havoc with shipping schedules."

"The tsunami damage could have been a lot worse," Keone said.

"Still kept us up all night, getting tourists out of harm's way," Angela added. "The people who live here know how serious these things can be. People on vacation, not so much."

"Keone, did that guy really try to sue you for carrying him up to the lobby at the Grand Wailea?" Janet asked.

"He tried," Angela answered for her partner. "But the pictures of his room saturated with seawater convinced the judge he was just a dumbass. Say, I like what you've done to the place, big guy."

Keone could hear the sarcasm. "Look, this house contains everything we own. Remember most of Julie's worldly goods were blown to pieces a year ago. And I never had much furniture."

Julie rescued her husband. "It works for now, Ange. We've decided to take our time and choose each additional piece to reflect our personalities. We've already added one critical item."

"Really? Old cheapskate let go of a dollar bill?" Ange said with a snicker.

"I'll have you know I let go of several pieces of currency. And not for myself either."

Julie led them all into her writing studio and pointed to her new writing desk. "It's adjustable. Keone knows I love to stand and sketch when I write my stories. Show them, Keone."

Keone decided to have some fun. He sat at the desk and, brandishing a pencil like a wand, he soundlessly touched a hidden release with his knee, then slowly stood waving his *wand* and commanding the writing surface, "Rise. Rise. Now tilt."

The desk surface was transformed into an angled drafting table.

Angela and Janet applauded, which drew Linda and Mahealani into the room. Keone had to repeat the performance for them, as he would for others, who cycled through the room during the evening.

With Keone continuously performing his trick, Julie answered the door to find Nancy Lister and her friend Kimmie, carrying huge, foil-wrapped platters.

Nancy gave Julie an awkward hug, before Kimmie rescued the teetering platters.

Julie led both friends into her new kitchen. "How's the job treating you?"

"Great," Nancy said. "Talking with customers and coworkers was the best medicine in the world after I lost Rob."

Julie nodded her understanding. After a few signing events in New York with her daughter Beth, Nancy returned to Maui. She seemed lost. Julie tried to encourage her to continue writing, but Nancy wasn't interested. "I only had one story in me and that was mostly written by Rob."

After a month, Nancy sold their condo and bought an apartment in the same complex as her friend Kimmie, who introduced Nancy to a variety of new activities and encouraged her to pursue pastimes she'd enjoyed before Rob died. The latter included playing golf with Angela, Julie, and Mahealani.

"I haven't thanked you two for that fabulous afternoon of shopping and sushi after golf last week. We all loved it." Julie hugged her friend.

"We pretend we're wealthy tourists. Until we get the bill," Nancy said with a smile.

It was good to see her smile again.

She and Kimmie removed the foil from each of the platters. A pungent, spice-filled bouquet permeated the kitchen and beyond. Audible sounds of delight came from the living room and the backyard.

"Now the party can get started," Julie said inhaling deeply. "Kimmie, your fiancé is a prince. I know how much effort it takes to haul in these giant fish on his kayak. Tell me you didn't stay up all night prepping and seasoning them before going to work."

"You know we love you guys," Kimmie said. "Besides, Lyle's gonna quit work early and stop by. It's Aloha Friday, *pau hana*, yeah?" She moved the platters to one of the tables set up for the buffet dinner. "Julie, Keone—you get the first tastes."

Keone ran in from the living room and pretended to fight with Julie to pull the most succulent morsels from the bones. The tender fish melted into tiny bursts of intense flavor on Julie's tongue.

"Dear gods, I've tasted heaven," Keone said. Then he yelled, "Everyone, you gotta try Kimmie and Lyle's Ono Grinds."

Julie, Nancy, and Kimmie escaped into the backyard with full plates ahead of the crowd.

ANOTHER BUZZ OF THE DOORBELL PROMPTED KEONE TO lope to the front door and swing it wide.

"Hey, big guy. Happy Housewarming. I brought seven growlers from the Maui Brewing Company. I needed help to carry everything." Tony Alcala walked past, followed by a lovely Hawaiian woman and two young men, each carrying the beer-filled glass jugs.

"I know dis one." Keone slapped a large paw on Tony's son's shoulder. "Howzit, Tim."

"Hey, Uncle Keone. This is my friend Ken, and that lovely

lady who came in with dad is Leticia. I think she may be trying out to be my stepmom."

"How do you feel about that?" Keone asked.

"'Bout damn time, yeah?" Tim said and led Ken to the food.

Tony returned with tall glasses of Bikini Blonde lager for Keone and himself. "Hey, you got a few friends, big guy. Here's to the new abode."

Keone clinked glasses. "Thanks, Tony. Been a hell of a fall and winter, yeah?"

"That little expedition you have coming up in April suggests spring might be kinda crazy, too."

"Let's concentrate on the good stuff tonight. Tim looks happy." Keone took a slow sip from his glass.

"Tim found someone who loves him and makes him happy. We're closer, too. Angela's advice made a difference."

"I'm glad. You both seem happier than usual. Does Leticia have something to do with that?" Keone asked.

"I don't want to jinx anything. We make each other happy. We'll see what happens."

"Tim seems to like her."

Tony just smiled and sipped his beer.

Keone walked his friend out to the backyard where people were seated on tatami mats in an arc around the small wooden platform. Kapena Billy Bones played and sang suggestions hollered out from the crowd. Billy and Julie had been in a writers' group together ever since she first came to the islands. Billy's books were more adult than Julie's but extremely fun.

Billy was currently playing a song synonymous with this important day of the week, *It's Aloha Friday*. Leroy Marder sang along in his unique, scratchy tenor. Though not a big fan of the corny tune, Julie added her voice to the chorus from where she was standing at the back.

Tony tapped Keone's arm. "I see Leticia, Tim, and Ken seated over there by the platform."

"Go. And have fun, yeah?"

Tony nodded and went off to join them.

Keone took the opportunity to snuggle up next to Julie. Her current bulk made sitting on the tatami mats an impossible dream, but her face was as lovely as he'd ever seen it. "I'm so lucky."

"We both are," Julie said. "How are Tony and Tim doing?"

"Good. They're both more relaxed than I've seen them in a long time."

"Relaxed is good. I'm glad for them and you. Now I think it's about time for a little surprise." Julie flashed a shaka at Kapena Billy.

"What?" Keone asked.

"Just listen to Billy."

Finishing his song with a final joyous chord, Billy waved his hands to quiet the crowd. "Okay, okay. You've all heard me before. It's time to celebrate this lovely new home with something special. Kāne and wahine, give it up for the best of the best. Comedian, juggler, and all-round fun guy—Ron Morton."

A chilling sense of déjà vu overcame Keone.

"Ron's on the Hawaiian Island cruises now," Julie said. "He jumped at the chance when I asked him to come to the party and insisted on doing his whole show for us. Happy?"

"Damn happy. Thanks, sweetheart, what a wonderful surprise." Keone scratched at the back of his neck. He was happy to see their talented friend again but hoped Ron's stint on the Hawai'i voyages would be over by April twenty-fourth. Having him on board would be a huge coincidence and a challenge. Keone could probably handle the challenge but hated coincidences.

A few days after the party at Keone and Julie's, a presence arrived in Honolulu.

I must scout each island for the appropriate place to send my children to Elysium.

That idiot juggler from the Greek cruise has moved to these islands. He lives in Honolulu with his family now. How ironic that he entertains on the very cruise I wish to take.

Maybe I should reward that fool for ruining my efforts in Athens, along with that big Hawaiian, if he dares confront me again.

The possibilities are intriguing.

46

Thursday, April 24, 08:00 a.m.

The Boyd-Kalama ranch emerged from the morning mist at its own pace. Angela saw this as an appropriate reflection of their island's special personality. Everything happens in its own time on Maui.

Mahealani had divided up the responsibilities for turning the ranch into an island fantasy. Boyd and the Kalama cousins did all the structural work. Keone's brothers prepared the spits and would do all the barbecuing. Dozens of side dishes would be carefully crafted by the women in the huge ranch kitchen.

Angela had a job, too. She helped Julie with the formidable task of cataloguing and distributing thousands of live plants from local flower growers around the outdoor settings for the service and reception. "I bet you're thinking about your own wedding," Angela said.

"Of course," Julie said. "Best day of my life. Hey, can I tell Keone where you're going on the honeymoon? We're trying not to keep secrets from each other."

"How's that going?"

"It's hard for Keone," Julie said. "He's not used to sharing information about his work that might frighten me. But he's trying. He's concerned about being away from me this weekend on a case, given it's almost my due date. But I can reach him by cell, so I'm not worried. With you and Linda away, too, Janet has offered to be available on a moment's notice."

"That's good. As for your request, you may tell him at the reception"—Angela paused—"that I'm making you keep our secret." She wasn't going to risk their privacy for anything.

"You're a hard woman, Ange. But it's better than nothing."

Ange nodded. She knew Julie understood better than most the impact of interruptions during a honeymoon. "Tony told me Keone's leaving right after the reception for some hush-hush case. But I still don't trust him not to spoil our honeymoon."

Keone and Tony had been a little vague about the details. Ange guessed they didn't want her to feel left out. She didn't. Linda's idea for their honeymoon was perfect. She could work on a case with her partner any time.

"I'm kind of glad he'll be gone. I won't have to sneak around to take you to your departure point tomorrow." Julie winked.

"Are you sure you feel like driving? I mean . . ."

"I can still fit behind the wheel, if that's what you're afraid to ask, and Kahului is close to the hospital if my water decides to break."

Angela glanced at her watch. "Whoa. I've got to leave for Marissa's soon to get ready. You and Janet are picking up Linda, right?"

"Yep. We'll be leaving in a few minutes to go by my house and get dressed. Then we're off to get Linda in Lāhainā."

"For such a modern woman, Lin's very traditional about some things. She was going to get a hotel room for her mother and stay there last night. I convinced her to let me stay at my sister's, so they could use the house. She says we can't see each other until I walk down the aisle."

"I think that's sweet."

"My mom picked Lin's mom up for breakfast this morning. Mama Rosa loves Linda's Mom, Fran. They're driving to the wedding together. Gotta go." Angela rushed to her car so Julie wouldn't see the tears forming in her eyes.

———

Keone slumped in his chair and sighed. The huge pile of paperwork on his desk was smaller, but not gone. He had to keep at it. Angela and Linda's wedding and reception were rapidly approaching. After that he'd be busy helping Andreos and Gurney protect six Canadian women, including his and Julie's friends Josie and Veronica.

He'd received no further word from Andreos, but Gurney forwarded his boarding pass. The agent arranged for Keone to join the cruise in Maui that evening after the ship docked in Kahului. He hated the idea of being at sea when Julie went into labor, but the doctor assured them that they had a few days at Julie's appointment yesterday.

Tony Alcala leaned into Keone's cubicle. "You almost ready?"

"Almost. Well, nearly almost. Thanks for offering to drive me to the ranch. Julie had to be there at the crack of dawn to help set up."

"No problem. I'm still taking you to the ship after the reception, yeah?"

"Yeah. But don't tell anyone else, especially Julie. She doesn't realize I'm leaving the island."

"I can't believe you're keeping another secret from her." Tony shook his head. "Haven't you learned anything?"

"We agreed that I would sometimes need to keep information about a case to myself, as long as I told her I needed to keep it secret."

"Whatever works for you guys. Hey, is your tutu still convinced the islands are in danger?" Tony asked.

"Hell, yes. She's got Julie believing only Pele can save us from destruction."

"Damn it, Keone. Why do all your cases have to involve the supernatural?"

Tony took Keone's silence as an answer. "Anyway, I guess you'll meet with Calliopoulos and Gurney on board tonight?"

"I could have waited until tomorrow and just joined the shore excursion. But that didn't feel right. I want to be there from the moment they arrive at my island."

"Understood. I've assigned back-up to each of the sites the three excursions with Canadian Olympians are visiting. Don't worry, I told them to be inconspicuous. Which one are you going on?"

"The one to Moloka'i."

"Good. That'll be the hardest to keep an eye on, especially with the mule ride down to Kalaupapa."

"Thanks to my uncle Kimo, we'll have some extra eyes on his island."

"How is that rebel uncle of yours? Still ready to secede?"

"Not so much secede as restore the lawful government. But I never said that." Like most citizens of this unusual state, Keone had mixed feelings as well as mixed heritage.

"Hawaiian sovereignty's a thorny issue," Tony agreed. "When those wealthy haole overthrew the constitutional monarchy in 1893, they had no legal authority—just rifles. Queen Lili'uokalani only yielded authority to prevent bloodshed."

"Our Hawaiian traditions must be confusing to outsiders.

We welcome everyone to our shores but don't believe anyone can own the land," Keone said with a smile.

"And Hawaiian residents from every ethnic group and economic class have risked their lives to protect the USA in both World Wars and all the ones since."

"Including both of my parents." Keone's eyes glistened.

"But we never forget where we come from." Tony put his hand on Keone's shoulder.

"I know, Tony. Even the most strident voices on every side of the issue know any real solution will involve some sort of compromise that respects tradition and accepts modern reality."

"With all the different cultures that have made Hawaii their home, smarter minds than ours will be required to figure out how to progress in the modern world without losing our souls."

"When you're right, you're right. Thanks for the break from the paperwork—and a reason to get back to it."

***

"I can't help but think back to your wedding today, Jules."

Julie was glad her sister broke the silence. After a happy series of greetings and hugs in Lāhainā, their passenger in the back seat had done nothing but stare out of the back window. "Good memories for sure, Jan. But I've seen what they have in store up at the ranch today. I do not exaggerate when I say, you ain't seen nothin' yet," Julie replied, hoping to get a response out of Linda.

Janet twisted around to address their passenger. "Linda, you're a bit quiet for a bride-to-be. Is everything okay?"

"What? Oh, sorry. I'm a little preoccupied."

"We were just with Ange. She looked very happy," Julie added, trying to keep the conversation going.

"She's putting on a good show. But I know she's disappointed."

"Her father?" Julie hadn't heard anything since Christmas about how he was adjusting to the idea of a same-sex wedding.

"Yeah. She's sure he won't come, even though they reserved seats for him and the rest of the family next to her mom. She dreads walking down the aisle and seeing those empty seats."

"Don't let that spoil your day. You two deserve nothing but happiness," Janet said.

"How are you doing, Janet? Ange and I haven't seen you and Mike since Christmas."

"We've been good. We've spent time with Julie's friend, Nancy Lister. We've both been reading her book."

"Ange worked on that case. It almost got her killed." Linda no longer gazed out the window.

"I know. It's all in the book. You helped Ange find the killer, didn't you?"

"All I did was read Rob's manuscript and point out a few possible clues."

Julie knew that Linda's discovery of a passage about Rob's army days was the key to identifying the killer. But Ange had never told Linda that detail. Given what happened later, she decided not to go there. "So, Janet, did talking with Nancy help you?"

"When Dave Walden killed my ex-husband, I felt guilty that I hadn't helped Sam more. I was so sure he was ill and would never get better. I needed to move on. I loved Sam before the accident—before he changed. I never considered he could be telling the truth. Dr. Drayton assured me Sam's story about coming back from the other world was just another delusion. But even if it was, talking to Nancy and reading her book gave me the courage to do something I needed to do."

"What was that?" Linda leaned forward.

"I went to talk with Keone about Sam's last moments. I had a dream where Sam, my Sam, came to me and told me to see Keone and tell him something."

"You talked with Keone? When? He didn't say anything to me." Julie was surprised.

"Last week, Jules. I met him at the station. I made him promise to let me tell you about it." Janet's face turned red.

"No, no. It's all good. What did he tell you?"

"First, he told me the same story about Sam having delusions and not saying anything coherent after he was shot. I told him about the dream and said what Sam asked me to tell him."

"What did Sam ask you to say?" Linda and Julie asked in unison.

"'Keone, you don't need to keep your promise any longer.'"

Julie could imagine the conflict her husband felt. "How did Keone react?"

"He closed his eyes and was quiet for a long time. Then he looked into my eyes and said, 'I believe you're right.'"

Julie relaxed her grip on the steering wheel. "So, he told you the truth."

"Yes. He told me everything. And I cried. But knowing Sam, my Sam, was a hero in the end . . . that he wanted me to move on . . . all my guilt and worries melted away."

"It's taken me a long time to reach the same conclusion," Julie said. "Reading Rob Lister's book and discussing it with Tutu helped me get past my resistance to accepting a few things I may never truly understand."

Julie drove into the entrance to the Boyd-Kalama Ranch, proud of Keone. Parking the car, she said. "Why don't we all enjoy this fantastic wedding, okay, Linda?"

"Let's do that," Linda said, her face glowing in anticipation.

47

Thursday, April 24, 1:00 p.m.

Josie couldn't believe she was in Honolulu. Last night she'd walked all over Waikiki trying to make herself tired enough to sleep. Six hours was a big time change to absorb. She'd finally dropped off at five a.m.

"When dat ship leave?" the cab driver asked.

"In an hour. I overslept. Can we still make it?"

"No worry. I get you dere in plen'y time. But you need a'hustle once we get dere."

Josie appreciated the advice. She liked the people here. They always seemed so helpful and happy.

She absorbed the views of the modern city of Honolulu as they sped along. It was exciting, but she looked forward to quiet time on the ship and on the less-populated, outer islands. She couldn't wait to see Veronica and the other girls.

Girls? We've been past that for quite some time now.

"Here we are. Have one lovely cruise."

"Mahalo." She used one of the two Hawaiian words she'd mastered and gave the man a healthy tip.

He'll never guess I'm Canadian.

When she reached the terminal, most of the passengers had already boarded.

I don't have time to look for Roni. Surely, she's already boarded.

"Josie?" A man's voice called to her.

"Ron? I didn't realize you'd be here." She loved the comedian and juggler from their earlier cruise.

How fun.

"I've been working here for a few months now. Even moved the family over. Josie, this is my wife Tori and our rug rats, Carl and Maria. I'm afraid I have to run. Come and see me on board."

Ron's wife was a lovely Latina with sparkling brown eyes and a melodic voice. "So wonderful to meet you. Ron told me how much he enjoyed you and your friends on that Greek cruise. You were in the Olympics, weren't you?"

"I won a bronze medal in kayaking."

"He said you were always having such a good time with your friend the diver . . . uh—"

"Veronica. We were hoping to meet here at the cruise terminal. But I'm late."

"You sure are. Ron's already headed for crew check-in. You better hurry, too. I'm so happy to meet you, Josie."

Josie lost track of Ron in the chaos of last-minute boarding.

The crew probably boards at a different place.

She had reached the terminal doors and was about to enter the building when she felt a sharp sting in her neck.

Mosquito? she had time to wonder before the dizziness arrived. Strong arms caught her before she could stumble and guided her away from the terminal building.

She waved her hand toward her desired destination, but watched it glide away.

48

Julie felt a soft caress on the back of her neck. Keone had arrived. He and Tony made it with minutes to spare. Not too many minutes, but enough. Tony gave her a hug and moved off to take his place. While they waited for the music to begin, she saw a movement out of the corner of her eye. Turning, she saw Angela's mother looking around hopefully. But the seats beside her were still empty.

Julie heard the music start, stood, and watched Angela begin her walk down the aisle. Angela sported her dress uniform, as did the man walking her down the aisle. Julie hadn't been told in advance who would have that honor. She only knew it wouldn't be Keone. He had another job.

The smile on Tony Alcala's face matched the one on Angela's as he deftly guided her toward the altar.

When Angela anxiously glanced toward her mother, Julie braced herself.

But was surprised and delighted to see the entire Beyers

family rise from their assigned seats. Angela's mother beamed from ear to ear and squeezed the arm of her stoic husband.

Angela's dad and brother must have arrived after the music started.

Tears sparkled in Angela's eyes and in those of her beloved Popi. Waiting up at the altar, Linda didn't try to hide her own tears.

Keep it together, Julie thought. And Angela did. The rest of the way to the altar, at least, where Marisa took her bouquet and Linda's. Angela and Linda clasped hands and turned toward the minister.

By the end of the ceremony, Angela wasn't the only one with tears in her eyes. Keone had wisely brought three handkerchiefs. Between the two of them, all three were used.

After the reception line, Julie noticed Tutu draw Angela over for a private conversation. She wondered if it had anything to do with the threat Tutu had told her about.

No. She's probably offering some ancient Hawaiian advice about how to create a loving home.

"Hey, Julie. Lovely ceremony, wasn't it?" It was Mahealani.

"You know I'm a sucker for a Hawaiian wedding, Lani. Good luck on your dinner surprise. No one has told them about it, not even Keone."

Mahealani gave her a thumbs-up.

Julie hugged her husband and more tears threatened to fall. Luckily, Tony and his son picked that moment to join them, with their same dates from the housewarming. These four seemed to spend a lot of time together, Julie noticed. She was happy for Tim. And for Tony.

After dinner, Keone rose and approached the microphone on the stage like it was about to bite him. He tapped softly to make sure it was working, then said, "Angela and Linda, congratulations. May you always be as happy together as you are at this moment. My sister and I have a little present for you."

With that, he whipped out the ukulele he'd hidden behind his back. Mahealani, in a beautiful golden dress, arrived on stage and Keone struck the first chord of the Hawaiian wedding song and began to sing.

For Julie, watching Mahealani dance was like enjoying a great work of art. Hula was an art form, but Mahealani made it a spiritual experience. When she danced, she was the definition of beauty and womankind. The chatty young woman from the golf course disappeared and a mature, confident professional took her place.

Julie walked quietly to the head table and put one arm around each of the new brides. "Not bad for a kid and a cop, eh?"

Angela was speechless.

"We knew Lani was talented, but . . . Keone. I had no idea." Linda said, through sobs. "They're breaking my heart right now —in a good way."

Julie's thoughts wandered back to the final night of their honeymoon:

They rode a gondola on the Grand Canal in Venice, their final stop before heading home. The gondolier first protested Keone providing his own music. Julie knew riders paid extra for an Italian with a guitar or accordion to serenade them but saw Keone quietly slip enough euros to the gondolier to end the discussion. Later, when the gondolier heard how sweetly Keone played his ukulele and sang, he offered to give the money back and thanked them for a unique experience.

Keone had sung the Hawaiian Wedding Song then, too. It was the first time he'd ever sung to her. His voice, clear and deep, brought tears to her eyes. When he finished, tears rolled down his checks.

"You got one of the good ones, you know," Angela added, bringing Julie from her reverie.

"You, too, Ange."

After the first verse, Mahealani had Ange and Lin join her on the small dance floor in front of the stage.

"I hope you don't expect us to hula," Angela said.

"No, a waltz is fine." They anxiously took a few steps arm in arm.

"Ladies and gentlemen, let's congratulate this lovely couple," Keone said as he played.

Everyone, including Popi, stood and applauded. Tears streamed down his face as he walked toward the couple. "I'd like to dance with my new daughter-in-law, if that would be proper."

"I would be honored, Popi," Linda said and kissed his cheek.

As Popi danced with Linda, her brother, Elgin, took Angela's hand. "You're my sister and I love you. I've been a total asshole, but even assholes can change for a person like you. Would you honor me with this dance?"

From these simple gestures, Julie realized Angela's family was giving their blessing in the only way they knew how.

After the wedding song, Keone turned the music over to the band. Julie gave him a kiss and hugged him in her arms. "You sing good, Kanaka."

"Not me. My heart."

Keone cradled her face in his hands, warm lips pressed to hers. She knew her husband would need to steal away with Tony to go work on their case by the sunset, but they had time for a few dances before then.

When she saw the sky begin to color in the west, Julie took Keone's hand in hers and walked to a Kiawe tree, away from the crowd. "I need to apologize. There's something I've been keeping from you because I was asked to. But knowing how hard you're trying to tell me everything, I asked Angela to let me break my promise. Even the fact that you're going to be busy on a case couldn't break her resolve."

"Ah. The honeymoon secret. I won't ask you to break your promise." A shadow passed across Keone's face.

"What is it?" Julie asked.

"I have been asked to keep a secret, too. For work. It kills me that I can't tell you."

"After that silly promise I had you make on our honeymoon, we agreed this would happen and that you could keep a secret about work, as long as you told me you were keeping it. Just promise to tell me all about it when the case is over," Julie said.

"That works. No secret secrets."

"No secret secrets, my love." Julie gave him one last kiss and watched him hurry to Tony Alcala's waiting car.

49

Thursday, April 24, 10:00 p.m.

From the cruise ship terminal in Kahului, Keone watched the liner enter the harbor and ease its way toward the pier. The stars glistened over the West Maui Mountains, and the full moon glowed brightly above the ʻIao Valley. The cruise ship gleamed white in the moon's reflected glow. The huge liner dwarfed the pier, but the captain gently nudged her against the dock. Keone had never seen anything so smooth.

He waited in the arrival lounge as the full docking process went on. His thoughts went back to his conversation with Julie after the wedding.

No secret secrets.

Once the docking process was complete, hatches opened on the side of the ship and crew members emerged. He knew the Olympians would stay on board until the next morning and looked forward to catching up with Andreos on the first leg of the journey.

"Sergeant Boyd, over here," a voice shouted from his left.

Special Agent Will Gurney was disembarking and waving Keone his way.

Where's Andreos? he thought but said, "Aloha, E komo mai. Welcome to Maui, Special Agent Gurney."

"Thank you, Sergeant Boyd."

Still couldn't manage a Detective Sergeant Boyd.

"I'm sorry to have to get right down to business, but we need to talk." Gurney led Keone to a small room used by security.

"Boyd, I'm worried about your friend Calliopoulos. He was the last passenger to board the ship. He explained that he wanted to keep an eye on the boarding and waited until the last moment because one of the Olympians hadn't boarded the ship. After we left Honolulu, I checked with the captain, and he confirmed one Canadian Olympian never checked in."

"Which one?" Keone felt that tingle again.

"The captain is obtaining the name now, but I left Calliopoulos with him because I needed to speak with you before you join the case."

"You have a suspicion?"

"Yes. I have found no solid evidence to suggest that Calliopoulos is not Thanatos."

An interesting way to say it.

"What evidence have you found that he is?"

"Only what you already know. He's been on Thanatos's trail since the first murder. Thanatos has only communicated with him and no one else. He was unable or unwilling to save the girl at the acropolis and sent you after the crewman. Yes, we always suspected the crewman was an accomplice. My suspicions of Calliopoulos are why I wanted him on this cruise, so I could keep an eye on him."

"But you lost him during boarding?"

"No, I never saw him. I was looking for him up until I had

to board. I figured he'd missed the boat until he showed up at my cabin."

"The missing Olympian could have missed the ship, too."

"I know. That's why we were allowed to sail here. But if anything happened to her, the captain is prepared to halt the cruise."

"What do you need from me?"

"I know you aren't likely to share my suspicions. Just from my brief interaction with Calliopoulos, I've begun to question them myself. But, please, as a fellow law enforcement professional, don't tell Agent Calliopoulos about my suspicions. And watch your back."

Keone knew murderers could be charming and hide their true natures, but Andreos? It would require a hell of a lot more than no evidence against him being a serial killer to change Keone's mind about his friend. But, for now, he'd play along with Gurney.

"Agreed, Special Agent."

"Thank you. We should board. Agent Calliopoulos will meet us in the captain's cabin."

Gurney facilitated their passage through security. Keone was relieved to see Andreos sitting next to the captain when they entered the cabin.

Andreos's expression reflected the urgency of the meeting. "We may have already lost one, Keone."

"Let's not get ahead of ourselves, Agent Calliopoulos. She may have just missed the ship. I—" Gurney was interrupted by a ring from his smartphone.

The agent walked to a corner of the room. When he got there, Keone's phone sounded, too.

It was Tom Freeman. Keone walked to another corner of the captain's cabin.

"Hi, Tom. What've you got?" Keone suspected he knew the answer.

"HPD has confirmed that the Canadian woman who did not board the ship arrived on Oahu yesterday. I just spoke to a cab driver who drove her to the dock. He swears that she made it in time to board."

"Do they know her name?" Keone felt that tingle at the back of his neck.

"Name is Mrs. Josephine Galliano."

"Tell me she just missed the boat," Keone pleaded, his heart in his throat.

"Well, HPD haven't found a body, but they haven't found her alive either."

Not Josie.

Keone's heart sank.

Can't think about that now. Need facts.

"When was she last seen?"

"Shortly before the ship sailed, she was seen talking to a performer from the ship and his family outside the terminal."

"Did they all get on the ship?"

"No, just the performer. A Ron Morton. I interviewed his wife . . . uh . . . Victoria. When she last saw Mrs. Galliano, she was heading for the terminal entrance."

"Thanks, Tom. I should get back to the captain and Andreos."

"I hope Gurney finally understands there's an actual case here."

"From the look on his face, I think he does. Aloha."

Gurney was still talking, so Keone sat beside Andreos, who looked up.

Keone quietly shared what Tom told him.

Ending his call, Gurney stretched his neck right and then left. He sat beside the captain, across from Keone and Andreos. "I'm sorry if I've seemed doubtful about Thanatos, Andreos. He may be here. A female Olympian is missing and there is some evidence that she may have been intercepted before boarding. I'll need your advice going forward. And yours, too, Detective Sergeant Boyd."

Keone felt sorry for the agent. Almost. He knew this was all part of his act. Gurney would see Andreos's late arrival as more evidence that he was Thanatos.

Gurney's suspicions would make this case even harder. But Keone had to be at the top of his game. They all had to be. Keone was concerned for the safety of all the Olympians. But Josie was a friend.

And Thanatos is here. I feel it.

He is here.

The heathen is on board.

Destiny is calling.

Five more of my children will make their way to Elysium in the coming days.

The heathen will make another journey.

Why do I bear less malice towards the other authorities?

They are merely flies to be swatted away.

But this one. This large Hawaiian has something.

I cannot put my finger on it.

A tingle at the back of my host's neck catches my attention.

Strange.

No matter. I have work to do.

50

Keone stared at the pier from the Lido deck. He'd have to head down to his tour in a few minutes. Then the fun would start. Watching out for the safety of two Olympians without being seen. At least Veronica Napoleoni wasn't on his tour. He hadn't spent a lot of time with the other athletes, but they might remember him from the Acropolis. He wore a baseball cap and dark glasses. At least here on Maui his skin color and build weren't unusual.

A moving vehicle caught his eye.

That looks like . . . Oh no.

The car pulling up to the dockside looked very familiar. Even more so when Julie exited the driver's seat to open the trunk for Angela and Linda.

He watched Julie drive off and the happy couple board before he shot down back stairs to the crew exit. He had to hurry if he was going to join his excursion group.

He knew he couldn't persuade the newlyweds to skip the

cruise. He'd just have to look after their safety as well as that of the Olympians. At least they weren't Thanatos's preferred targets.

When he arrived, the bus to the airport for the flight to Moloka'i had just finished boarding. Andreos was talking to the driver, who stood beside the bus.

"All safely on board. The driver kept the first seat open for you at my request. My excursion to Hāna leaves in one hour." Andreos gestured to an adjacent coach.

"Thanks for keeping watch. I have some unexpected news. I just saw my partner and her new bride board the ship. I took the back stairs. I couldn't let her see me or she'd suspect something and want to help."

"Would that be a bad thing?"

"Not necessarily. But she's on her honeymoon."

"How ironic," Andreos said.

"I know. I'll keep her unaware as long as I can. How did you and Gurney convince the captain to continue with the cruise? He seemed pretty adamant about company policy after a suspected passenger death."

"Gurney spent the night waking people in Washington. I believe a call from the Attorney General to the president of the cruise line broke the deadlock at five a.m. The key was that Josie never checked-in and was therefore not officially a passenger when she disappeared. And they still have not found a body."

"I hope Gurney doesn't fall asleep on watch today."

"Keone, I am sorry I did not contact you before the cruise, but Agent Gurney threatened to keep me from coming if I did. He cannot stop us from talking now, though. See you this afternoon." Andreos approached his own tour bus and talked with the driver.

Keone was relieved he didn't have to concern himself with

Gurney's suspicions during the tour to Moloka'i. He suspected Gurney would be tailing Andreos's bus.

Who's watching the other Olympians?

He couldn't think about that now—he had two of his own to watch today. He was glad the captain agreed to keep Ron Morton busy on the ship. He liked Ron, but the talkative entertainer could also blow Keone's and Andreos's covers.

A tingle at the base of his skull.

No. No way.

Keone grabbed his cell phone. "Tom, I need you to check some people out without letting Gurney know. I'm sure it's a non-starter, but I need to be sure."

Keone boarded the bus and glanced at the bow of the ship. What he saw there sent a jolt through his body. In beautifully scrolled lettering, the name of their ship glared at him.

Pele's Fire.

"WE'RE HERE," LINDA CALLED TO A LAGGING ANGELA.

"Is your cruise somehow longer than mine?"

"What?"

Angela struggled to the cabin door with Linda's huge suitcase. "Or did you just decide to bring a few anvils with you?"

"Funny. Really. You're a riot, Alice," Linda replied in a passable Ralph Kramden imitation.

Angela smiled and brushed Linda's cheek with a kiss as she passed. Damn, she loved this woman. She thought of something Nancy Lister said at the reception. *You* can *fall in love with your best friend. I did.*

Linda squeezed her new wife's arm. "I love you with all my heart. Now get lost."

"I know. You want to take your sweet time putting everything away."

"And?"

"And I'd get in the way. Okay, okay. I'll go explore the ship. But we're meeting in the Lido bar in a half—

Linda slowly shook her head.

"All right an hour, but no more."

Linda waved Angela out the door with a flourish and closed it behind her.

Angela shrugged and walked over to a cross-sectional map of the ship on the corridor wall.

She'd only seen cruise ships in movies. Given her preference for action films, the ships tended to sink or get hijacked. But they were still impressive. Angela looked forward to exploring this giant, floating hotel from top to bottom.

An ornate, glass-sided elevator brought Angela up to the observation deck. From there she climbed stairs to reach three additional levels. There was one more level, but that stairway was blocked with a chain and a sign reading: Crew Only. A crewman came down the stairs and disconnected the chain. Detective Sergeant Beyers might have tried to talk the man into letting her have a peek, but on this cruise, Linda expected her to be Angela, off-duty and committed to fun.

On the way down, Angela toured each deck and spotted every off-limits area. She was still a detective, after all. The spa level was amazing with all sorts of equipment, baths, and a running track. The showroom was larger than she'd expected as was the main dining room. On another floor she found a twenty-four-hour buffet and a cluster of specialty food outlets.

By the time she reached the Lido deck, she'd concluded the security on the ship was very tight. Angela doubted this was normal. But with no experience to judge against, she accepted it.

Angela made her way aft along the Lido deck, noting the pools and hot tubs were sparsely occupied. She guessed most passengers were going on shore excursions today. The water in the pools looked cool and inviting, but she had more ship to cover.

Completing her inspection tour, Angela returned to the bow and its well-stocked bar.

Why not? she thought. *I'm off duty.*

She ordered a Mai Tai. Two women sitting beside her at the bar talked about the same thing that caught her eye: ship security.

"They've got more security on this ship than the other one. They're trying to play it cool, but they're taking the threat seriously," a short brunette said to her tall, blonde companion.

"Patty, I'm worried about Josie. She would never cancel at the last minute. We've been talking about this trip for a month. I tried to call her husband when we were still at sea but got voicemail. I'll try again this morning. I figured with the six-hour time difference Vic should be home from work by about eleven a.m. Hawai'i time."

"I'm sure she's okay, Roni. The Purser said she must have missed the ship. If so, she can fly to Maui and meet us here. She'll probably be in the bar sipping a Mai Tai with me by the pool when you get back from Hāna."

"I hope so. But I can't help thinking this is how it started last time."

When the brunette named Patty headed to the pool, Angela approached her blonde companion, drink in hand. "Aloha. Did I hear that you're going to Hāna?"

"Yes. I'm looking forward to visiting the Seven Sacred Pools. Have you been?"

"Oh, yes. I live here. There are more than seven. And the sacred part is a little shaky. But they are lovely pools connected by beautiful waterfalls. You'll have a great time. I'm Angela." Angela offered her right hand to the stranger.

The blonde took her hand and flashed an engaging smile. "I'm Veronica. This place is so beautiful. How can you ever leave?"

"I generally don't. This is my first cruise. I'm on my honeymoon. How about you?" Angela probed gently.

"This is my second. The other one was in the Mediterranean."

I bet it included Greece.

"The Mediterranean. How exciting. Is it as beautiful as they say?"

"Oh yes, what I saw of it. We had to leave before the end of the cruise."

Had to leave early. I wonder if she's an athlete?

"That's too bad. Did someone in your party get sick?"

"Something like that." Veronica nervously glanced at her watch. "Look at the time. I better scoot if I'm going to catch my tour. Maybe we can talk more later."

"I'd like that, Veronica."

Didn't Keone meet a Veronica and a Josie on his Mediterranean honeymoon cruise?

One thing she shared with her partner was a distrust of coincidences.

Wasn't it interesting that Keone left Maui the same night the cruise left O'ahu.

Another coincidence?

51

Friday, April 25, 4:30 p.m.

A tired Keone returned to the ship and waited on the dock, pleased the two Olympians under his care returned safely to the ship. He texted Gurney his report and blind copied Andreos. Gurney sent a terse acknowledgement, but Andreos sent his cabin number and suggested Keone make his way there.

Keone climbed to Andreos's cabin using stairways restricted for the crew's use. He couldn't risk one of the Olympians, Ron Morton, Angela, or Linda spotting him, not to mention Thanatos.

After one knock, Andreos opened the door, ushered Keone into the cabin, and scanned the passageway. "We have a situation."

"One of the other shore excursions?"

"No, they all returned safely, like yours. The one woman who never left the ship is accounted for as well."

"Is this situation related to Agent Gurney?" Keone had to be careful.

"Yes. He was supposed to keep an eye on the women who toured Lāhainā, but I saw him as I re-boarded my bus at Hāna after lunch to leave for the seven pools." He looked at his notebook. "That was one p.m. The Lāhainā excursion does not return until five."

"Andreos, I—"

"I believe Gurney thinks I am Thanatos."

Keone said nothing.

"I also believe he has told you to be careful of me."

Keone remained silent.

"I will never ask you to betray a promise, Keone. But I wanted to tell you, face-to-face, I am not this monster we seek. If you believe me, I need you to help me guard the other women while Gurney watches me. We will need another pair of eyes."

"I agree with you," he said, but thought, *Sorry, Ange.*

AT THE EARLY DINNER SEATING, ANGELA WAS PLEASED and surprised that they were seated with the woman she'd met earlier in the day, Veronica.

Another coincidence?

Angela took the seat next to Veronica, which put Linda next to a sturdy brick of a woman with mildly Asiatic features. The fifth and sixth chairs at the table were empty.

Veronica smiled with recognition when Linda introduced herself and Ange. "I've already met Angela. I understand you two are on your honeymoon."

"Yes, we are," Linda replied.

Angela saw Lin tense slightly, prepared to defend herself.

"On my last cruise, the couple at our table were newly-weds. You two have that same glow about you." Veronica smiled.

Linda relaxed. "I knew I liked you. You're Canadian, aren't you?"

"Guilty as charged. So is my friend Osha next to you," Veronica said, then asked, "How'd you guess?"

"The way you pronounced *about*." Linda made the word sound like *a boat*.

"That word is such a giveaway," Veronica said. "I try to avoid it when I'm around Americans. Come to think of it, that couple from the other cruise were from Maui, too. What a coincidence."

"Yes. Isn't it?" Angela was certain it was anything but. "Was that the Mediterranean cruise you mentioned this morning? Were you on that one, too, Osha?" Angela asked, trying to bring the woman into the conversation.

"Yes, she was," Veronica answered for her friend. "She raved about the food for weeks after we got back."

Osha glanced at Veronica and nodded.

Why isn't she letting her friend speak for herself? I'm sure it was Keone's cruise. Maybe the cruise line asked them not to talk about it. Angela's eyes scanned the dining room.

Linda picked up the conversation. "We get a lot of Canadian tourists here on Maui. What province are you from?"

"Quebec. I live in Montreal. So does the person who should be sitting there." She pointed at the empty fifth chair. "My friend Josie missed the boat in Honolulu. We were hoping she'd catch up to us here, weren't we Osha?"

The other woman laid down her breadstick and nodded seriously.

"Have you tried to contact her?" Angela tried her best not to sound like a detective.

"I've been trying since last night and all day today. I even tried her husband. I . . . I . . . just get voicemail."

"Are you sure she arrived in Honolulu? Were you on the same flight?" Angela asked gently.

"No. My flight was full by the time Josie got around to booking. She's a bit less, uh, organized than me. Do you think she missed her flight, too?" Veronica seemed hopeful. "If she had to come a day late that would explain everything."

"Of course," Linda said. "She couldn't answer her cell during a trans-continental or trans-Pacific flight. Then she'd have to get an inter-island flight. Maybe she couldn't make it in time for Maui and plans to surprise you on the Big Island." Linda reflected Veronica's new-found optimism.

Angela continued to scan the tables for a familiar face. Her gaze briefly settled on the starboard-side windows. The lovely view of Kahului Harbor and Wailuku was occasionally interrupted by people strolling on the deck. Then one large form blocked the window for more than a moment.

I knew it.

Angela excused herself and went toward the ladies' room, before quickly changing direction and walking on deck to confront Keone Boyd. He'd moved away from the windows.

"Spill, big guy," she said and punched him firmly in the arm.

"How much have you figured out so far?"

"Really? You want to test my detective skills after keeping me in the dark and crashing my honeymoon? Okay. My tablemate is a Canadian. Her name is Veronica. She has a missing friend named Josie. Her only other cruise was in the Mediterranean. Her tablemates on that cruise were a newlywed couple from Maui. By her physique, I'm guessing she was an athlete in her youth. Maybe an Olympic athlete? Happy now?"

Keone smiled.

"Why do I suspect Veronica is not at our table by accident?"

"Guilty as charged, Detective."

"How many casualties so far?"

"One missing on O'ahu."

"Josie." Angela's heart sank.

"I'm afraid so. I see someone else is missing from your table. A woman named Patty Ferguson is supposed to be there. She's another one of the athletes. She's supposed to have stayed on board all day."

"I met her today with Veronica. She was heading to the pool. Do you think she's missing, too?"

"I doubt it. She was seen on board after all the excursions returned and the computer shows she never left the ship. Plus, Thanatos always kills in port. We're hoping he just gave today a miss."

"Like he did on the other cruise. Do you want my help looking for Patty?"

"Well, you know what she looks like, and a little bird told me you spent a good deal of this morning casing the joint, while I was off on a shore excursion. Besides I'd hate to barge into the lady's spa or sauna. Any good hiding places?"

"A few. Most aren't accessible to passengers, though."

"You now have full access to the ship. Thanks to me, and the captain, the entire security staff now knows you by sight."

"I can't tell Veronica or Linda or Osha, can I?"

"Not yet. But if Linda figures it out, I won't make you lie to her. Welcome to my world."

"Is it Thanatos?"

"Yes, I think so. So does Andreos."

"Agent Calliopoulos is on board. I'd love to meet him."

"You will. Any messages you have for me, give to Andreos." Keone slipped her a piece of paper. "Andreos's cabin number and my own. And his cell number. You have mine. One last thing. We shouldn't be seen together."

"Oh? Why?"

"It's complicated."

"Isn't it always? Who else is looking after the women?" Angela's curiosity was piqued.

"An FBI special agent, but he's . . . uh . . . distracted. Andreos and I will need your help on The Big Island. If I'd known you were going to take this cruise, I would have warned you not to. I'm truly sorry, Ange."

"I should have let Julie tell you the damn secret. Oh hell, let's just nail the bastard."

52

When Angela returned to their table, she appeared a bit queasy to Linda. "Are you okay, Ange?"

"My stomach's just being annoying."

Veronica glanced out the window. "We haven't left the dock yet."

"I know. I'm sure it's nothing, but better safe than sorry. I've got a prescription in the cabin."

Linda didn't hesitate. "I'll come with you."

"Don't be silly. Enjoy your meal. I'll probably be fine by the time you get back to the cabin. Then we can rock this ship."

Intrigued by their tablemates, Linda felt conflicted. She also rarely missed a meal, especially one she'd already paid for. "I don't know, Ange."

"Look. We have our phones. I'll call you if I need you."

"You better. I mean it."

"Maybe we can all get together later for the show. I happen to know Ron Morton. He's a great entertainer," Veronica said.

"Sounds good." Angela gave a thumbs up and walked to the elevator.

With Angela gone, Linda decided to play detective. "Was Ron on the Mediterranean cruise, too?"

"Yes. His shows were amazing, and Ron is a kick offstage, too. He kept us in stitches on our excursion to the Amalfi Coast and Pompeii."

Osha stopped eating long enough to add, "He did a special show just for us in Athens. But that didn't end too well."

Veronica's smile wavered slightly.

"Angela told me you left the cruise before the end. Why was that?"

"We were told not to talk about it." Veronica's voice became stern.

"I'm sorry, Roni, I didn't mean to pry." Linda felt her cheeks warm with embarrassment.

"Three of our teammates disappeared during the cruise," Osha answered.

"Osha." Veronica fumed.

Not making me feel better, Linda thought.

"Oh, Roni, it's been almost a year. Don't worry, Linda. The guy responsible is dead. He fell onto the stage in the middle of Ron's performance on the Acropolis. The sound his head made when he hit that marble stage—yuck!"

"Ron passed out. The man's body landed right next to him." Veronica shivered.

"I'm so sorry." Linda felt something. "Jeez, I'm shaking all over and I wasn't even there."

"The ship's moving. We're pulling out." Osha pointed out the window.

"Mind if I take a quick look outside?" Linda said, hoping to change the mood.

"Not at all. I'll come with you. You don't mind, do you Osha?"

Osha speared another hunk of prime rib and waved them on.

Linda and Veronica stood at the railing and watched the ship slowly pull away from the pier. After a little while, Linda asked, "What was Osha's Olympic sport?"

"Shot-put. She's an Inuit, never been more than a few miles from her tiny village before the Olympics. Her family didn't want her to compete, but she won them over and then won a silver medal."

Linda knew about trying to win over parents. "I noticed six chairs at our table. Do you know who belongs to the other empty one?"

"Our friend Patty. She was with me when I met Angela but stayed on board today."

"I'm sorry she skipped dinner. I'd love to meet her."

"You will. She just decided to eat at the smoothie bar in the spa tonight."

Linda frowned.

"Don't worry. Patty's not in the spa for exercise. She's getting a full beauty treatment. Soaks, aroma therapy, cucumber facial, the whole nine yards." Veronica laughed.

"Oh. I could get into that. I'll have to tell Ange." Linda turned to go back inside.

But Veronica touched her arm. "Look, Linda, I'm sorry about my reaction when Osha talked about the other cruise. It's just . . . I pray it's not all happening again."

"What's not happening again?"

"People disappearing on a cruise. Last time, they turned up dead."

"Not this time," Linda assured her. "Fate wouldn't dare mess with my honeymoon." Linda assumed a boxing stance, presumably to punch out fate.

"I wouldn't mess with you," Veronica said with a grin. "Look, dessert is being served."

Linda had an idea as three chocolate mousse cakes were laid before them. "Say, why don't you come to our cabin after dinner?"

"I'd like that," Veronica replied. "We've just met, but I feel like I've known you and your wife for years, like our friends Keone and Julie from the other cruise."

Linda was speechless. She just watched as Osha inhaled her dessert.

"Nice to meet you, Linda. I've got a date in the spa to get pampered. Not much of that where I come from. See ya," the stocky Inuit said as she got up from the table.

Veronica turned to Linda. "I envy Osha's focus. I haven't taken a bite of my dessert."

"I like her style." Linda said, a heaping spoonful of chocolate decadence finally en route to her own mouth.

KEONE SEARCHED THE LOWER DECKS, WHILE ANGELA TOOK the upper.

Having Angela here could turn out to be a blessing. The killer had seen Keone before and probably Andreos. William Gurney looked like central casting's idea of what an FBI agent should look like. But Angela was a wild card.

Andreos caught up with him on the fifth deck. "Your partner found the girl in the spa."

"Is she—?"

"She's fine. Detective Sergeant Beyers offered to stay, but the woman's friend, Osha, arrived, so I suggested to your partner that she return to her cabin."

"I'm relieved Thanatos still avoids killing at sea."

"Are you not concerned by the theories of Special Agent Gurney?"

"Andreos, assholes rarely have great theories." Keone smiled.

"Did you know that your partner is following up on a theory of her own?"

"No."

"Did you also know that we have cellular service throughout the cruise?"

Taking the hint, Keone called Angela's cell. The line was engaged so he left a message to call him ASAP.

"I believe she may still be on the line with someone named Lindsay," Andreos said. "I heard your partner ask her to do a *deep dove* on someone from our Greek cruise after I escorted her back to her cabin."

"Deep dive," Keone corrected.

They arrived at Keone's room to find Gurney waiting by the door.

"We found the girl," Keone began. "She's safe in the spa with a friend."

"Good work, Detective Sergeant Boyd."

Hallelujah. He can be trained.

"Have we received any further information from Honolulu?" Andreos asked.

"Yes. I have photos of the missing woman on my tablet."

Keone's phone rang before he could join Gurney and Andreos. He didn't need to see pictures of Josie and appreciated the excuse to leave the cabin. He walked down the hall far enough to be sure he was out of earshot.

53

Keone was relieved to hear Angela's voice on the line. "Hey, Keone. I'm standing in the hall. Lin's got Veronica with her in our room. She's pretty shaken up about being unable to contact Josie or her husband."

"What a coincidence. I'm standing in a hall, too. As for the inability to contact Josie's husband, Gurney told me that the FBI's with Vic Galliano in Montreal. For the moment, his phone is being monitored, just in case Josie was kidnapped. I know it's unlikely, but they have to cross all the t's and dot all the i's. Any call that is obviously from a known caller is sent straight to voicemail."

"Understood. Why did you ask me to call?"

"That little bird told me you have a theory about Thanatos."

"I guess Andreos heard me talking to Lindsay. She's helping Tom Freeman with the assignment you gave him."

"Have they learned anything yet?"

"Not much. Lindsay said she'd call as soon as she has

anything significant. I'd just hung up when Linda and Veronica got to our cabin."

"I've got to get to a meeting now, but we'll get together and compare notes as soon as I finish."

Keone ended the call and returned to find Gurney and Andreos arguing.

"We should just take the remaining five off the boat when we dock in Hilo," Gurney said.

"We'll never have a better chance to catch Thanatos."

"Lower your voices." Keone didn't need to shout to exert his authority.

"We *know* he's on the ship, Keone," Andreos said in a normal voice.

"How?" Keone asked.

"Agent Calliopoulos got a note from him this evening," Gurney replied and held a sheet of paper out to Keone.

The note was handwritten on a portion of today's dated dinner menu. Keone recognized the handwriting.

My Dear Agent Calliopoulos,

Welcome back to the game. I suppose you've realized by now that I was busy in Oahu.

You need not look for a casualty on Maui, though. There is none.

I could have taken young Patty on the ship, but my next child will leave for Elysium from the true home of Hawai'i's greatest god.

I respect you as a detective, and will not harm you or your family, as I promised. But you should not have involved that heathen. If you send that big Hawaiian after me, I promise a *less pleasant final destination for him than for my children.*

Thanatos

"Maybe we should talk to the captain again?" Gurney offered.

"We have no definitive evidence that Josie has been killed or even injured," Andreos said.

"No, but the note suggests he did something on Oahu, even if he doesn't mention Mrs. Galliano by name," Gurney noted. "And we still have five Olympians to watch with only three law enforcement agents and a serial killer on board."

Keone knew Gurney even doubted whether all of those agents were on his side. *I bet he thinks Andreos wrote the note.*

"You are correct, Special Agent. Tomorrow, two Olympians will travel together on the Merrie Monarch Excursion, but the other three have separate plans. One will travel to the Hawaiian Volcanoes National Park, one to the Parker Ranch, and the last to visit family friends in Kailua/Kona. We would need at least four people to watch them all." Andreos looked directly at Keone as he spoke.

"Will, if I could vouch for a fourth law enforcement officer on board, would you consider waiting to talk to the captain until after tomorrow's excursions?" Keone made a point of using the FBI agent's first name.

"I'd have to meet and approve of the officer personally," Gurney replied.

"Meet me in your cabin in an hour." Keone allowed no time for Gurney or Andreos to react before leaving the cabin.

"WHAT THE HELL, KEONE?" LINDA SAID WHEN SHE opened the cabin door.

Angela pulled her partner in and shut the door. "So much for not being seen together."

"Keone? I don't understand. When did you get here?" Veronica looked overwhelmed.

They all listened quietly as he explained why he was on the cruise. He told them the truth about Josie Galliano and wasn't surprised that Veronica broke down at the confirmation of her friend's disappearance.

He comforted her in his arms and felt tears form in his own eyes. "I know it looks bad, but agent Calliopoulos got a note from Thanatos just now. Although he threatened harm to you and your friends, he didn't mention Josie. In the past he's always bragged after he sent one of his children to Elysium."

"But, Keone, he could just be trying to misdirect you," Veronica said between sobs.

"True. But the whole Honolulu police department is searching for her, and until I have evidence to the contrary, I'm going to hang on to a little hope."

"Me too," Veronica said. The woman seemed determined to collect herself as she walked to the bathroom, washed her face, and then returned.

When Keone finished his complete report, Veronica said, "How can I help?"

"Mostly by going on the Merrie Monarch Festival shore excursion tomorrow as if nothing has happened. Normally, we'd try to replace both you and Osha with policewomen in disguise, but there isn't time and—"

"I'm tall, pale, and blonde. Probably a bit uncommon in the Hawai'i PD," Veronica interrupted, completing Keone's sentence for him.

"I won't lie to you. This will be dangerous. I'll try to

persuade Special Agent Gurney to allow Angela to go with you, dressed as Osha. Thanatos doesn't know her, and there's no one I trust more to keep you safe than Detective Sergeant Beyers."

"I'll do anything you ask to help catch that maniac," Veronica said, a fierce resolve behind her words.

"Andreos will be on the volcanoes tour with another Olympian, Agent Gurney will keep an eye on the one visiting family friends in Kona."

"And you're the logical one to go to Parker Ranch," Angela said.

"Well, you're pretty good on a horse, partner, but I don't think I could pass as Osha." Keone grinned.

"What about me?" Linda asked.

"You're a civilian," Keone said.

"A civilian who was an Army Ranger in Afghanistan. No way I'm sitting this out." Linda's back straightened, daring anyone to challenge her.

"That was years ago," Angela said.

"I can still whup your butt."

Keone went over to Linda and put his arm around her. "I don't want to be responsible for your first fight as a married couple. But Gurney would never approve."

"Does he need to know?" Linda asked. "I'm already scheduled for that excursion and friends with Veronica and Osha."

"Well, no, but—"

"Keone, I could honestly use Linda's help." Angela surprised Keone with her willingness to have Linda with them, then realized, *She wants to keep her close with a serial killer loose.*

"Let's go see your FBI guy." With that Angela led Keone out of the cabin.

54

Angela halted their progress in a hallway and turned Keone around to face her. "I heard back from Lindsay and Tom."

"About Andreos?"

"Yes. And some others." Angela took out her notebook.

"Not here. My cabin's just along this corridor." Keone pointed left.

He waved Angela inside. "What have you got for me?'

Angela began her report. "Do you remember when you told me about the juggler?"

"Sure, when we went after Dave."

"Every time you mentioned Morton's name, you scratched the back of your neck. You only do that when something's bothering you."

"I didn't know you were watching me so closely. Good catch, Detective."

"I decided to do some digging. Well, I asked Lindsay to do some digging for me. She informed me you'd already asked Tom to check on Andreos and Gurney but not Ron Morton. I got reports from them on all three. Turns out Morton's from Seattle." Angela opened her notebook.

"Did you forget he helped us catch the guy in Greece?" Keone asked.

"I did not. But, Keone, Ron is more than he appears. And your gut's been trying to tell you that."

On the Greek cruise, Keone never considered the funny, happy guy a suspect. He honestly liked Ron. "What do they have on him?"

"Lindsay, Tom, and their FBI contact, Tomiko Yamada, checked with all the cruise lines involved and discovered Ron was on all of the cruises where Olympians were killed, not Andreos."

"Why didn't we catch that?" Keone controlled his anger. "Surely, Europol and the FBI checked that out."

"Ron Morton is just one of four stage names used by Roald Petersen. And he, unlike Andreos was on all the more recent cruises where Olympians were killed."

"Of course. I knew Andreos wasn't on those other cruises. And damn it, Josie even asked Ron about stage names on our tour to Pompeii, but he never answered." Keone could kick himself. Then another piece clicked into place.

"Ange, I just remembered where I'd seen the crewman that fell onto the stage at the acropolis before. He was the crewman that picked Ron up from our tour of Pompeii." Keone's mind continued to make connections. *Another coincidence—that wasn't.*

Angela took advantage of the pause to continue. "Petersen was born in Oslo, Norway, and moved to Seattle with his parents when he was two years old. His parents changed his name legally to Ronald when they all received citizenship. His father was a juggler, too. Apparently a great one. By age eleven, Ron was performing with his father. Despite his age, Ron's glib delivery and lack of any accent made him a natural front man for the act."

"Any friction between father and son?" Keone asked.

"There's no record of any. The only criminal record Tomiko found was juvenile and that was sealed on his eighteenth birthday. Father and mother died of natural causes when Ron was sixteen. No arrests as an adult. Performed under the other names since his parents' deaths, never Petersen."

"We need to see that juvenile record, Ange."

"Tomiko is working on that, but it's not that easy. She's also got a handwriting expert checking the notes from Thanatos against four samples we've obtained from people on this cruise."

"Who?"

"They'd already ruled out the Canadian athletes and their families. They're focusing on Andreos Calliopoulos, Ronald Morton, William Gurney, and Keone Boyd."

"Does Gurney know?" Keone asked.

"Yeah. Tomiko's been working with him. Thinks he's a jerk. That's why she put his sample in, ostensibly as a control. I think she likes to piss him off."

"I can understand that."

"If he's not pissed off at her, he might be pissed off that I went behind his back," Angela noted.

Keone glanced at his watch. "You'll find out. It's time to introduce you to Special Agent Gurney."

"Andreos will be there, yeah?"

"Yeah. Let me do most of the talking, though, okay?"

"You got it, partner."

"WE NEED TO TALK," WILL GURNEY SAID, ESCORTING Keone and Angela into his cabin.

Gurney led them to a couch where Andreos sat quietly, then sat in a chair across a coffee table from them.

Keone wanted to spare Angela the agent's wrath, and spoke in his calmest voice. "Angela was just telling me some interesting information her friend in the Honolulu PD found out about Ron Morton."

"I know. Detective Sergeant Beyers, we all owe you a huge debt of gratitude for looking outside the box the FBI and Europol were stuck in. My colleagues at the bureau and I never considered the juggler as a serious suspect."

"Neither did I or my superiors at Europol," Andreos said.

"You can add my name to that list. I still can't get my head around Ron as a cold-blooded killer." Keone felt the tension in his neck relax, glad Angela received the gratitude she deserved for her initiative.

"I helped Agent Tomiko Yamada get Petersen's juvenile file unsealed. Your hunch was good." Gurney lifted a fax from the coffee table. "Here's what Agent Yamada found out. At age thirteen, Ronald Petersen exhibited some strange emotional behaviors. A child psychologist referred him to a specialist who diagnosed the boy with a rare form of multiple personality disorder. The doctor worked with him for two years. At age fifteen, the doctor declared the alter ego gone. One year later, his folks died of natural causes. Ron finished high school with good marks and went on to college but dropped out to work full time on his comedy juggling act. He changed his stage name to avoid any appearance that he was benefiting from his family's reputation. At age twenty-five he married Victoria Gonzales. Shortly before their wedding he had his name legally changed to Ronald T. Morton. They have two small children."

"Interesting, but I don't see any motive in all of this," Keone said.

At this, Andreos spoke up. "The psychiatrist who worked with Petersen, a German national named Schwartzmann, has since moved to Bern, Switzerland, where he has a large practice. One of my agents is contacting him and will report back to me before morning."

"Still no motive," Keone noted.

"Agent Yamada also reported results from the handwriting analyst," Gurney said. "The only match was with Ron Morton, with eighty-three percent confidence. They also report, with ninety-nine percent confidence, that Keone, Andreos, and I did not write those notes from Thanatos."

"In light of this information, I believe we need to come up with a potential plan of action." Keone leaned forward to see if Gurney or Andreos had anything to say.

No one spoke. But the two agents nodded.

"Okay, then. I've been thinking about a possible scenario for tomorrow that may or not make sense. After I lay it out, I would like each of you to comment. But let me lay the whole thing out before you do, okay?"

Nods all around.

"I suggest we deploy enticing targets for Thanatos. Targets that are in effect traps. A key element of one of these traps involves Detective Sergeant Beyers impersonating a Canadian shot-putter named Osha. In this role, she can keep an eye on Olympian Veronica Napoleoni during the Merrie Monarch Tour. The rest of us would then be free to look after the other Olympians on the other three tours. I apprised Ms. Napoleoni of the risk, and she has volunteered to participate. I would appreciate everyone's thoughts on this suggestion, including yours, Angela."

Gurney spoke first. "My support of this plan would depend

on what Andreos's agent discovers and what plans Ron Morton has for tomorrow."

For the first time, Keone thought Gurney sounded more like a team member than an impediment.

"I tentatively support this approach, too, and agree with the importance of the two pieces of information Special Agent Gurney mentioned," Andreos added.

Thanks, Andreos.

"I am willing to go undercover as the shot-putter and provide security for Ms. Napoleoni. I don't say the plan is perfect, but it represents a significant chance of ending the career of this maniac," Angela said.

Atta girl, Tita.

"With your approval, I believe we should prepare to go forward. We can reconvene after we've obtained the necessary data to make a final decision to move forward, modify the plan, or abort it. Are we agreed?" Keone asked.

Nods all around.

"I'll follow up on whether or not Morton is booked on any of the excursions on the Big Island, and if so which," Gurney offered.

"I shall return to my room and await the call from my agent," Andreos added. "I shall contact you when I have something more to share. I fear it could be quite late given the time difference."

"Detective Sergeant Beyers and I will go to her cabin and help prepare her and Ms. Napoleoni for tomorrow's excursion, and I will keep her informed of everything I hear from the two of you." Keone stood up and left the cabin, Angela close behind.

Part Five
Belief

"Some things have to be believed to be seen."

— Madeleine L'Engle

55

Angela opened her cabin door to find two familiar women standing by the couch. But something was different about them.

"No way," Keone said.

"Don't you recognize us?" Veronica's voice said.

Keone laughed. The voice seemed to be coming out of Linda's mouth.

"Don't laugh. We put a lot of work into this." Linda's voice came out of Veronica's body.

The transformation was eerie. Linda wore Veronica's cocktail dress and spiked heels on her feet. But the real trick was the long, honey-blonde hair. Meanwhile, Veronica seemed inches shorter in flats and the short spiky hairdo normally sported by Linda.

"What the hell have you done?" Angela roared. "Are you out of your minds?"

Keone closed the cabin door behind them. "I appreciate all the effort, but I agree with Angela. It's too dangerous."

"How is it any more dangerous than me going as myself?" Veronica asked.

Angela took a moment to realize that it was Linda asking.

She does look like Veronica.

Angela considered the possibilities. "Look, what you're suggesting is not a terrible idea. Think about it though. Keone will never be able to get Gurney to go for this."

"Does he need to know?" the real Veronica asked.

"Yes, and so does Andreos. I'll need to talk with both of them and see what I can convince them to accept." Turning back, Keone added, "None of you will leave this cabin until I get back. Oh, and Ange, you might have these magicians work on your Osha disguise. They're pretty damn good."

56

Saturday, April 26, 12:25 a.m.

Keone knocked softly on Andreos Calliopoulos's cabin door. Finding the door ajar, Keone entered with Gurney on his heels. "You called?"

"I did. My agent in Bern called me with his report." Andreos closed the cabin door behind them.

"We guessed," Keone said. He liked Andreos, but the Greek's politeness could become wearying after midnight.

"How was the interview with Dr. Schwartzmann?" Gurney asked.

"Herr Doctor refused to share much about his private consultations with Ronald Petersen, our Ron Morton. He called Ronald a very kind boy with a difficult medical problem that they succeeded in overcoming together."

"We already knew that," Gurney said.

Andreos ignored the interruption. "Dr. Schwartzmann told my agent, Jean-Pierre, that the disorder has been referred to by many names over the centuries. A split personality, multiple personality disorder, even demonic possession has been blamed for what is now recognized as dissociative identity disorder (DID). The doctor went on and on about the great strides he had made in recent years with DID patients. Jean-Pierre had almost given up on getting any valuable information for our investigation when he decided to take, um, a shot in the dark, yes? He asked the doctor if he knew the name Thanatos."

"And the answer to that question is why you called us here," Keone said, his impatience fading.

"Dr. Schwartzmann was quite familiar with the name. Thanatos was the alter ego he helped Petersen control when he was fifteen years of age." Andreos stared calmly at the other two men.

"Did the doctor ever communicate with Thanatos?" Keone asked.

"The doctor told Jean-Pierre he had spoken with Thanatos one time only. He described Thanatos as having delusions of divinity. Thanatos believed himself the Greek god of nonviolent death. He told the doctor he could possess Ron at his whim, without Ron's knowledge." Andreos paused long enough for Gurney to slip in a question.

"You two know more about Thanatos than I do. Does this track with what you know?"

Keone responded, "Thanatos is a real Greek god. I looked him up, but Andreos knows more about him." *Did I just say* real *Greek god?*

"What does a god of non-violent death do, Agent Calliopoulos?" Gurney still seemed unconvinced.

"I am glad you asked. According to Greek mythology, Thanatos provided people a peaceful and exquisitely pleasant, some would say erotic, transition to the afterlife simply by gesturing with his hand." Andreos waved his hand towards Keone's throat.

Message received.

"What afterlife did the Greeks believe in?" Gurney asked.

"Their paradise was called the Elysian Fields or *Elysium*," Andreos replied.

"That's our man." Keone was certain at last.

"Our Thanatos has mentioned Elysium in his messages." Andreos leaned toward Gurney.

"Even the MO fits. He just happens to have some kind of double-pointed needle in his hand when he waves it," Gurney said.

Good, Agent Gurney. Very good.

"If we know for certain who Thanatos is, our crazy plan might just work," Andreos said.

"Morton is scheduled to take the excursion to the Merrie Monarch tomorrow," Gurney added. "Now we know who and where."

"Uh, given the switcheroo I told you two about earlier, I'd like to suggest our crazy plan become just a tad crazier," Keone said and went on to explain Veronica and Linda's identity swap.

"No. I won't risk two civilians." Gurney shook his head so hard, Keone thought it might detach and fly around the room.

"I don't like the idea any more than you, Will. But we have a good idea who Thanatos is, where he is now, and where he is going tomorrow. We'll never have a better opportunity to catch him in the act. We can't stop now." Keone intentionally used the agent's first name.

"We can stop whenever I damn well say so," Gurney shouted.

Andreos glared at Gurney. "At least you must no longer

waste your time and effort following me. Oh yes, I knew you suspected me. My former supervisor at Europol probably encouraged you in your false assumptions. But I assure you that since the handwriting results cleared both me and Detective Sergeant Boyd, I have had a very intense conversation with my new superiors. They have offered me their full support on this case."

Gurney seemed to shrink at the revelation.

"Keone, you go convince your partner to put her new bride in jeopardy. Agent Gurney and I will continue to work on the details for our plan for tomorrow—including ersatz Olympians to take the place of those on the other tours."

FAR BELOW THEM IN THE CREW QUARTERS, RON MORTON woke to hear a strange sound coming from his own mouth. A voice, deep and resonant with a slight European accent, seemed to be speaking to him.

Hello, Ronald. My name is Thanatos. I thought we should meet, at last.

Ron struggled to speak. With great effort, he was able to say, in his own voice, "I know that name. Dr. Schwartzmann told me Thanatos was a piece of my mind that tried to control me. He got rid of you."

The other voice replied. *Obviously not, Ronald. I simply left you for a while. I am able to inhabit any human body. Yours became the most desirable for me once again when you began your career with the cruise lines. Your profession was very help-ful. Entertainers, unlike other crewmembers, hop from one ship to another, like a bee pollinating many flowers.*"

"I don't believe you," Ron managed to say through his fear.

I do not need you to believe me, Ronald. Conversely, I

believe you . . . are very tired right now. I believe our conversation is at an end. And I believe I will be using this flesh sack tomorrow.

Ron struggled not to succumb to the exhaustion he suddenly felt. A question foremost in his thoughts came out of his mouth. "Why tell me now?"

57

Saturday, April 26, 10:00 a.m.

Angela watched a human struggling in the tentacles of a giant, lumbering demon with red eyes. He reached out with another tentacle and stroked Angela's neck before leaping into a flaming pit. A massive earthquake then knocked Angela off her feet, causing her to wake up, drenched in sweat and tangled in her bedsheets.

Keone had worn her down last night—no, early this morning. She didn't share Keone's opinion that she looked enough like the Inuit shot-putter, even wearing a wig with straight black hair, makeup, and padding. What if Morton didn't wait until the Merrie Monarch to act? Could she protect both Veronica and Linda? Was one of them the person in her dream?

After showering and donning her disguise and getting made up by Veronica, Angela stared from the balcony of their cabin past Hilo Harbor. Her eyes wandered up the lush green slopes and focused on the peak of Kīlauea Volcano. After her nightmare, she wondered if the Merrie Monarch Tour was Thanatos's true target.

Linda and Veronica applied the final touches to their makeup, and Angela had to admit they looked believable—more believable than her. A knock on the cabin door ended her contemplations. Sergeant Angela Beyers had a job to do, and she would do it to the best of her ability.

Angela opened the door to find Keone and Agent Gurney.

Gurney spoke first. "Agent Calliopoulos is headed to meet his excursion group in the lounge."

"Where is his group going?" Angela knew Keone had told her last night but couldn't remember.

"A tour of Kīlauea Volcano," Keone said, now inside the cabin. "By the way, good morning, *Osha*."

"Right. Kilauea." Angela's thoughts crept back to her dream.

No, damn it, she banished the thoughts. *I'm on duty.*

"We're ready," Linda announced as she and Veronica came in from the bedroom.

"You two look great." Angela ran her fingers through her wig. "I wish I could say the same about myself."

"You look just like Osha," Veronica said from Linda's body. "You're both the same height and . . ."

"And degree of brown. I know."

"Don't worry, I'll be with you all the time," Keone said. "You have my sincere promise that I'll take care of you."

"I thought you were going to Parker Ranch."

"We caught a break there. The athlete who was going to Parker Ranch is now going to Kona with the one who had friends there," Keone explained.

"So Special Agent Gurney will watch them both?" Veronica asked.

"No, I'll travel with your tour," Gurney said. "I asked

Special Agent Tom Freeman from DEA to fly over and meet the ship in Hilo. He'll follow the women to Kona and keep an eye on them."

Angela's eyebrows shot up. "When did you set that up?"

"After we left Maui. I was going to have him watch the woman in Kona so I could watch Andreos. Of course, there's no reason now." Gurney still looked embarrassed about his mistake.

"I'm guessing all of the other Olympians are also body doubles, yeah?" Angela asked.

Keone smiled.

"Any other changes?" Angela couldn't hide her frustration. She hated last-minute changes almost as much as coincidences.

"A minor one. Since I will be with the tour, I will take Keone's place during the final step of the plan. I'll spirit Veronica away from the restroom at the arena. Although to anyone watching, I'll be helping an ill Linda get back to the ship."

"Why change that now?" Keone asked.

"When I finally tried to get to sleep, at five a.m., I began to wonder what would happen if Morton decided to leave the tour at some point. Suppose his target is in Kona or at the volcano and he just wants us to think otherwise." Gurney sounded more like a colleague than ever.

"He's right," Keone said, looking at Angela. "I'd have to follow Morton and that would leave no one to collect Veronica at the arena. If we're wrong about Morton, you'd still be in danger."

"All right. But please, promise me this is the last change," Veronica said.

"I promise." Gurney flashed a rare smile.

As Angela, Linda, and Veronica walked toward their bus, Veronica whispered under her breath, "There's our killer."

Ron Morton headed their way. Angela breathed a sigh of relief when Agent Gurney appeared between them and Ron. The agent smoothly engaged the juggler in conversation before he could get close enough to the girls to spot anything out of the ordinary.

"You're the juggler from last night's show, aren't you?"

Taken by surprise, Ron answered, "Yes. And you?"

"I'm Will Gurney from Pocatello, Idaho." The agent stuck out his hand. "What you did with those Indian clubs last night was truly amazing. I bet those suckers need to be perfectly balanced."

Angela was impressed. Gurney wrapped his arm around Ron and turned him away from the bus long enough for the three of them to board and claim seats at the rear. Ron and Gurney boarded together last and sat in the very front of the bus. Angela suspected the FBI Agent and the entertainer would be joined at the hip for the rest of the tour. She decided the agent might deserve a little more credit than she'd given him.

Angela saw Ron and Gurney joking and laughing as they got off the bus at their first stop, the Moana Loa Macadamia Farm. By the time the three of them got off, Ron and Gurney were nowhere in sight. Angela continued to be impressed by how well the agent distracted their suspect. She even took a moment to search for Keone among the staff at the farm.

"Do you notice how many people on the staff here are big Hawaiians?" Linda asked with a wink and a grin.

"I admit it. I was sure Keone would stand out in any crowd and certainly would never get past this detective's eagle eyes," Angela said.

"What do you bet they have a lot of big Hawaiians working at the botanical gardens, too?" Veronica smiled and chuckled.

Angela guided Veronica and Linda to re-board the bus early. She hadn't seen Ron since they started the tour.

When Agent Gurney boarded last, he was alone.

One of the farm workers came on the bus and showed Gurney a pink phone. The agent studied the device for a little while, then handed it back to the worker and pointed to Angela.

"You must have dropped this on the trail, miss." The worker subtly showed her an HPD badge.

"Oh, thank you so much. I'm such a klutz." Angela made a show of giving the man a five and slipped the phone in her purse.

After the man left and the bus pulled out, Linda whispered, "That's not your phone."

Angela glared at her, then out the window. She saw Ron Morton sitting in the back of a cab. A few minutes later, the cab took off, followed by an old Toyota truck that pulled out of the lot just ahead of their bus.

Keone.

Thank God Gurney thought ahead.

The bus exited the lot and headed in the opposite direction from the cab and the truck. Angela removed the pink phone from her purse. It had a text message on it:

Suspect claimed to be sick and got in cab to go back to ship.

I'll follow – K.

Gurney stays with you.

Stick to plan.

Angela deleted the message and thought of possible reasons for Morton's departure. One possibility stood out in her mind.

What if all Gurney's attention spooked him?

I WAIT TO FULLY RECLAIM THE MORTAL'S BODY UNTIL THE *excursions depart.*

At a nut farm, I make it vomit. What a smell these creatures make.

That helpful FBI agent asks if I am all right. I use the mortal's voice to tell him I am ill and must return to the ship. He even signals an attendant to help me to the cab. I know the attendant is a disguised policeman, who listens while I tell the driver to take me back to the ship.

I don't need to glance back to know the heathen will follow. As we pass the entrance, a much-used vehicle pulls out of the parking area. I don't need to use the juggler's eyes to know the heathen turns in our direction. He is careful not to close the gap.

Mortals. Even the changes they make to their plans fulfill my aims.

"Driver, I've changed my mind. Let's go to Volcano House."

RON MORTON KNEW HE WASN'T FULLY CONSCIOUS BUT could hear his own voice saying, "I don't feel well. I must get back to the ship."

He heard no other sounds for some time until he heard his voice again. "Driver, I've changed my mind. Let's go to Volcano House."

Silence returned.

Thanatos must be in control. Why can't I hear his thoughts? Why can't I hear other sounds?

Ron hated feeling so helpless. He knew the mind in control of his body was blocking him out. But how did he know this?

Were they still connected? If so, there might to be a way to regain control.

In the total silence, Ron focused his thoughts. He searched for any glimmer of that other mind.

58

The primeval beauty of the botanical gardens outside Hilo reminded Angela of everything she loved about Hawai'i. Friendly guides shared the stunning flora of this magical place in a setting of waterfalls, lava tubes, and breathtaking ocean views. With Ron Morton gone, she could almost forget why they were there. Almost.

Standing on a sheer cliff, watching the crashing surf eat away at the black lava shore, Angela realized they made a tempting target. What if Morton and the killer were two different people? What if Thanatos was working with an accomplice again? A killer could be standing right next to them.

No. Morton is our guy.

As Angela moved Veronica and Linda away from the cliff edge, she worried more about Keone.

Where's Morton leading him?

Has anyone heard from Andreos up on Kīlauea?

She hated having so many unanswered questions. Spotting Gurney a few feet away, she decided to get some answers.

"Will you look at that?" Angela directed her statement

toward the agent. "A tree is actually growing out of this cracked coconut."

"That's amazing," Gurney agreed in a loud voice. He added in a whisper, "Haven't heard anything more from Keone. Have you?"

"No. What about Andreos?"

"He checked in a few minutes ago when his tour arrived at the Volcano House. The woman with him is safe and enjoying the tour. The one she's playing and the one you're playing are on a plane scheduled to leave for Canada as soon as Veronica joins them."

"What about the two Tom's watching?"

"They did some shopping in Kona. Now, Tom's following them to the family friends' house. He'll collect them there and take them to the airport unless Morton heads his way."

"Do you still want to collect Veronica outside the arena in Hilo?" Angela asked.

"Keone said to stay with the plan. When they go to the restroom, I'll wait outside and take her to a waiting taxi, driven by a lieutenant from the Hawai'i PD. He'll take her to the airport for the Canada flight, and I'll return to my seat in the arena. Linda can continue to play Veronica."

"I guess Keone's right. Who knows, Morton could double back."

Gurney's body language telegraphed he didn't believe the killer would double back any more than she did. But what else could they do?

Gurney lagged behind as she and the others continued up the trail.

Linda moved close to Angela. "Any changes?"

"No. We'll keep Roni with us until the bathroom break. Just be careful."

"It helps that none of the other athletes are with us. How are they doing?"

"Fine according to Andreos. He checked in with Gurney from Volcano House. I guess we just enjoy the flowers for now." Angela wasn't convinced, but she'd do her job.

Ange felt the phone Keone left for her vibrate in her pocket. She wasn't certain she could hear it in her purse out here. Another text:

On Morton's tail.

Heading to Kīlauea Crater, not ship.

We may have spooked him.

Wish I knew if this was his Plan B.

Told Andreos to keep an eye out.

Keep with plan.

Ron may be Thanatos, but he's worked with an accomplice in the past.

Tell Gurney to keep with the plan, too, but not where I'm headed.

Want him to stay focused. You, too.

The last line surprised Angela.

Did Keone still have concerns about Gurney staying on task?

Was he afraid Gurney might head up to Kīlauea if that's where the collar would be made? Could that be the real reason Gurney changed the plan, so he'd be in on the collar? Would the agent really leave us swaying in the breeze if he thought he'd miss the arrest?

Angela decided following Keone's instructions was exactly what she would do.

59

Saturday, April 26, 2:30 p.m.

Keone predicted his quarry's destination correctly. Morton's cab pulled into the parking lot at Volcano House. What he didn't expect was for the cab to block the driveway while Morton paid the driver. With no other option, Keone continued past the entrance and tried to avoid eye contact. Ron Morton did the opposite. The entertainer beckoned with his fingers and winked, before sprinting into the surrounding forest.

Damn confident for someone with nowhere to go.

Keone made a quick U-turn and was nearly hit by an oncoming tour bus.

Can't let him get to me.

He returned to the spot where the taxi continued to block the driveway, parked the truck on the other side of the road, and ran to the cab. The driver was unconscious. Morton must have given him a little taste of the needle. Keone called

Andreos on his cell and ran toward the spot where Morton entered the pine forest.

Andreos's voice came on the line. "What do you have for me, Keone?"

"Morton's here. Have Hawai'i PD take charge of your *Olympian*. You need to get out to the parking lot. I think Morton gave some magic juice to the cab driver who brought him here. He has a pulse and his cab's blocking the entrance."

"On my way. I'll try to save him. You go after Morton."

"I'm on it. He ran into the woods just south of the parking lot."

By the time Keone ended the call, he'd found a trailhead. He spun around in a half-circle, spotting smaller paths going off in multiple directions.

Think, Keone. What was Morton wearing on his feet?
Loafers.

Keone remembered a moment back at the Macadamia nut farm. He'd thought about Ron struggling up the steep winding trails at the botanical garden in leather-soled shoes.

Most of the paths had marks from tennis shoes or hiking boots, but one set was different. He just hoped it was Morton's.

Or is he Ron Morton anymore? Maybe I'm chasing Thanatos.

Starting down the trail, Keone took a last glance at the parking lot. He saw Andreos reach the cab and throw open the driver's door.

Keone's boot hit a root and he lost his balance. He rolled with the fall but cursed himself for being so stupid.

Hurry down a trail and look behind you. Good move, dumb ass.

He hoped his quarry didn't hear him fall, whatever name the man/god was using now.

Keone picked up his pace, dodging the pine and ironwood

trees that grew right up to the edge of Kīlauea crater. He wasn't exactly running anymore, more jogging briskly. Along with the trees and their roots, Keone had to deal with a slippery carpet of pine needles interspersed with the jagged seams of black lava flows. He had to be close to Ron by now. Morton would make slow progress with those slippery leather soles of his. Keone wanted to confront him before the sun dipped below the peak. The shadows would create too many hiding places.

Crack.

A branch fell a few yards behind him.

No. He couldn't have gotten behind me.

This time Keone halted his forward motion and yanked out his machete before turning his head. A sharp pain stung his neck. He'd been outsmarted.

Not behind me, beside me. He must have tossed that branch to get me to turn.

Keone spun to face the killer, machete in hand. His arm fell limp at his side. The machete fell into the pine needles and so did he. He noticed how soft they were against his body as he relaxed into their caress.

Keone heard a demonic laugh above him. Forcing his eyes to open, he saw the tall skinny body of the juggler. He tried to focus on the contorted face but couldn't recognize Ron in the blur.

Is this the face of a god?

The green and brown images faded around him. Keone fought against the shadows closing in.

Is that another voice? A normal voice yelling . . . yelling what. sounds like, "No."

His final thought was of Julie. Then, nothing.

"No!" Ron screamed, but the sound he heard was softer. His voice, but muted.

Where did that come from? I did not say that.

The mortal.

In my excitement, I allowed him to creep to the surface and join my thoughts.

It won't do you any good. I'm in control.

Are you enjoying your tiny peek into the massive consciousness of Thanatos, little man?

How about some agony?

"Aaaaaugh"

Now hold your tongue, mortal. Or should I say my tongue?

60

Saturday, April 26, 3:00 p.m.

Their tour arrived at the Edith Kanaka'ole Multi-Purpose Stadium for the Merrie Monarch Festival well before the evening's performances were to start. A young woman wearing a brightly flowered dress and an aromatic lei of plumeria and tuberose met the bus, introduced herself as Fantasia, and gave each tour member a lei and a light kiss on the cheek. Fantasia led the group to an outdoor craft fair that accompanied the festival. Booths offered books, craft goods, cultural demonstrations, and workshops related to the Big Island of Hawai'i, the reign of the Merrie Monarch, David Kalakaua, and the festival in his honor. The largest, an *official* gift shop/museum, sold posters and DVDs of previous events. The tour members wandered through the various booths picking up gifts and learning about Hawaiian traditions.

That was fine with Angela. She wanted to see if she could bump into a couple of people she knew would be here today.

Mahealani Boyd was, of course, here to judge the hula competition. And, after her wedding ceremony, Keone's Tutu had told her she would be here too and that they would see each other. She searched each booth without luck, arriving at the gift shop.

Failing to find Tutu or Mahealani, she decided to scout around for someone who could give her an update on Keone and Morton. She spotted a particularly husky docent that she recognized from a law enforcement conference two years ago on Maui. He was Hawai'i PD then, and she bet he still was. "How much for the DVD of last year's Festival?" she asked, in a louder voice than necessary.

The docent leaned in and whispered, "No word on Morton or Boyd so far."

"Mahalo."

"When you enter the arena, your usher will give you another update." Then in a normal voice. "That's twenty-five dollars."

"You should be ashamed of yourself. What a racket." Angela rolled her eyes before drifting off to a designated area of lawn where the rest of the group was enjoying drinks and pupus.

THROUGH THE FOOLISH JUGGLER'S EYES, I GAZE DOWN AT the huge heathen on the forest floor. His breaths are coming slower now. They sound like metal scraping glass. The driver might survive his smaller dose, but not the heathen.

You fool. You thought you would catch me at that pagan festival. Oh, I shall still have your precious Veronica, but that can wait a bit. I am on this mountain to tempt a greater target.

Only when god faces god can my true majesty be displayed.

The heathen draws his last breath. The throbbing in his neck stops.

Time to move on.

61

The usher guided Veronica, Linda, and Angela toward their seats. But Ange tugged on the usher's arm to make him hang back a little.

"Update?" Angela whispered.

"Last we heard that Greek cop was searching for Sergeant Boyd and the suspect on Kīlauea," he whispered, then in a regular voice, "Here you are. A perfect view."

Angela spotted Mahealani Boyd sitting with the other judges. She seemed so mature for her age. Very serious in her analysis of the competitors. After the switcheroo, Angela hoped to talk with her during an intermission. Angela knew Keone's sister's presence enhanced her partner's concern about an attack at the festival. She wondered if it might have influenced Keone's plan to watch over them during their tour. She hoped Andreos was watching over him on the volcano.

Angela swept her eyes slowly across every section of the arena, while Roni and Lin happily enjoyed the top-level hula performances. Their scheduled visit to the restroom loomed about ten minutes away. Staying in her seat would be the hardest part of the plan for Angela. She watched Will Gurney slowly climb the stairs and take his seat on the aisle two rows up from them.

Gurney finally impressed me today. I'm glad he's here to deliver Veronica safely to the Hawai'i PD for the trip to the airport.

At the prearranged time, Linda and Veronica rose from their seats and eased past Angela. She gave Veronica a little squeeze, knowing she wouldn't see her again. After they descended the stairs, Will Gurney inconspicuously rose to his feet and stretched for a few seconds before following. Everything was happening the way it was supposed to. Angela still resisted an urge to kick Gurney in the butt to make him move a little faster down the stairs. Veronica was in his hands now, not to mention the love of her life.

Linda returned to her seat ten long minutes later, still disguised as Veronica. She gave Ange a thumbs up. For the first time, Angela allowed herself a smile.

With Morton at Kīlauea and Veronica on her way to the airport, is there really any reason for me and Linda to stay here?

As if in answer, Mahealani took the stage. Her music was a slow, sensual, but purely Hawaiian melody. As she swayed, it was easy to understand why she was a champion. Angela became completely absorbed in the timeless message of Lani's hula.

The usher from earlier knelt behind her and broke the spell. "Where the hell is Agent Gurney?"

She glanced behind her. The agent's seat was empty. He should have returned from passing Veronica on to the local cops by now.

"I saw him connect with Veronica outside the bathroom while I was still inside," Linda said.

I hope nothing happened to him.

"Where did he go after he dropped Ms. Napoleoni off with your guys?"

"That's just it. He never showed up."

"Damn it. Get her back to the ship." Angela pointed at Linda. Without waiting for an acknowledgement, she flew down the stairs and out of the arena.

Angela burst into the parking lot, eyes sweeping the scene to spot a dirty, white-panel van exit onto the highway. She approached a police vehicle and flashed her badge. "Keys."

Without hesitation, a Hawai'i PD cop tossed her the keys to the four-wheel ATV.

I sure as hell hope Veronica's in that van. But where's Gurney and who's driving the van? Unless . . .

Oh shit.

Angela gunned the ATV's engine and burned rubber swerving onto the highway on the hunt for Special Agent William Gurney. Son of a bitch.

62

Using this tired, human body to climb is tedious, but I must maintain my disguise until I reach my goal.

On the other hand, using a machete to slash through the undergrowth is a novel experience for me.

It was nice of the heathen to bring one along when he pretended to be a worker at the nut farm.

How quaint of Gurney to phone. Like he did when he phoned to update me on the Hawaiian cruise. A god sees everything. But he felt it was necessary to inform me that his portion of the plan was on schedule. No matter. I shared my defeat of the heathen with him.

He was not as pleased as I expected, almost sad.

The tiny mind of the mortal, whose skin I wear, is also sad. Overwhelmed with hopelessness.

Mortals.

Gurney will meet me at Pele's altar with the lovely Veronica.

By meeting there, I challenge the strongest of these false Hawaiian gods to face me.

She will probably cower in fear. But a battle with her might provide an interesting diversion while I wait.

I hope Hades' reception to the underworld provides a stark contrast to my gentle means of sending the big Hawaiian there.

My brother is known for his warm welcomes.

———

ANGELA PRAYED SHE'D GUESSED RIGHT ABOUT THE VAN'S destination. She fought to keep the supercharged four-wheel centered on the narrow switchbacks. Pushing the accelerator to the max on the short straightaways, she caught a glimpse of the white van a few switchbacks ahead.

Her inability to raise either Andreos or Keone by cell phone continued to worry her. She hadn't bothered to call Gurney.

The bastard. I'd just started to trust him.

She punched a different name on her cell.

"Freeman."

"Tom, it's Ange. Tell me all the Canadians are at the airport."

"All but one. If Ms. Napoleoni doesn't get here soon, she'll miss the flight," Freeman warned.

"Listen to me, Tom. You make sure that plane takes off on time with the other Canadians on board. I'll take care of Veronica Napoleoni. And let everyone know, Gurney works for Thanatos." She ended the call before he could comment.

At least she was finally certain she was heading in their direction. All of them: Veronica, Gurney, Keone, Andreos, and Ron Morton. Now it was clear to Angela that Morton and Thanatos were one and the same person. That made Gurney his newest accomplice.

Could that lunatic have surprised Keone?

Thanatos wouldn't be satisfied to incapacitate Keone. He'd kill him.

Dear God, don't let Keone catch up to that maniac alone.

Angela slowly closed the gap with the white van, her experience in Hāna paying off. She'd cut Gurney's lead to barely a minute, watching carefully to make sure he didn't disappear on a side road.

Eventually, the van didn't appear at an expected switchback. Angela stopped her vehicle and made herself wait a full minute to make sure. When the van still didn't appear, she knew the hardest part of the chase had begun.

Off-road, her advantage over the clunky van should be decisive. But only if she found the precise spot the van left the highway.

63

She waits for me in front of a ruined temple. Hawaiians call such temples heiau. They formed these substantial structures from carefully carved and positioned blocks of lava.

She does not sit on the temple proper but on a nearby slab that bears some of the cat-scratching they call petroglyphs.

I admire her beauty. Her garments ripple with real fire, appropriate for a goddess born of volcanoes.

In response, I expand beyond my earthly guise and glide to a point about one hundred yards from her.

I'm impressed. She doesn't quail at my magnificence.

"Greetings, noble Pele," I say in my native tongue.

"And to you, so-called Thanatos of Olympus," she responds in ancient Greek.

Again, she surprises. Pele understands the language of the true gods. For this I shall give her one chance to survive.

"I have important business on your lovely island. You may assist me, depart, or perish. The choice is yours."

"We have watched you conduct your business on our sister

island of O'ahu and find it distasteful. You may depart at once or cease to exist."

The calmness of her statement piques my interest and anger.

"You are the guardian of a tiny realm. I am an Olympian. Your powers are trivial compared to mine. Must I end you as I ended that heathen below?"

Slowly Pele stands. Her body seems to increase in size and brilliance with the act. "You are foolish to believe the size of a realm determines its importance."

I feel the earth beneath me quake. A wave of intense heat assaults my back. I turn to see a glowing rift split open a few feet behind me.

Pele must be ready to play.

I cast powerful energy from my arms toward the unsuspecting goddess.

"Let the games begin."

64

Saturday, April 26, 4:35 p.m.

Will Gurney was surprised to experience a complicated mixture of emotions on his drive up Kīlauea volcano.

He was honored to be the only mortal able to understand that Ron Morton's body was inhabited by the god Thanatos. He also believed in UFOs and Bigfoot, but he never shared these beliefs with the bureau.

Still, Keone dead.

Gurney had come to respect the big Hawaiian. He'd honestly tried to impress him.

But his master made the decisions and Thanatos was a god. His god.

Time to move on.

Gurney glanced in the back of the van to see if Veronica had recovered from the strong sedative he'd given her. He noticed some faint twitches interrupting her regular breathing. She'd be coming around in a few minutes.

"Can you hear me yet, Veronica?"

No answer.

"You're probably still in dreamland. But, just in case, let me tell you what's in store. Your savior Keone is dead. My lord took care of him while I collected you. I know you liked Keone. No matter. You must never question the will of the gods. Thanatos waits for you on the mountain. Don't worry, he has a gentle touch. That touch will fill you with ecstasy beyond any earthly experience. He may appear to you as a mortal. Be assured, he is not. Thanatos is the god of non-violent death from Mount Olympus. He chose you and your friends because of your success in the Olympic games held in his homeland. Yes, the gods still watch those. You have been chosen for special treatment. Thanatos will gently launch you on your long journey to Elysium."

Still no response, but it felt good to talk.

"You probably think I'm some kind of phony, but I'm not. I really am an FBI agent and was assigned to this case by my superiors. Mind you, gods can arrange a lot of things."

No sound from the back, just regular breathing. Gurney began to wonder if he'd given her too much sedative.

"I was friends with a human named Ron Morton in college. He dropped out to pursue his career as a comedian and juggler. I went on to get my law degree and join the FBI. I loved the training and my initial assignments. But the Bureau is very close-minded about things that are beyond its philosophy."

She should be awake by now.

They'd turned off the main road some time ago and were now bumping along the rustic track to where they would park before their climb up to the heiau to meet Thanatos.

"I'd already come to despise my job before Ron reappeared in my life last year. Too many friends had been shown the door for going all *X-Files*. At first it was fun just to catch up with Ron about old times. But soon Thanatos revealed himself to me. I realized Ron was just a vessel. The poor man had no knowledge that Thanatos was stealing his mortal form more and more frequently. I became his worshiper and assistant. The greatest choice I ever made. You'll see."

He stopped the van. "Sorry, dear, we'll have to walk the rest of the way."

VERONICA FELT LIKE SHE WAS WAKING FROM A DREAM. She could only make out noises at first, then a voice. Agent Gurney seemed to be rambling on about Mount Olympus.

She kept her breathing regular and opened her eyes a sliver. She was tied hand and foot, the ropes looped around the metal plates in the interior of . . . what? A van. They were bumping along on a rough road.

Veronica tried not to make a sound as she worked to free her feet. The knots were tight. Luckily, her diver's flexibility allowed her to move her limbs in unconventional ways.

Gurney continued talking. "You probably think I'm some kind of phony . . ."

No. I think you're an asshole. And I'm going to have a surprise for you when you unlock that back door.

Veronica managed to get one leg free and began working on the other, ignoring Gurney's fanciful depiction of what was about to happen to her.

Think I'll pass on that, she thought, freeing her other leg, and starting to work on her wrist restraints.

Gurney stopped the van and said, "Sorry, dear, we'll have to walk the rest of the way."

The restraints bit into her skin. Every effort to twist free brought searing pain.

Gurney turned off the engine. The front door opened and closed.

Time was up.

No need for pretense now. She knew Gurney couldn't see her as he walked to the back of the van. With one last desperate effort, she freed her hands. No time to worry about the gag in her mouth.

She heard the key in the lock and braced herself. When the latch clicked, she threw her body at the door.

But the agent wasn't there. He must have suspected she'd try something and stepped back. She looked up, helpless, from the gravel roadbed. Gurney strolled over and cocked his arm to punish her for her audacity.

Veronica braced herself, prepared to feel a fist smash into her face. Instead, a familiar voice yelled, "Freeze! Hands in the air, Gurney."

65

Angela motioned with her free hand for Veronica to crawl over to her. When Gurney started to turn, she shouted. "Give me an excuse to shoot, shithead."

"I don't believe I will, Sergeant. You're alone up here and I'm not. I can wait," Gurney replied with a thin smile.

"That's Detective Sergeant, asshole." She gripped her Glock with both hands and aimed it directly at Gurney's heart. "Ease that pistol out of your belt with your left hand and hold it by the barrel."

Gurney did as ordered.

"Now, toss it as far as you can over those bushes and drop to your knees."

The pistol flew over the bushes and the special agent dropped like a rock but continued talking. "Sorry about Keone. I'm afraid my lord took care of him. Permanently."

No. Not Keone. The bastard's lying.

Angela removed the cuffs stashed inside her disguise and approached the kneeling Gurney. "I'm intrigued. Please tell me how skinny little Ron Morton took out a two hundred and seventy-five-pound Hawaiian? Did he juggle him to death?"

"He killed him quite gently, just like all the others. Thanatos told me that he watched Keone take his last breath and counted the final beat of his heart."

She grabbed Gurney's arm and twisted, knowing she hurt him. Wanting to. "Didn't your mother warn you not to believe everything a Greek god whispers in your ear?"

An odd dizziness caught Angela unawares. The earth beneath her feet seemed to drop a foot.

An earthquake? Now?

Gurney chose this moment to spin and knock her gun away.

She heard Veronica scream in the distance.

Angela wrestled with the taller Gurney, striving to regain a firm hold on one of his arms. She'd almost succeeded when a sharp blow knocked her to the ground.

Gurney leapt for her gun before she could recover.

Angela struggled to stand, watching Gurney swing the gun around and aim at her chest.

Before he could fire, Veronica leapt on the agent's back and screamed like a banshee. Gurney swung around, flailing his arms backward, but Veronica dodged his swings.

Gurney swung his right hand, which still held Angela's weapon, at Veronica's skull, missing by mere inches.

Angela recovered and launched herself at Gurney's mid-section. At the same moment, Gurney reared back his head.

Angela heard a sickening crunch as she connected with Gurney.

It took her a moment to realize the sound came from Victoria's nose and not Gurney's rib cage. Veronica's limp form slid off Gurney.

The agent, staggered by both blows, shook his head to clear it.

Angela didn't hesitate, wrenching her gun from his hand.

But Gurney wasn't finished. He put a vice-like grip around Angela's throat with his right arm and reached around to the back of his waistband with his left. When his hand reappeared, Angela saw the index and middle fingers were sheathed in silver with two needles protruding from their tips.

She had no angle. No time for a shot.

Angela dropped her gun and grabbed Gurney's left wrist with her right hand, stopping the needles inches from her neck. Gurney swung his right knee into the back of Angela's, knocking her to the ground. The agent fell with her, pinning her right hand to her side.

Angela swung her left hand behind her neck, barely stopping Gurney's wrist before he could plunge the needles home. The awkward angle put the detective at a disadvantage. Angela felt Gurney's hand edge closer to her neck. She imagined a slight tingle before a gunshot exploded to their left.

At the distraction, Angela rolled onto her back. With her stronger right hand free, she twisted Gurney's wrist with both hands and jammed his needle-tipped fingers into his own neck. The two remained in this position until Gurney went limp. Angela pushed him away.

"You okay, Tita?"

Angela had never been happier to hear a familiar voice. "Hey, aren't you supposed to be dead?"

"I was for a little while." Keone retrieved Angela's gun and handed it to her. "I was very fortunate, though. A brilliant Europol agent arrived, bearing an antidote to Dr. Morton's divine sleep elixir. He also restarted my heart with a very painful fist to my chest and kept it beating until the drug kicked in."

Andreos appeared from behind Keone. "That is one annoying thing about antidotes. They require circulation to do their magic. I am relieved this version worked."

Andreos moved to Veronica and examined her wound. "She is unconscious, and her nose is broken, but she will recover. Angela, could I trouble you for something with which to wrap Madame Napoleoni?"

Ange ran to the ATV, returning with a thick blanket. She helped Andreos wrap Veronica's limp form in the blanket before Keone picked up the athlete, carried her to the van, and laid her gently on the front seat.

When he turned to find Angela at his elbow, Keone said, "I'm sorry I couldn't just shoot Gurney, but I couldn't risk hitting you."

"No problem. The distraction was enough," Angela said, but her mind added, *barely.*

"I'm glad Veronica's gonna be okay." Keone wisely changed the subject.

"It's hard to keep that lady down. She fought Gurney like a tiger before you got here. I'm kinda glad you're okay, too, big guy." Angela punched Keone's shoulder and walked over to where Gurney lay sprawled in the pine needles. She knelt beside him and felt for a pulse, knowing she wouldn't find one. "Got any more juice, Andreos?"

"I had three doses. The cabdriver required one and Keone required two. I am afraid Agent Gurney must face the consequences of his own actions." Andreos shrugged.

"Ange, there's one more thing I need to tell you about . . . about the time between when I passed out and Andreos brought me back," Keone said.

"Since, at the time you mentioned, you were legally dead, I would like to hear this, too," Andreos said.

"I heard someone else's thoughts—in my head. I'm sure it was a man, and his thoughts had an accent like Andreos, but much stronger."

"Was it Calla?" Angela could hardly speak.

"Didn't say. But he did tell me he was a fisherman and asked me to give his best to a descendant—an acquaintance of mine." Keone looked directly at Andreos.

Angela returned to the ATV, located the first aid kit, and brought it to the van. "I'll take care of Veronica. I believe you two have some unfinished business to attend to. Ron or Thanatos or whoever he is expects to meet Gurney and Veronica at the top of that trail. You better get moving."

Andreos opened his mouth to object.

Keone pulled the Greek along toward the trail. "We started this together. Let's finish it together."

Keone noticed flashes of light coming from the trail above. What in the world was waiting for him up there?

66

How does she deflect my lethal energy? How can the fire from her hands cause me pain? Impossible.

We have been struggling for ages. Does she never tire?

I feel myself slide back a few inches toward the fissure as the goddess approaches with her hands outstretched. Molten lava flows from those hands and the crevasse behind me.

Time to unleash my full fury. No more restraint.

Powerful energy waves surge from my fingers and push back the lava on all sides. My azure waves soar toward the goddess to end her.

"Die, bitch."

The earth continues to shake.

KEONE AND ANDREOS PUSHED THROUGH THE LAST OF THE bushes screening the heiau from view. What they saw astounded them. Keone jerked back and nearly knocked Andreos off the mountain before grabbing his arm.

"Who is that old woman?" Andreos asked, easing himself from Keone's grip.

Keone didn't see an old woman. He saw the goddess Pele. The beautiful glowing form continued toward Ron Morton, who seemed to be struggling to stay upright at the edge of a glowing fissure. Flames shot from the tips of her fingers.

The fires of Pele, Keone thought.

Morton started shouting.

"Stay away from her," Keone yelled.

"Mr. Morton is not yelling at the woman," Andreos said. "I believe he is arguing with himself."

67

Saturday, April 26, 5:25 p.m.

This time it was Ron Morton's voice that rang out across the volcano. "Noooo! You will not harm anyone else. Ever again."

"How are you speaking? I destroyed your mortal form when I assumed my true form."

"I'm afraid not. My human body still holds you," Ron replied.

"But I am a god."

"You aren't a god. You're just a screwed-up piece of my mind that a doctor helped me seal away years ago."

For the first time in his long life, Thanatos was confused.

The god's perceptions blurred and transformed. He no longer glowed in his massive spiritual form. He was once again in the juggler's puny body.

Pele no longer shone either. She had shrunken to the form of an old woman, her ankle-length silver hair blowing in the wind. She looked like she could be Keone's grandmother.

Tutu reached out to pull Ron back from the edge of the molten fissure and managed to link her fingers in his. "Let me save you, child," she said in English, tears in her eyes.

"Thank you for trying," Ron gasped through the acrid smoke. "But I must end this. I know I'm not responsible for what he made my body do, but he's still in here. I feel him. I can't keep him confused much longer."

Keone watched Tutu try to pull Ron toward her. But Ron slipped her grasp, turned, and fell into the glowing crack.

Off balance, Tutu fell backward. Keone rushed to her side and caught her, then carried his grandmother away from the rift's bubbling lava, shielding her from the searing heat with his body.

After spurting out its anger, the rift narrowed to a thin line as Keone carried the slight form of his Tutu over to Andreos.

"Look." Andreos pointed to something protruding from the crack in the mountainside. The hilt of Keone's machete was all that remained above the sealed rift, a tiny glowing cross pointed to the sky. Then it too melted, sealing the last remnant of the fissure.

Keone carried his grandmother in his arms down the slope, crashing through the brush toward the place where Angela and Veronica waited.

Andreos placed his fingers on the old woman's wrist. "Her pulse is strong."

Tutu's eyes opened before they reached the gravel path. She gazed at her grandson.

Keone spoke in Hawaiian, "What were you doing up there, Tutu?"

"Pele's will."

"But, Tutu, that man was very dangerous. He thought he was a god. He killed a lot of women."

"Oh, my sweet keiki. Pele is not simply a woman. And that man was not a god."

ANGELA CONTINUED TO WIPE VERONICA'S BROW WITH A damp rag, hoping Andreos and Keone had found and dealt with Morton.

Veronica's eyes opened wide, and she threw her arms out in defense.

Angela grasped her wrists and whispered, "You're safe. Gurney's dead. It's me, Ange."

The Olympian's arms relaxed and circled the detective's shoulders. "You saved me."

"Only after you saved me."

"Keone?"

"He's okay. Andreos resuscitated him after Thanatos poisoned him."

"Thanatos?"

"Ron Morton. Keone and Andreos have gone up the mountain to take him down for good."

"But what if he really is a god?" Veronica said, as a large shape crashed through the bushes and toward the van.

THEY WERE BOTH QUITE RELIEVED TO SEE THE SHAPE WAS Keone carrying an old woman in his arms. Andreos trailed behind with an astonished look on his face. He walked directly to Veronica.

"Ms. Napoleoni, I am so happy to see you are back with us," he said. "I must apologize to you for something."

"First tell me, is Ron dead?"

"Yes. I'm afraid he is. He could find no way to end Thanatos without ending himself. Keone's grandmother tried to save him at the end, but she couldn't."

"Thanatos deserved to die for what he did to my Olympic sisters. What he did to Josie." Veronica started to cry.

"That, I'm afraid, is the one thing I need to apologize for. Thanatos did indeed kill many of your Olympic sisters, but not Mrs. Galliano."

"What?" Angela asked.

"I apologize to you and Angela, and your friend Linda for this as well."

"How?" Was all Veronica could think to ask.

"You remember Agent Gurney making much of me being the last person to board the ship in Honolulu, yes?"

"Yes," Keone said, joining the conversation after setting Tutu in the van.

"I was so certain Thanatos would act at the first port that I waited around and searched the dock area. That is where I found Mrs. Galliano and administered the antidote. I was with your friend the DEA agent, Freeman. When I saw she would recover, I worked out a little scheme with him so Thanatos and his new accomplice wouldn't suspect that we had perfected the antidote. I couldn't even tell Keone, given his suspicions of me at that point."

"Josie is alive?" Veronica asked, her heart filling with joy.

"Very much so and safe at home with her husband. That's why we couldn't let them answer their phones for a few days."

"Did you know all along that Gurney was the accomplice?" Keone asked.

"No. But I must admit that I never found myself fully able to trust him." Andreos smiled.

ON THE DRIVE TO KONA AIRPORT, KEONE SAT IN THE BACK of the van, and Andreos drove with Veronica at his side, chatting on her cellphone with Josie.

In the back of the van, Keone had made a nest with blankets where he could speak with his Tutu. Since they spoke in Hawaiian, their conversation was private.

"Tutu, I saw the fires of Pele up there. They seemed to surround your body and made you grow and glow. But Andreos only saw an elderly woman. How is that possible? Are you Pele?"

"Keiki, I have told you that a spirit resides within us. I call it Pele because of how I was raised. You must find your own name for it. My brother Kono calls it the 'aina. Julie feels it too, but she calls it God. Names are not important. You saw what you saw because of the spirit within you. Andreos saw what Pele let him see."

Before he could say any more, Keone's cellphone buzzed, displaying the time as 6:00 p.m.

"That's Mahealani. After she tells you her news, tell her I'm all right, and we'll meet her at the airport," Tutu said.

As he listened to an urgent voice, Keone saw his Tutu break into a huge smile.

Epilogue

Saturday, April 26, 11:30 p.m.

Julie Boyd sat in the birth position in a delivery room at Maui Memorial Hospital, holding her sister's hand and panting. She couldn't wait for the doctor to tell her it was time to push. She was more than ready. She felt huge.

A massive form in green scrubs entered the room and took her other hand just as the doctor said, "Okay, Julie. Let's try a push when the next contraction arrives, okay?"

She saw Keone's eyes widen above the mask on his face. Then he gently squeezed her hand and said, "Right here with you, my love. Got a call from my sister. Sorry to cut it so close."

Then the contraction arrived, and everything began to move swiftly, culminating in a beautiful baby boy being placed in her hands.

A few days later they were safe and warm at home. Julie sat on their new couch breast-feeding tiny Keahilani Ka'imi Boyd. The boy's proud father sat beside her, calmer than she had ever seen him. Keone was different since he returned from the Big Island.

Oh, he'd told her about his assignment and his shock at finding Tutu on the Big Island. The old woman had travelled with Mahealani to the Merrie Monarch but sneaked off on the last day to visit a heiau dedicated to Pele.

Keone had also given Julie the official account of what had happened on Kīlauea. Ron Morton suffered a recurrence of his childhood dissociative identity disorder. When he finally realized what his other self, Thanatos, had done, he became despondent and committed suicide. An FBI special agent, who served as Morton's accomplice, was killed trying to murder Veronica Napoleoni, who was now safely back home in Montreal with her husband and their dear friends the Gallianos.

Keone even told her the details about Josie's unsuccessful murder and the nearly successful attempt on his own life by Thanatos and on Angela's by his accomplice. Julie would be forever grateful to Andreos Calliopoulos, whose quick actions saved both Keone and Josie, and a Hawaiian cab driver.

Julie knew there were pieces missing. She also knew Keone and Angela would share everything with her over time. She studied her husband's face and thanked a higher power that he was sitting beside her, safely home again.

"I'm glad the cruise line booked Angela and Linda on this week's cruise of the islands and put them up at the Royal Hawaiian until it sails," Julie said, watching Keone take a slow draw from his mug of Kona coffee.

"They deserve an uninterrupted honeymoon cruise. So did we." Keone gingerly placed his cup on the folding table propped up beside their couch. "Julie, I need to tell you something. The official account is only part of the story. I want to tell you the rest."

"I know, sweetheart. And I'm glad you want to tell me. I'm sure some of what happened is probably a little hard to believe, as usual. But I don't want to hear any more about the case. I have a different question for you."

"Sure. Anything."

Julie switched to flawless Hawaiian. "Keone Kaʻimi Boyd, are you finally ready to accept who you are?"

Keone looked shocked. "How much do you know?"

"I know about your reading and your sessions with Tutu. I know what I believe about Sam Loftus and Rob Lister. And I know what Tutu believed about Thanatos and Pele. What I need to know is what you believe—about yourself."

"I believe that I am Hawaiian and that a spirit, Pele or God or the ʻaina or something spiritual with no name at all, lives inside me, as it does in my Tutu and in you and in our little keiki."

"I believe that, too." Julie gazed into the face of their baby. "And, my little keiki, that's why your name means Seeker of the Fires of Heaven."

Keone started to say something, but Julie put a finger to his lips. "It's enough."

They put Keahilani in his crib, went to their bedroom, and fell asleep wrapped in each other's arms.

It was enough.

Acknowledgments

Here, at last, is the revised third novel in the Maui Mystery series. A lot has transpired since the initial publication of this story as *Pele's Fire* in 2019. Most notably, the wonderful folks at Babylon Books have given me the opportunity to rewrite and professionally publish all three books in my Maui Mysteries Series. The first, *Eyes of the Beholder,* was released in 2022. The second, *Voice of the Victim,* was released in 2023. Now this third book in the series, renamed *Soul of a Sleuth,* is available.

A great tragedy struck my beloved Valley Island. The lovely township of Lahaina was devastated by a terrible fire in early August of 2023, and it will take many years for folks there and in other areas on the island ravaged by fires to fully recover and rebuild. An effective way to help them is to send a donation to one of the organizations below or many, many others:

Maui Strong Fund: This major effort is coordinated by The Hawai'i Community Foundation at the website: https://www.hawaiicommunityfoundation.org/strengthening/maui-strong-fund.

Peoples Fund of Maui - Launched by Oprah Winfrey and Duane Johnson after the fire Peoples Fund of Maui is a component of the EIF, the Entertainment Industry Foundation and can be found at the website: https://www.eifoundation.org/partners/peoples-fund-of-maui/.

Maui United Way: a long-established group that is helping fire victims. It can be found at the website: https://www.mauiunitedway.org .

Lahaina Action Committee: another long-established group, which sold my early Maui Mysteries in their gift shop, are an excellent resource for multiple groups supporting the fire victims. A list of resources helping Maui fire victims can be found at this webpage:

https://visitlahaina.com/maui-fires-resources/

Although my wife Christy and I returned to the mainland in 2016 after eight years living on Maui full time, we still return to the Valley Island every chance we get. Our last visit was in December of 2023. Although I'm no longer able to experience Maui every day, I remain sensitive to capturing the honest essence of my favorite place in the world during the decade we lived there. We are very fortunate that our son was wise enough to continue to live and work on Maui full-time and provide a place for his less wise parents to stop over. We return as often as possible to visit him and our many dear friends on the Valley Isle, including the talented writers of Maui Writers, Ink, many of whom read and commented on this and my other attempts to bring a bit of Maui magic to you.

I've been blessed with a multitude of wonderful authors who read and commented on this book during its earliest incarnations as *Ports of Call* and *Pele's Fire*. These included Selma Mann, Laurie Hanan, Elaine Gallant, Lara Bernhardt, R. J. Johnson, J.A. Ludwig, and Ken Andrus. Detective Lieutenant Audra M. Sellers, Maui Police Department provided valuable input on Maui Police Department structure and law enforcement procedures for all the Maui Mysteries. Ron Pearson, a fabulous entertainer and dear friend, and his amazing wife Tanya, helped me understand the life of an entertainer and his family. And five voracious readers have helped me improve this work as well as my others: Doug McLellan, Darrel Allen, Fran Boughey, Deyna Puckett, and Jim Miller.

I again thank my mentor and dear friend Bill Bernhardt. A prolific, best-selling author, publisher, and wonderful teacher. Bill has provided direct feedback on each of my books and inspiration for all my endeavors.

For this completely rewritten version of the story, I thank my alpha readers Christy Ludwig and J.A. Ludwig for a meticulous reading and critique of what I optimistically referred to as the final draft. I also thank my beta readers Elaine Gallant, R.J. Johnson, Ken Andrus, Betsey Kulakowski, and Lara Bernhardt for valuable feedback that improved this book more than I could have ever hoped. Any errors that remain are mine.

I began this novel in 2014, and the Maui it describes is the one I experienced at that time and resolved to keep it set when it was written. The cane fields are gone now, as are many of the restaurants, and the version of lovely Lahaina Town that I experienced, but the spirit of this blessed island remains the same.

I am grateful to Babylon Books for sticking with me through all three books and supporting me at every turn. The quality of the eBook and paperback versions are testament to their dedication. I was also blessed to have fantastic editors in Lara Bernhardt and Ally Robertson, who made my stories so very much better. And I can't begin to thank Maria Navillo Saravia and her colleagues at BeauteBook for another mysterious and enticing cover.

I first wrote the story that became *Soul of a Sleuth* in 2013 – 2014. It describes Maui as it was then. I hope that memories such as this will help to guide those working so hard to recapture the magic that was Lahaina Town.

My greatest thanks, as always, go to my family of Christy,

Jennifer, and Jonathan, who teach me something new and exciting every day.

About the Author

James Richard (Rick) Ludwig, Ph.D. spent forty years in the academic, health care, biotechnology, and pharmaceutical disciplines. Rick also maintained a writer's journal since his junior year in high school and populated it with short stories, poetry, and essays throughout his life.

Although a published author of multiple scientific papers and textbook chapters between 1975 and 2008, writing for a popular audience presented a unique challenge. Rick spent the first year of his retirement, converting all his writings, including his original writer's journal (1967-2008), to digital format. Since then, he has written full-time and completed multiple manuscripts. *Soul of a Sleuth* is the third novel in his Maui Mystery Series published by Babylon Books. The first was *Eyes of the Beholder* (2022). The second, *Voice of the Victim,* was published in 2023. Rick is currently working on the second volume of his autobiography, which he is writing for his wife and children.

Rick participated in the 2009 Hawai`i Writers Conference in Honolulu, Hawai‘i, served as Volunteer Coordinator for the 2013 Aloha Writers Conference in Kapalua, Maui, and attended best-selling author William Martin's Retreat workshop during that conference. Rick participated in best-selling author William Bernhardt's Level 1, Level 2, Level 3, and advanced writers' workshops between 2010 and 2016. Since 2015, Rick has presented seminars as part of the Rose State

Writers Workshop (2015), the Red Sneaker Writers Workshop (2018), and the WriterCon Conferences (2020 and 2022), all held in Oklahoma City, OK.

Rick is married with two grown children, Jonathan and Jennifer. He divides his time between Maui, Hawai`i and Southern California with his wife of forty-three years, Christy, with whom he is learning to relax and enjoy the game of golf.

You can follow Rick on his website: rickludwigauthor.com or send him an email at rickludwigwrites@gmail.com.

www.ingramcontent.com/pod-product-compliance
Lightning Source LLC
Chambersburg PA
CBHW022308310726

48973CB00001B/266